Any Day Now

ROBYN CARR

Any Day Now

MIRA

MIRA

Recycling programs
for this product may
not exist in your area.

ISBN-13: 978-0-7783-0807-2

Any Day Now

For questions and comments about the quality of this book, please contact us at CustomerService@Harlequin.com.

www.MIRABooks.com

Printed in U.S.A.

A Message from Robyn Carr

The characters I can't help but love

When I'm writing a novel, things don't always work out as planned. Then again, some things work out even better than I expected. It's always a journey, and I like to watch the story unfold just as the reader does; even if I didn't want to, there's no way I can think of the entire story before I write. Nothing would get done that way.

I might think about the leading characters for a while and get to know them before writing them, but that's only a couple of the people who give a series depth and longevity. Those characters with supporting roles usually begin with a sentence or two, and sometimes that's all I need—at first, anyway. There are times a character just disappears because they've refused to carry the story ahead. They lack vitality and so are left on the cutting room floor, so to speak.

But sometimes characters grow in my mind and become so interesting to me, they breathe. It happens that I fall deeply in love with them. On occasion they get their own book. There are a couple of examples that come immediately to mind. Preacher from the Virgin River series was nothing more than a sketch in *Virgin River*—a big, bald man with black eyebrows, a diamond stud in one ear, a scowl on his face—and when someone said, "He's terrifying," the main character, Jack, said, "Nah, he's a pussycat." *Zing*, that was it. I was going to write a whole book using this terrifying man and name him, of all things, Preacher—a huge, frightening, powerful man who is gentle as a lamb. Unless he needs to be otherwise. And, boy, did he step up.

In *What We Find*, because it's the first book in my new Sullivan's Crossing series, a big cast was required. And there were some surprises—I love when that happens. One character who captured my heart was Tom Canaday. He first appeared in a couple of sentences: "a single father of four who worked any job that paid—raising four kids alone can be an expensive business!" It didn't take me long to start wondering how this lovely man ended up alone. While working on *What We Find* I learned that Tom has been slow to move on after his divorce—he wanted to be married for life. It turned out his divorce was hard on him and he wasn't treated very well. So, by the time *Any Day Now* came along, Tom was under my skin. He's the kind of man I wanted to know better—good friend and neighbor, an involved father proud of his kids, a faithful son and loyal brother, uncomplaining, gives to the community. It didn't take a genius to figure out that Tom was in need of a good woman, a woman nothing like his ex-wife.

A woman for Tom began to come into focus. I hadn't noticed her before and neither had Tom. I loved the look of her, rosy-cheeked with dark curly hair, a robust figure and a great sense of self; an independent woman who had been raising her two sons on her own. And, like Tom, she'd been around the town all her life and put great stock in being a good friend and neighbor. Her name is Lola and, also like Tom, she's had to work hard to make ends meet. Although they've known each other forever, they meet on a new playing field—single adults, parents, long overdue for a meaningful relationship, people who thought all hope of one day finding a lifetime companion was past for them. New love for mature adults has never been so lush, so ripe. When I first saw them come together, it was a sigh-worthy moment. At that moment there were no two people I'd ever known who were more ready for love.

But I had a bigger problem to solve than Tom and Lola. I had to find a character strong enough to carry a whole novel. A woman, I thought. She should come from *What We Find* to give my readers that continuity they want. And yet there didn't seem to be a woman in *What We Find* who'd sparked that curiosity and possibility. Then I thought about Cal's youngest sister, Sierra Jones. It was a leap of faith—she didn't even appear in *What We Find* and all that was said of her was that she struggled with addiction. But I knew, as all writers know, there was more to her. As the pages stacked up, I was introduced to this extraordinary young woman with untapped strength and brand-new confidence. Once I put Sierra with some of the familiar faces around Sullivan's Crossing, she fit perfectly and I was able to watch her growth, her self-discovery. Cal and Maggie are happy to have Sierra nearby to round out their family, and Sully has found himself a new surrogate daughter. Sierra, thirty years old and beautiful inside and out, finds herself with a new home and new friends. It's all she's ever really wanted.

One of her new friends is firefighter and paramedic Conrad "Connie" Boyle. As I watched them and wrote about them, Connie noticed Sierra. Really noticed her. While Connie was getting to know Sierra, I was getting to know Connie. On the outside, he's a hero—saving lives for a living. It was not a complete surprise for me to learn that he's a hero on the inside, as well. It was so lovely, so gratifying to watch Sierra bring out the best in him.

I'm very glad you've come back to Sullivan's Crossing with me in *Any Day Now*. You're going to have a good time watching these couples discover the happiness they feared was out of their reach.

I hope you come to know and love them as well as I do.

Robyn Carr

Any Day Now

Home is the place where, when you have to go there,

they have to take you in.

—ROBERT FROST

Chapter 1

SO, THIS IS WHAT A NEW LIFE LOOKS LIKE. SIERRA Jones opened her eyes on a sunny Colorado morning to that thought.

She had given this a great deal of consideration. Colorado had not been her only option but she decided it might be the best one. Her brother Cal, with whom she shared a deep bond, was making a life here and he wanted her to be part of it. Sierra needed a new place to start over. A place with no bad memories, where she had no history and yet, had a strong emotional connection. Her big brother was a powerful pull.

When she was a child, it was Cal who'd protected her, loved her unconditionally, cared for her, worried on her behalf. He was eight years older but had been more than just her brother. He had been her best friend. And when he'd left home, or what passed for home when she was ten years old, she'd been adrift.

When she'd finally made up her mind to give this place a chance, Cal wanted her to come directly to his house. His house in progress, that is. But that didn't sound like a good idea; there was only one bedroom finished so far. And, more important— she wouldn't be a burden to anyone, and absolutely did not want to be in the way of a new couple who were just feeling their way into marriage. Cal and Maggie had been married less than six months and were living in the barn they were converting into a house. Sierra thanked them kindly and said she'd prefer to find her own lodgings and live on her own. A very important part of creating a new life was independence. She did not want to be accountable to anyone but herself.

That's what she'd told them. The truth, hidden protectively in her heart, was that she was afraid to depend on Cal again as she had when she was a little girl. He had a new family, after all. She remembered too well the pain from her childhood when he'd abandoned her. It was awful.

Independence was a little frightening. But, she reminded herself, she did have her brother near and willing to lend a hand if she needed anything, just as she was more than eager to be there for Cal and Maggie. She was thirty years old and it was high time she built a life that reflected the new woman she was becoming. This was a joyful, challenging, exciting and terrifying change. If a little lonely at times...

She had a short checklist of things she wanted to settle for herself before seeing Cal. First—she wanted to look around the area. Timberlake was the town closest to where her brother and Maggie lived and she thought it was adorable. It was a little touristy, a little on the Wild West side with its clapboard shop fronts and Victorian-style houses, surrounded by the beauty of snow-topped mountains and long, deep fields. The first day she spent in the small town there was a herd of elk cantering down the main street. One big bull was bugling at the cows and calves, herding them away from the town and back to grazing land. They were at once majestic and klutzy, wandering in a little confusion through the cars. An old guy standing in front of a barbershop explained to her that with spring, they were moving to higher elevations, cows were giving birth, grazing was found in different areas. And in the fall, he said, watch out for rutting season. "Those bulls get real territorial."

That was all it took for Sierra to begin to hope this would be the right place for her, because her heart beat a little faster just watching that grand herd move through town. The old guy had said, "You don't see that every day."

She'd found a comfortable, clean, cheap hostel that would let her pay by the week and they were just starting to get an influx of students and adventurers who wanted to take advantage of the Colorado springtime. She'd have to share a bathroom, but it wouldn't be the first time; she wasn't fussy and it would make decent housing until she could find something more permanent. The owner of the hostel, a woman in her sixties called Midge, had said there were rooms and apartments being let by local homeowners all over town.

The best part about the hostel—there were people around, yet she would be on her own.

She'd found a part-time job right away—the diner needed early-morning waitstaff help a couple days a week. They'd lost their main morning waitress and the owner's wife had been filling in. As it happened, Sierra loved the early morning. The money wasn't great but it was enough to keep her comfortable and she had a little savings.

The most important thing she'd researched before coming to Colorado was locations and times of AA meetings. She even had an app for her phone. There were regularly scheduled meetings everywhere. In Timberlake and in all the small towns surrounding it from Breckinridge to Colorado Springs. They were usually held in churches but there were some in community centers, in office buildings, hospitals and even clubhouses. She would never be without support.

Sierra was nine months sober.

Sierra had reconnected with Cal about seven months ago, right before he and Maggie married. He'd visited her twice since and called her regularly. He'd begun lobbying for her move to Colorado a few months ago. For the eight years previous they'd been in touch but not much a part of each other's lives and for that she had regrets. Those years had been especially difficult for Cal; the past five years had been brutal. His first wife, Lynne, had suffered from scleroderma, a painful, fatal disease, and had passed away three years ago. Cal had been a lost soul. If she'd been a better sister, she might've offered her support.

But that was in the past and the future was her opportunity. She hoped they could rebuild the close relationship they'd once had and become family again. Right before she'd started the long trek south to Colorado, Cal had shared a secret—he was going to be a father.

Sierra was thrilled for him. He would never know how much she looked forward to a baby. She would be an auntie. Since she would never have children of her own, this was an unexpected gift.

Cal Jones lay back against the pillows, his fingers laced behind his head, sheet drawn to his waist. He watched Maggie preen naked in front of the full-length mirror, checking her profile.

"We got a thing going on...me and Mrs. Jones..." he said, his voice husky.

She really didn't show much yet. Just the tiniest curve where her waist had been. She kept smoothing her hand over it. "I passed the dreaded first three months with no issues," she said. She beamed at him, her eyes alive. "I'm not sick. I feel great. I'm going to tell my dad it's okay to tell his friends now."

"Don't be too surprised if you find he already has."

"I wouldn't be at all surprised."

He watched her with pride. Thin as a reed with that little bump that he put there, her smile wistful and almost angelic. She wanted the baby as much as he did; she thrilled with each day it grew in her. This baby had healed something in her. And it filled him with a new hope. She was more beautiful now than she'd ever been.

"Mrs. Jones, you have to either get dressed or come over here and do me."

She laughed. "I already *did* you. Magnificently, I might add."

"I said thank you."

She reached for her underwear, then her jeans, then her sweatshirt. The show was over. Now he'd have to wait all day to have her alone again.

"It's time for you to get to work—I need a house. Tom will be here anytime. I'm going over to Sully's store," Maggie said. There was much cleanup and restoration to do at her dad's general store and campground at Sullivan's Crossing. It was the first of March, and it wouldn't be long before the campers and hikers started coming in force.

Cal and Maggie were living in the barn they were renovating into a big house with the guidance of Tom Canaday, a local with some amazing carpentry and other building skills. Tom had good subcontractors to help, speeding up the process. Maggie and Cal had married last October and, while the roof and exterior were being reinforced and sealed, dormers added to what were once haylofts, the wiring refreshed, the interior gutted and windows installed where there had been none, they'd been living at Sully's, in his basement. Tom, Cal and a few extra hands had finally finished off a bedroom and functional bathroom along with a semifunctional kitchen. That bedroom on the ground floor would eventually be Cal's office when the house was finished. The proper master bedroom would be upstairs. They had a good seal on their temporary bedroom door so they could sleep there and not be overcome by sawdust or the dirt of construction. They'd been in residence two weeks, thanks to warmer weather and a good space heater.

Maggie spent most of her free time at the store helping her dad. Then there were those three or four days a week she was in Denver where she practiced neurosurgery. On her practice days she stayed at the Denver house she'd owned for several years. During her days away, Cal and Tom did the things that were noisiest, smelliest and messiest—the pounding and sawing,

cutting granite and quartz, applying the noxious sealer, install-
ing the floors, sanding and staining. Every time Maggie came
home it was like Christmas—she'd find new stairs to the second
floor, a bathtub, a new kitchen sink, ceramic tile on the kitchen
floor, half a fireplace. But the most precious addition of all was
the Shop-Vac. That little beauty kept dirt, sawdust, spillage and
debris manageable. It was their goal to have the house finished
before the baby came, due in October.

Tom Canaday was at the house, his truck backed up to the
door, before Cal had finished making Maggie breakfast—very
likely by design. Cal got the eggs back out and started making
more breakfast.

Tom brought his twenty-year-old son, Jackson; something he
did whenever Jackson had a day free of classes. In the cavern-
ous great room they sat at a long picnic table. Tom had thrown
it together and it became the table they ate at, spread plans on,
used as a carpenter's bench, a desk when they held meetings.
They met with subcontractors there, spread material samples or
design renderings on it, looked through catalogs. It was truly
multipurpose.

Once Maggie had gone to Sullivan's Crossing, the men were
still seated at the picnic table, finishing a second cup of coffee
when there was a knock at the door.

"She forget something?" Tom asked.

"Maggie wouldn't knock," Cal said, going to the front door.

Standing just outside on the step, was a pretty girl with light
brown hair streaked with honey. She had peachy skin and a
pretty mouth stretched into a smile. She wore tight jeans with
fashionably torn knees, but Cal guessed hers weren't purchased
that way. Her hoody was tied around her neck. The sight of her
made his eyes glitter with happiness.

"Well, you finally got around to me," he said. He lifted her
off the ground with his hug. "How are you?"

"Good. Brand-new. I love this place."

"You might get a little tired of it this month—March is pretty sloppy."

"Yeah, that happens," she said.

He looked beyond her to the little orange VW parked on the road. Not new, that's for sure. He thought he saw a piece of twine holding the front bumper in place. Then he looked back at his sister. "The pumpkin," she said with a smile.

"You must've looked hard for that thing," he said.

"She came at a good price."

"Hard to believe," he said facetiously. He always forgot how beautiful she was. She was thirty now but still looked like a girl. He put a finger under her chin and tilted her face to look into her clear brown eyes. "How are you feeling?" he asked softly.

"Never better," she said. "Really."

"Are you going to stay here until you find something?" he asked.

She shook her head. "Found something already. It's temporary, but clean, safe, comfortable and convenient. The hostel in town. It'll keep me very well while I look around some more."

Sierra looked past him. Wires were hanging from the ceiling and sticking out of walls, building debris was scattered everywhere, stacks of wallboard, tarps, doors leaning against walls, piles of supplies from plumbing fixtures to hinges. "Love what you've done to the place, California."

Someone cleared his throat and Cal turned to see Tom and Jackson staring at Sierra with open mouths and wide-eyed wonder. "Oh, sorry, guys. Tom, Jackson, this is my sister Sierra. Sierra that's Tom and his son, Jackson. We're building together. Remodeling the barn. Like I told you the last time we talked—it's going to be our house by the time the baby comes."

"Amazing," she said, looking around the massive interior. "Put up some walls, California. You don't want to be living in an arena."

"Right," he said, smiling. "Listen guys, Sierra and I have

some catching up to do. I want to take her over to Sully's to see Maggie. I'll be gone for a couple of hours but I'll be back. You okay without me?"

Jackson grinned. "Sometimes we're better without you."

"Way to pump my ego," Cal said. "See you in a while." He pulled the door closed and steered Sierra toward her car. "Can I drive?"

"The pumpkin? I guess... But she's very sensitive. You'll have to be gentle. Don't grind the gears or pump the brakes." She pulled a key out of the pocket of her tight jeans. "But why?"

He grabbed it. "Indulge me. I want to see how it handles on these mountain roads."

She slid into the passenger seat. "Okay, but no matter how much you love her, you can't have her."

The first thing he did was grind the gears. "Sorry," he said. She groaned.

He was smoother then, driving around the foothills. There were a lot of sharp turns, uphill and downhill grades, narrow roads that briefly widened and some amazing mountain vistas. At a widened lookout, Cal pulled the pumpkin right up to the edge and stopped.

"Not bad, Sierra," he said. "Kind of creaky, isn't she?"

"She likes me better," Sierra said. "I have a sweet touch and you're a clod."

"It suits you, this little orange ball. How was your drive down?"

"Pretty. A little rainy. Colorado is beautiful."

"I worried, you know. Thinking about you making that drive all alone when I could have ridden with you..."

She laughed outright. "God, I needed to be alone more than you'll ever know! Do you have any idea how rare time alone was for me the last nine months?"

"That wasn't one of the things I thought about," he admitted. He'd spent all his energy fearing her relapse. Or worse.

"I've been living with people for nine months, first in rehab and then in a group home. It taught me a lot, I'm the first to admit that. But it also drove me crazy. For a long day on the road, I could actually hear the inside of my head. My first day in Timberlake there were elk right in the town. On the main street, weaving through the cars."

"I've never seen anything like that. I've heard it happens but never saw it." He gave her knee a pat. "Tell me if there's anything you need. If there's anything I can do to make this move, this transition, easier for you."

She shook her head. "Nothing at the moment. I planned it very carefully, down to the tiniest detail. If I need anything, I'll be sure to let you know."

"You're being very brave," he said. "You left your support system and came all the way to—"

"I have a phone, Cal. I'm in touch with my sponsor and will be going to meetings now and then, looking for a local sponsor. I'm in touch with a couple of the women in recovery I lived with the last six months. We shore each other up and…" She took a breath. "And I'm not fragile, all right? See—no sweaty palms. It's all cool. I'm excited about being here."

"You never said what did it? What finally got you in rehab?" Cal and his late wife, Lynne, had tried an intervention, offering support if she'd consider sobriety, but it was a failure. Sierra wasn't interested. She said they were overreacting.

"Listen, something you should understand, I didn't know I had a problem, okay? I should have, but I didn't. I thought I drank a little too much sometimes, like everyone. I kept meaning to do better but it wouldn't last long. I mean, I hardly ever missed work, I never got a DUI, never got DT's when I didn't drink and even though I did things I regretted because of alcohol, I thought that was my fault, not the booze. I decided to give rehab a try but I honestly thought I'd go into treatment and learn that everyone else had a problem and I was actually just an idiot who didn't always use good judgment. But it didn't work out that way. Now I know all the things I should've known a long time ago." She chuckled and looked out at the view. "Imagine my surprise."

"I thought you were doing a lot of drugs," he said.

"Hardly ever," she said. "I didn't need drugs. I was busy drinking."

He was quiet for a long moment. "I'm really proud of you," he finally said. "Nine months is good," he said.

"It's excellent, to tell the truth. And I'll be honest, in the early days I wasn't very confident of nine days. But here we are. Now you—tell me something—what does it feel like, knowing you're going to be a daddy?"

He felt his face grow into that silly smile he'd been wearing lately whenever he thought about Maggie. "Unbelievable. Overwhelming. I was getting used to the idea this wouldn't happen to me."

"But it's not a surprise, is it?" she asked. "The baby?"

"Nah, we wanted a family. Maggie's way more fertile than she bargained for—it happened right away. We're still getting used to the idea, but it feels great. You'll see someday..."

She was shaking her head. "I don't think so. Don't get me wrong, I look forward to being an auntie but I'm not all that into the mommy scene. I didn't grow up looking after little kids like you did."

"You saying you don't like kids?" he asked.

"I love kids," she said. "When they're someone else's. But... Can I ask a personal question?"

"Sure. Be gentle with me," he said, but he smiled when he said it.

"Do you ever worry about the schizophrenia thing?"

Their father, Jed, was schizophrenic and he wasn't medicated. Rather, he was self-medicated—he smoked pot every day. It kept the delusions a little quieter. Jed was, quite honestly, crackers. And schizophrenia sometimes ran in families.

"I worry about everything, including that. It appears Jed didn't inherit his disease or pass it on, unless someone's holding back information. But I have Maggie. She's much more logical and pragmatic. She began listing things we could worry about—the list was long. It covered everything from childhood cancers and illnesses to teenage pregnancy and she suggested, firmly, that we deal with each problem as it appears. You have to remember, Maggie handles catastrophic head injuries and brain tumors for a living—you can't scare her. And if mental illness is one of our problems, trust me—we'll be managing it in a different way than Jed does." He paused. "How are they?"

"I saw them briefly before I left and they're exactly the same. Mom said she was glad I was going to be around you, that you probably needed me. I have no idea where she got that idea. I told her not to tell anyone but Sedona and Dakota where I was. I don't know who would ask but I want to cut ties with that old life. I mean, I still have my Des Moines support, but we don't give out information on each other. Mom was fine, Dad was getting ready for a big security briefing of some kind. In other words, he's in Jed's world. You call them, don't you?"

"I haven't talked to them in a couple of weeks—I've been busy with the barn. I'll check in. Sierra, are there debts to clear or something?"

"No," she assured him. "I just don't need anyone from rehab or my old party days tracking me down. I'm good."

"If you have issues like that, tell me. Better to straighten it out than ignore it."

"I don't have those kinds of issues, Cal."

"Okay. But if I can help… Just get settled."

"I worry about them, too, Cal," she said.

"But there's nothing we can do," he reminded her. "Let's go find Maggie. She's dying to meet you in person."

★ ★ ★

Sierra drove the pumpkin, following Cal's directions to Sullivan's Crossing. As she oohed and aahed at the scenery, she thought one of the great things about rehab had been learning she was not the only person with a totally screwed-up family. Given the fact that her sister Sedona and brother Dakota were living functional and what appeared to be normal, conventional lives, it seemed to boil down to her parents, and all because Jed didn't want to be treated for his schizophrenia and Marissa, her mother, didn't push him. Crazy parents weren't unusual in rehab. In fact the number of people who had been drinking or drugging their way through delusions was astonishing.

She had told a small lie. She'd told it cheerfully and with good intentions. Truthfully, she wished she could have children. But there were multiple problems with that idea. First, she had a very bad history with men—she chose the worst ones imaginable. And second, not only did she have to deal with schizophrenia in the family tree but also addiction, which also tended to run in families. How could she risk cursing a child with such afflictions? Add to that, you'd have to trust yourself a great deal to be a good parent and she wasn't even close. Self-doubt was her constant companion.

"You get to see this scenery every day," she said to her brother. "I was mainly coming here because you and Maggie are here but it's an amazingly beautiful place."

"I wonder if you ever get used to it," he said. "I still can't believe I'm lucky enough to live here."

"How'd you end up here?" she asked.

"You know," he said. "Wandering. Trying to find myself, sort of."

"Sort of?"

"I was roaming. It's in our genes. Plus…" He hesitated. "I was looking for a place for Lynne. A place for her ashes. I gave her my word—I'd leave her in a beautiful place and then I'd let her go."

"And did you?" Sierra asked.

He was quiet for a moment. "I found a beautiful place. By that time I'd met Maggie. And my life started over." He reached over and touched her knee. "Your turn to start over, kid."

"Yeah," she said, suddenly feeling tired. Scared. It came upon her at the weirdest times, that fear she'd turn out to be a failure. Again. "Right. And looks like a great place to do that."

"I think of this as home," Cal said. "We never really had a home."

"We had the farm," she said. "Sort of."

"You had more of that than I did," he said.

Their parents, who described themselves as free spirits, hippies, freethinkers and nonconformists, raised their family on the road, living in a bus converted into an RV, but it was really just a disguise. Jed was sick and Marissa was his enabler and keeper. Marissa's parents had a farm in Iowa and they landed there quite often, all of them helping on the farm and going to school in Pratt, Iowa, a small farming community. Then they'd take off again, on the road. By the time Sierra was eight they'd settled on the farm full-time, taking care of the land for Grandma after Grandpa passed away. Cal finished high school there.

Then he left to seek his fortune, to go to college with the help of scholarships and loans. She had been only ten. He passed responsibility for her on to Sedona, next oldest. When Sierra was twelve, Sedona left for college. She got herself a full ride and went to a hoity-toity women's university back East and though she called, she rarely visited. When Sierra was fifteen, Dakota left, enlisting in the Army at the first opportunity. Then it was just Sierra. Sierra with Jed and Marissa. Counting the minutes until she could get away, too.

Not long after they all left her she discovered beer and pot.

The Crossing, the place where Cal had found his woman and his second chance, did not look anything like Sierra had expected. It was a completely uninhabited campground. Little dirt pads were separated by trees, the foliage just beginning to turn leafy. The sites were dotted with little brick grills here and there. The picnic tables were all lined up by the side of a big old store with a wide porch that stretched the length of the building. There was a woman sweeping the porch—had to be Maggie. She stopped sweeping, stared at them, smiled and leaned her broom against the wall. She descended the steps just as they got out of the little car.

"Sierra!" she said, opening her arms.

"How did you know?"

She hugged her and then held her away to look at her. "You couldn't be anyone else. You belong to your brother as if you were his twin. Maybe I'll have a daughter and she'll look exactly like you."

Sierra blushed. "Would that be a good thing?"

"That would be perfect," Maggie said.

Difficulties strengthen the mind, as well as labor does

the body.

—SENECA

Chapter 2

SIERRA LEARNED SHE'D ARRIVED AT THE CROSS-
ing in the middle of some serious cleanup. A skinny old guy
named Frank was cleaning and stocking shelves; his wife, Enid,
was giving the kitchen and pantry a good scouring; Sully was
cleaning the rain gutters and when he was done with that he'd
begin repairing and painting picnic tables. Maggie was going
to hose down the porch, and then she was intent on raking up
the patch of garden behind the house so they could get planting.

But everything stopped when Sierra arrived. They gathered
on the porch. A table was wiped off, warm buns and hot coffee
were brought out for a little visiting, getting to know Sierra.

"Don't you do too much," Cal said to Maggie. "Just take care
of the bump."

"We don't let her do too much," Enid said.

"I got my eye on her," Sully said.

"Don't know what all the fuss is about," Frank said. "Women
been doin' it since Eve. Exercise is good for her. What?" he asked
when he noticed everyone was glaring at him. "I just speak the
damn truth!"

"That's a first," Maggie said. "I agree with Frank."

"And I bet Frank just stays in trouble, don't you, Frank?"
Sierra said.

"Young woman, I been working like a farmhand every day it don't rain," Frank informed her.

"'Bout damn time," Sully said. "Tom Canaday is rounding up some boys from that county road crew he works with. Some fellas who need a little extra cash and can bring their own equipment. They'll give the grounds a good grooming, clean out my trench for the runoff from the snowpack melt and cart off some heavy trash when they leave. I can fix and paint the picnic tables, spruce up the lavatory, showers and laundry room. And while the yard crew is here, I'll get 'em to till up that garden."

"I always thought running a campground would be easier than this," Sierra said.

"Mud season," Maggie informed her. "When the snow melts and the rain plagues us, there's a lot to do to restore the place before the campers start showing up again. We're coming up on spring break and Easter weekend and from Memorial Day through summer, it's full almost all the time."

"Maybe I can help out," Sierra said.

All eyes turned to her. It was quite a while before Sully spoke. "Could you use a little extra money, girl?"

"I was thinking of being helpful," she said. "I have a job, but it's only part-time. I'm happy about that—I want some time to explore and...you know...get settled in. I'd be happy to help out."

"That's very sweet," Maggie said. "Are you going to stay with Cal and me?"

"In the construction zone?" she asked. "Thanks, but I have a place."

"Oh?" three people said at once.

"A hostel in town," she said. "It's very nice. It's next to a bookstore. It's across from the diner, where I'm going to work a few mornings a week."

"Midge Singleton's place?" Sully asked.

"That's it," Sierra said.

Sully leaned forward. "Girl, that woman will stack bodies end on end, stuff as many people as she can in that place."

"It seems decent enough. She seems very nice," Sierra said defensively.

"I didn't say she wasn't nice," Sully said. "I've known Midge over thirty years. She opened up that place when her husband died a long while back and she means to make a good living on it. You got extra beds in your room?"

"Just one," Sierra said. "For a female in my general age range. She promised to let me have the room alone as long as she could and that's just how a hostel works. I'd like to think she means that..."

"I'd like to think that, too," Cal grumbled.

"Here's another option," Sully said. "You go ahead and try that hostel, but watch your stuff. Let Midge lock things up for you—she'll do that. If you don't like it so much, I have empty cabins. There's a shower and bathroom in each one."

"That's awful nice, but—"

"You can have one of 'em if you want," Sully said. "I ain't gonna put another camper in your bed with you, no matter how full up we get."

Cal laughed and Maggie winced. "What's the rent on one of those cabins?" Sierra asked.

"Well, let me think," he said. He rubbed the back of his neck. "Bathroom needs regrouting. Picnic tables need paint. Porch on the store and at the house need sealer painted on. Garden needs work and tending. And there's stocking daily in the store. Fifteen or twenty or so hours should cover a week. Easy. Then there's always the rumpus room, which is free. But you'd have to share a bathroom with an old man."

"Rumpus room?" she asked.

"Our old apartment," Cal said. "It's in the basement. The pipes clang sometimes but it's comfortable. And no roommates."

They visited for almost two hours when Sierra noticed that

Sully was getting a little fidgety. Very likely he wasn't used to sitting around, swilling coffee and yakking. "I think it's about time I got Cal back to the barn and to work or Maggie will never get her house. And, Sully, give me a couple of days to figure out my schedule and the town and I'll come around to lend a hand."

"I'm capable if you have better things to do," he said, standing up from the table and giving his jeans a yank up into place.

Out of habit, Sierra picked up cups and napkins along with Maggie, carting them back to the kitchen. She stopped to look around a little bit, intrigued by the supplies that ranged from food to ropes to tools. There was even a bookshelf full of second-hand books.

"This place is a popular stop off for campers and hikers," Maggie said. "Through-hikers who have taken on the Continental Divide Trail count on this place to restock and rest for a day or two. There's even a post office—they can pick up mail here."

"Are there a lot of them?" Sierra asked.

"All summer," Maggie said. "They're amazing. It's quite a conquest, the CDT."

"Is it a long trail?"

"It's 3,100 miles from Mexico to Canada."

Sierra gasped. "Are you *kidding* me?"

Maggie shook her head. "It's a pretty interesting group that passes through here in summer—everyone from hikers and rock climbers to families camping for vacation. There are quite a few RVs and fifth wheels here from spring through fall—lots of people enjoying the wildflowers and then later, the autumn foliage. It's a beautiful place."

"You're so lucky to have grown up here," Sierra said.

"I didn't grow up here. My parents divorced when I was only six. I didn't see my dad for years, then only as a visitor. I lived for some time here. I've always loved this place. And now, I'm going to raise a family here." She absently ran a hand over her stomach.

"Pretty soon, too," Sierra observed. "I hope you get the barn remodeled in time."

"Hopefully before the first snowfall on both. I'm going to have to make sure Cal gets a plow..."

Sierra went back to Timberlake and continued her exploration of the town. The hostel was right next door to The Little Colorado Bookstore and, like everyone in the Jones family, she felt the promise of books pulling her in. Books had always been their salvation, their only means of learning while they traveled, the only real entertainment they had.

This store was tiny and packed to the rafters, specializing in books about Colorado—livestock and ranching, wildlife, history, mining, plants, crops, insects, anything and everything Colorado and its history, including lots of maps. They also carried fiction pertinent to the state. She learned that it wasn't a busy store, but the customers were steady. The owners were the Gibsons—Ernie and Bertrice, a couple in their fifties. They were more than eager to tell her all about the store, founded by Ernie's father a long while back. They liked to work the weekends when tourists were around because they were experts on both the state and the merchandise.

They also did a big mail-order business—people contacted them from all over the world to find specialty books and other collectible volumes, valuable maps and papers that the owners had curated over the years.

The store had four leather armchairs spaced around the stacks where people would sit to page through special books and there was a long table in the back of the store where patrons could look at maps or loose papers. She noticed a man tucked back in a corner with a big book of maps balanced on his lap. He must have been in his fifties or maybe older, but he had a familiar look about him. His hair was sparse on top but he had a ponytail. He wore a T-shirt with a peace symbol on it, the popular local fashion of khaki shorts, hiking boots with white socks and a pair of glasses balanced on his nose. With a start she realized he looked a little like her father, at least in style—he had that aging hippie aura about him.

Growing up with Jed had been filled with challenges, but Sierra loved him deeply. He was like a lost boy at times and while he could go off on manic delusions for days on end—complex theatrics in which he was the star physicist or inspired prophet—she had always found him amazing. She was a teenager before she understood that inside his mind must be a maze of confusion. But Jed had always been a gentle man. They were all so lucky that way. He was nonviolent and, if you ignored the fact that his behavior was crazy as a loon, highly functional. And he was sweet to Sierra. She was the baby of the family and Jed and Cal both doted on her. It was kind of magical in a way. Jed was nuts and Cal was like the white knight, always making sense out of chaos.

The man in the chair looked up at her. *Grumpy.* So Sierra did what she did best—she smiled at him. He smirked but she knew she had melted him a little bit. Since she was a little girl she'd known how to charm her way out of a bad situation.

She walked around town a little bit, stopping in at the diner for a midafternoon ice cream. She chatted with the waitress Lola, a fortyish woman with two kids. Lola had been working in that diner for years—when she was married with small children, when she was divorced and a single mother, now still single, working two jobs and trying to finish her education by going to school part-time. Lola gave Sierra the gossip on the diner—what the boss was like, which fry cooks were dependable, who on the kitchen crew would back her up. She also told her where to buy the khaki shorts and white golf shirts that would be her uniform at the diner.

Sierra wandered the town after that, dropping in at the drugstore, checking out the small grocery. She noted two law offices, a small storefront clinic, a hair salon and barbershop. There was a furniture store—custom designs. There were three small art galleries, one liquor store, one jewelry store, a bank, a consignment shop that tied up some time as she browsed, two churches and the fire department. The guys were washing down one of the rigs in the drive—nice eye candy. The police department was just across the street from the fire department.

The next day she drove to Leadville to buy her uniform and spent the day looking around that town. She found a bigger bookstore and a great little grill that served wonderful burgers. She then drove out to the barn to check in with Cal who was up to his eyebrows in what appeared to be crown molding. There was a lot of hammering and sawing going on upstairs and Cal was painting the molding. She told him all about Timberlake and Leadville as if he didn't know for himself. Maggie came back from Sully's, dirty from gardening, and informed Sierra she would be joining them for dinner, then went off to shower and change.

The next few hours proceeded like a beautifully choreographed dance. Sierra ran the Shop-Vac around while Cal cleaned up his paintbrushes and folded up the tarps. Tom and his son came downstairs covered with sawdust and Sierra laughingly vacuumed them off. Tom and Cal had a beer, and some corn chips and salsa were put out. Sierra had a Diet Coke with Jackson while Maggie, refreshed, fixed herself orange juice. Cal began to putter in the kitchen getting chicken ready to put on the grill. Tom and Jackson left and the three of them were like a small, cordial family. Maggie told Sierra to be sure to check on Cal while she was in Denver working. The dinner of chicken and vegetables, casually thrown together, was delicious and nutritious. Then the dishes were cleaned up. It was like the fantasies Sierra had. Fantasies of a family, of feeling normal, of belonging.

She watched as Cal was kissing Maggie's neck and rubbing

her belly. Then she remembered it wasn't really hers. It was their life and she was a guest.

Sierra borrowed trouble and darkness. It was a bad habit. A dirty little secret she kept. *Deep inside you're very lonely and unhappy*, her inner voice reminded her.

"I have to get going," she said. "Thanks for dinner and everything."

"Don't run off," Maggie said.

"Don't you have to get up early and head for Denver?" Sierra asked.

"Not that early," she said.

"Get some sleep," Sierra said. "I'll see you in a few days."

As she drove back to Timberlake she asked herself, *Can I make this work? Must I always feel like some weird outsider?* She knew that Cal and Maggie weren't doing that to her.

When she got back to town, still early in the evening, there seemed to be a lot of activity in the hostel. Sure enough, a group of young girls had come in and they were loud. There was lots of laughing, shouting, talking at the top of their voices. She got to her room and saw a duffel on the second bed in her room, but the rambunctious girls were just a room or two away. Well, Sierra wasn't going to undress for bed in that case. Most of her belongings were in her car and she had only her backpack with her. She'd go back to her car in the morning for fresh clothing and shower and change then. This was the downside of staying in a hostel—it was a busy young people's kind of place and one traded privacy for cheap housing.

She sat on her bed and dug around in her backpack for something to read. Out in the car she had several books on recovery that were nearly memorized by now. She didn't feel like that tonight. She pulled out her copy of *Pride and Prejudice*. It was battered all to hell. Sierra carried three novels—*Pride and Prejudice, Forever Amber* and *Gone with the Wind*. That pretty much established her as a tragic but hopeful romantic. It had been hard to leave *Wuthering Heights* behind and that was telling. No happy endings for Sierra. Not yet.

The noise escalated and Sierra hoped someone would complain. Mrs. Singleton didn't stay the night in the hostel—she had her own small house in town. The young man who was left in charge for the night was pretty social; he might not mind the noise. Or the girls. When Sierra had checked in there were no single rooms and Mrs. Singleton said that chances were good no one would need a bed in a double and if anyone did, it would most certainly only be let to a woman.

She opened her book, midway, hungry for a little of Mr. Darcy's evolution from aloof snob into a real hero. She put her smartphone on one of her music downloads, her earbuds in her ears and settled in to ignore the noise of girls having fun. She didn't last long. Less than an hour passed when she went downstairs and told John, the young man in charge, he'd have to do something about the noise.

"I've talked to them a couple of times," he said. "College girls. I don't want to ask them to leave if I can avoid it."

A little bit later one of the girls stumbled into the room. She looked about eighteen. And she was drunk.

"Roomie!" she greeted with a slur.

"Crap," Sierra said. "You're drunk!"

"Jes a little," she said, then hiccuped. She held out a fifth of whiskey. "Wanna little?"

Before Sierra could even answer, the girl fell on the bed. Facedown. Dropping the fifth so it spilled onto the rug.

"That's that, then," Sierra said, looking back at her book.

But the girl *stank*. The room smelled of whiskey. And she was, of course, snoring like a freight train. The odds were good she'd end up sick.

Sierra packed up her things. She went downstairs and right out the door without saying a word to John. She'd work it all out later, ask for a refund. Right now she was feeling like this whole idea, all this bloody do-it-alone crap, was the biggest mistake of her life. She was on the verge of tears, but Sierra never cried. She punished herself by holding it fiercely and stoically inside. She could call Cal and Maggie, but she didn't want to. What would they think? That Sierra the emotional cripple was going to hang on to them forever and they'd never be free? That three days in Timberlake and she was falling apart? So much for independence! She'd always be the baby to Cal even though she was thirty and had done some hard living.

She sat on a bench outside the dark barbershop and called her old sponsor and former roommate, Beth. The phone went straight to voice mail. She said, "Just me. Everything is fine." Then she disconnected.

Well, so much for that.

Her phone rang immediately. Beth.

"It's late," Beth said. "What's wrong?"

"I'm just a little screwed up. My head is on wrong. I'm staying in a hostel and got a drunk roommate—she can't be twenty-one. Not that that ever stopped me. But I can't be in that smell. I'm sitting on a bench on the main street of this little, dinky town and the only action is down the street at the only bar and grill and I can't think. I can't move. I don't want this to be a mistake. Maybe I'm not ready. Jesus, it doesn't take much to send me off the rails, I guess."

"When did you last go to a meeting?" Beth asked.

"It's been a while," she said. "I'm not really settled in yet..."

"I guess you're not if you're staying in a hostel. Weren't you going to be with your brother?"

"I never intended to stay with him," Sierra said. "He's just married six months or so and they're pregnant. I'd be in the way. I want to see him a lot, not live with him. I have to figure this out."

"Here's what I want you to do. If there's a meeting tonight—go to it. Then I want you to go to a motel. Worry about money later. Hit the first meeting of the day tomorrow. It might even be a two-meeting day. No more hostel business—you don't want to be living with a bunch of college kids on a vacation bender..."

"The lady said they were strict..."

"Uh-huh," Beth said. "Another thing that never stopped you. Talk to someone at a meeting about a sponsor. You shouldn't fly solo in a new town. You should have someone you can call if only to go for coffee in the next few hours. Are you hungry? Tired?"

"Nothing like that. Just depressed. Why, I have no idea! My brother and sister-in-law pulled me right in, this place is beautiful, some drunk girl stumbled into my bedroom and stank up the place. That's a good reason to be irritated not depressed!"

"We don't need a reason," Beth reminded her. "Find a safe, warm place tonight and call me in the morning. Find a meeting."

"I will," Sierra said.

"I'll wait while you look," Beth said.

Sierra gave a heavy sigh. She checked her phone app—a meeting locater. She did a little clicking. "Looks like I missed the last one...ten o'clock in Leadville, a thirty-minute drive. Midnight meeting in Denver—a long drive. But there's a seven o'clock in the morning. I hate being the new kid."

Beth laughed. "Come on, there's a long list of things to hate."

"I want to be strong," Sierra said.

Beth laughed again. "Good luck with that. That one never works."

We don't pray for control, Sierra recited silently. *We are powerless.*

"Think you can make that early one in the morning?"

"Yeah. Sure."

"Can you find a place to stay?"

"Yeah, there are places around. And there's always my brother. One night wouldn't kill him."

"Or you?"

"Or me," she said. "Okay, I think I have a handle on it now..."

Beth asked her to recite exactly what she was going to do. The little grocery was still open. She'd get some snacks, maybe a premade sandwich if they had some. Chips and a soda, maybe a cupcake or something. She'd find a warm, safe place to stay for the night, hit an early meeting, but by morning she'd feel a lot better and have a good plan.

It was amazing to her how fast that feeling of hopelessness could come over her. It was usually like this, a stack of relatively small issues—being the third person at a table, the odd one; her brother kissing his new wife and the envy she had that he had somehow managed to rebuild his life. She suddenly thought, *I will never have that.* Then the noise of partying in the hostel; the drunk girl. Any one or even two of those things wouldn't have screwed up her head. Sierra was, if anything, resilient. She knew how to hunker down, breathe deeply, offer up a prayer or two, get through it. She worried that maybe she was given to some mental illness. Not the same as Jed's—she didn't have imaginary friends. But she believed she leaned toward depression.

She'd voiced that in a meeting once and at least five people said, *Duh.*

Impossible as it was for her to comprehend, she was still grieving the loss of her crutch, her best friend, her savior. Of course that crutch broke under her weight, that friend betrayed her, the savior cast her into hell.

She pulled her sleeping bag out of the trunk and put it in the pumpkin's small backseat. Then she went to the grocery; they were just closing up so she turned on her fake smile and begged a favor, a few snacks if she could be quick.

"Got the munchies?" the clerk asked snidely.

A huff of laughter escaped her. "I'm not high!" she said, incredulous. "I'm staying at the hostel and there's nothing to eat!"

"Make it quick," he said. Clearly, he did not believe her.

"Sorry for the inconvenience," she said, heading for a refrigerated section that contained a few deli items. She grabbed a sandwich, a couple of hard-boiled eggs, a large Kosher pickle, and added a soda and bag of chips on her way out. As an after-thought, she added a couple of candy bars. She wasn't even hungry, but she'd be damned if she'd be caught with nothing on hand. Just having some supplies made her feel more secure. There was no way she was going to Cal and Maggie, though she knew they'd be happy to find her a space. It was so important to her that Cal and Maggie think she had it together.

She decided to go to the Crossing. That Sully, he seemed like a pretty simple, straightforward guy. He wasn't too deep or complicated, she could see that. And it was a campground. She'd camp. It wasn't too cold, given her sweatshirt and sleeping bag. Her flashlight was charged, she had food and drink, there was a public bathroom… She'd snuggle up in the backseat, read her book and snack and if she ran into any trouble, like a bear or something, she could outrun it in the pumpkin. Or she could lay on the horn until Sully woke up.

That's right, Sierra. Wake up a little old man to fight off your bear.

But nothing would go wrong. In the morning she'd just tell him the hostel filled up with college kids and she wasn't the partying kind. She was more the kind to have a quiet and private night. Best to ask about that cabin; she'd be more than happy to work around the Crossing for a room.

Her first surprise was that she could even find the Crossing—it was awfully dark on these back country roads. It was after ten and she didn't pass a single car. Fortunately there was a bright moon and Sully had some lights on at the grounds. There were a couple of small campers and a car parked by one of the cabins and even in the dark she could see progress had been made on the cleanup in just a matter of days.

She parked right between the store and Sully's house where he would see her car first thing. She didn't want to shock or worry the old guy. Then she crawled into the backseat, snuggled into her sleeping bag and looked at her phone. She still had plenty of charge for the night. She pulled out her nifty little book light that fit around her neck like a necklace shining in front of her. Her bag of groceries sat on the car floor on one side of the bump, her open backpack on the other. If nature called in the night the light on her cell phone would get her to the loo.

She pulled out *Pride and Prejudice* again. Just like her other favorite romances, the hero was very masculine and a little cruel. Just like real life, Sierra-style.

Her throat hurt a little as she fought the release of tears. She denied herself tears. It was her penance for all her sins—the pain of holding in the tears. Someday, when she'd suffered enough, she imagined the floodgates would open and she'd cry till she drowned. But not tonight. She drank some soda to take the ache away. It wasn't long before she nodded off in her book, cozy as a bug in a rug.

She was roused in what seemed like seconds by a tapping on her window. Startled, she woke to see Sully tapping with his flashlight. It was still dark. Was he frowning? Beau, the yellow Lab, had his forelegs up on the door, panting excitedly. Beau seemed to be smiling. She opened the window a crack.

"Coffee's on," Sully said. He walked into the store.

The keenest sorrow is to recognize ourselves as the sole cause of all our adversities.

—Sophocles

Chapter 3

SIERRA TOOK A BRIEF DETOUR THROUGH THE bathroom, backpack over one shoulder. She washed her face, brushed her teeth and ran a brush through her hair.

She wondered if Sully was angry. It was a campground, after all.

She wandered into the store. In the back was the kitchen and a short breakfast bar with just three stools. Sully stood behind the bar, which also served as the checkout point for purchases. He was staring into a steaming cup of coffee. Behind him at the back door Beau was inhaling his breakfast in great, greedy gulps, tail wagging.

Sierra climbed up on a stool a little sheepishly. Quiet.

Sully took a swallow of his coffee, then slowly turned toward the little kitchen. He brought her a cup of coffee, then pushed the cream and sugar toward her.

"You mad?" she asked.

He didn't look at her. "Ain't worth a damn before my coffee."

"Ah," she said. So she left him to it. She stirred some cream and sugar into her cup and took a slow, luxurious sip. Excellent coffee, she thought. It would be slightly more excellent if the sun was at least up. Maybe if they became friends she could point out to him that he might like the morning better if he slept until the sun at least began to rise. As for herself, it was as she had predicted. She felt fresh and new. Apparently her demons decided to sleep in.

"How's your neck?" Sully asked.

"My neck? It's fine. Why?"

"You were sleeping like a pretzel. Wasn't it a little cold?"

"Nah, I was toasty. I had my sweatshirt on and my sleeping bag is great. I wouldn't have slept in the car if it was predicted to freeze."

"You Joneses," he said. "You really know how to make do."

She laughed. "You were right about Mrs. Singleton's hostel. It filled up with college girls who were oh-so-happy to be on a vacation. They were loud. And I scored a roommate—surprise, surprise. She was drunk and passed out on the bed. I used to be a lot more flexible."

"That so?" he asked.

In for a penny, in for a pound, she decided. She was going to be asking for a cabin if he proved tractable. And he was Cal's father-in-law. "Well, specifically, I was usually the one who passed out. Sobriety is kind of...startling. And at times inconvenient." She took another sip. "You know about me, right?"

"Know what about you?" he said, refilling his half-empty cup.

She told him her story, the abbreviated version. She was a recovering alcoholic, sober nine months. She'd been reunited with Cal while she was still in rehab, right before Cal and Maggie got married. She was in AA, the second A standing for *anonymous*. "But I figured Cal would have mentioned something about me," she added.

"Not a lot," Sully said.

She gave a short unamused laugh. "Someday I'm going to learn to play my cards close to my vest like that. Did you or didn't you know?" she asked directly.

"He mentioned you were in the hospital and he wanted to

visit you before he and Maggie married. I think he wanted to know if you inherited your father's malady. The mental illness."

"I wanted to know that, too. I didn't."

"I guess that's lucky, eh?"

"It's not too late," she said.

"That so? And how old was your dad when he succumbed?" Sully asked.

"As close as we can figure out, he was in his early twenties. But he had some symptoms he and everyone around him tried to ignore. Like he was... Well, he was brilliant. I think under his schizophrenia he's still brilliant. It's just all twisted up."

"Your brother seems pretty smart. Is it possible those two things aren't really connected?"

"Huh?" she asked.

"The smart and the crazy?" Sully asked.

She just shrugged. She'd asked herself that a lot. Because it was horrible to be afraid of intelligence, especially one's own intelligence.

"I got the feeling they aren't the same thing—smart and crazy. There's some autistic kids from a group home come around in the summer. Not a one of 'em could pass an IQ test of any kind and some of 'em are just downright brilliant. You know? Memories like steel traps, math skills you wouldn't believe, musical talents that knock me over. They're a hoot, you should know 'em."

"Do you know them?" she asked.

"Some," he said. "I get on with the autistic kids just fine. That's probably because I ain't all that smart to start with but I have a talent or two. Not like them, that's for sure. We open the grounds up to some youth groups now and then. You just don't know how trapped they feel till you see 'em on the trails or in the lake—they cut loose." Then he grinned in a way that showed the pure joy in him.

And Sierra fell in love. Right then.

"Who told you you weren't all that smart?" she asked him.

The smile stayed. "Girl, no one had to tell me. More coffee?"

"No, this is good enough. I don't want to get the wiggles. Listen, about that cabin…"

"It's all cleaned up and ready for you," he said. "I knew you'd come around. Besides, I think this place helps."

"Helps what?"

He looked reluctant to answer. "I don't know—helps what ails you. I see it happen all the time and people need all different things. Your brother, for example. I had no idea what he needed but he hung around, made himself useful now and again even before I needed a hand. And eventually he stole my daughter right out from under my nose. It worked for me, way back when I came home after the war. Course it took a while before I managed to get what I needed. I wasn't that much older than you."

"Oh? I'd love to hear about that," she said.

"Well, I think it's boring to everyone but me. I'll tell you one or two things if you'll eat a sticky bun."

"Deal," she said, smiling.

"Let me fetch one and put it in the microwave," he said. "It's better warm."

He took a moment to do that. Then he took her cup away and refilled it anyway, bringing the coffee and pastry to her.

"My grandpa built this place. He left it to my dad. My dad planned to leave it to me. I didn't have much interest in it, to be honest. I had bigger plans. But my dad needed me home, I could see that. My mother died while I was in Vietnam and the Red Cross got me home for that but it wasn't till I was in my thirties that I found a wife and brought her back here. But she was a terrible wife and I was an even worse husband. In spite of that, we had Maggie. It took six years before my wife got fed up and left me." He raised a thick, graying eyebrow. "Bored yet?"

She licked icing off her fingers and shook her head.

"She took Maggie. I'm the first to admit I was crap for a father. I sulked, yelled, wandered off without a word sometimes, argued over anything, didn't know beans about school lessons or homework, had no patience, drank too much whenever I got irritated and I got irritated pretty often. I had a tone of voice, I'm told, that would scare bears off. I treated my dogs better than my family and it made no sense because I loved my family. Well...well, the truth is, I didn't love Phoebe all that much after the first few months. But then, she didn't love me much, either. We were wrong for each other from the start. I brood while she fusses. She needles and I yell. Then I sat out here in the store and drank until she was asleep.

"But I loved Maggie and I wanted to do right by her. So I had to start my life over. I reckon you have some experience with that, eh?"

Sierra nodded and licked the sweet icing off her lips. "How'd you do it?"

"The hard way. I fished a lot, worked till I dropped, suffered in silence, forced myself to do things I had no use for like making a bed and washing clothes. It was one thing to keep up the grounds for the customers—even I wasn't too stupid to know I needed money to eat. But taking care of myself? Cleaning my own surroundings? That took willpower. It was a pretty horrible process. But there were some things I had to do if I'd ever have my family back." He rubbed a hand along the back of his neck. "I wasn't too keen on having Phoebe back. Jesus, that woman's the biggest pain in the ass. But I thought maybe if there was a God she'd get hit by a bus or something and Maggie would come back. I was bound to be ready if that happened. I tried to read." He laughed at himself. "I was never gonna be as smart as Maggie or even that damn Phoebe but I was determined not to be a complete dunce." He took a drink of his coffee. "I hung up the beer mug. No fanfare, no meetings, no bugles or drumroll. Just retired the mug."

She swallowed. "Are you a friend of Bill W.'s?"

"How's that?" Sully asked.

"Are you an alcoholic?"

"Hell if I know," he said. "It probably depends on who you ask. I didn't have a thing to drink for years, then I had a beer on a hot day and old Frank, he said I was a damn fool to even think about it. When I was a younger man I drank too much now and then...more than now and then. I was certainly headed for trouble. It was only a matter of time and I knew it. Nowadays I have limits. What I learned—what I wanted to tell you about—I learned I didn't have to go through all the agony I went through, and I'm not talking about liquor."

"What are you talking about?" she asked. What she wanted to ask was, "What does this have to do with me?"

"I didn't have to do it all alone," he said. "No matter who reached out to me, offered a hand, pulled up a chair to talk a spell, I froze 'em out and went my own way. It was every bit as terrible as I hoped it would be. I wanted to suffer, I guess."

"But you and Maggie are together now..."

"It took a few years before I was in good enough shape to see her, to take care of her. She's still pissed about that, by the way." Then he laughed. "She's a pistol. I guess she comes by it naturally. According to Maggie I didn't fight for her. What she'd want with a father like me, I have no idea. But by the time Phoebe let her come to visit I'd laid most of my ghosts to rest."

"How?" she wanted to know. "If you didn't go to rehab or meetings or counseling or—"

"Did I say I never went to meetings or counseling?" Sully asked. "Maybe not the same ones you go to. There's a group of Vietnam vets that look out for each other. That's where I first met Frank and I ain't got shed of him since! We try to do some nice things for the community, keep an eye out for our brothers. When I found out I was part of a group, things got better. Easier. Just so you know, little girl, you're part of a group. You got people here."

Sierra felt that raw scrape in her throat again and took another drink of her coffee to soothe it.

"And another thing—you got the land," Sully said. "Now I'll be the first to admit, I tend to take it for granted, but you get out there on the trail a little bit and you pray to whatever entity you want, whatever great being made these mountains and forests and I'm not kidding, answers come. I didn't just make it up. All these lunatics that march through here all summer while they're taking on as much of the CDT as they can manage will tell you the same. Your brother did that, didn't he." It wasn't a question. "He got out on the trail and had a little nature, then he was square. His head wasn't a corkscrew anymore."

"Sully," she said, laughing, maybe inappropriately. "He was looking for a beautiful place to let his wife's ashes go."

"He musta found it because he snatched up my daughter the minute he got back."

"You're not unhappy about that, are you?" she asked.

"Hell no. Those two are giving me a grandchild! If you want the truth, the last man Maggie got herself involved with, I actually *feared* what it might be if they had a child together!"

"I can't wait to hear that story," she said.

"That one ain't mine to tell," he said.

"Something tells me you'd take pleasure in it," she said, finishing the last of her sticky pastry and licking her fingers.

"The thing that irritated me the most about Maggie's last fella, he didn't seem to take any notice of how lucky he was that Maggie gave him the time of day. Arrogant fool. I bet he's suffering now."

Sierra grinned. "Despite what you say, I bet you were a wonderful father."

"I'd like to meet your parents," Sully said.

"*My* parents?" she asked. "Oh, Sully. Hasn't Cal told you about Jed and Marissa? They raised us mostly in a converted school bus! On the road. Sometimes we picked vegetables to make ends meet. We hardly went to school. Jed has a serious screw loose.

Last time I saw him he was wearing an aluminum foil beanie on his head. He was the first person to give me a joint!"

"Yet the lot of you came up good. I met your other brother and your sister at the wedding. How do you suppose the lot of you managed to be so normal? And smart?"

She shrugged. "Aside from Cal, maybe we're not. Sedona is so controlling we can't visit longer than two days and Dakota—no one knows Dakota. He's been to war so many times, he's gotta have some serious issues. Then there's me..." She decided to take another drink of her coffee rather than expound.

"You're a little hard on yourself," he said. "That's okay, I understand that. But put that on your list of things to work out—what you got in your childhood to prepare you for this life. And, what you might do to give yourself a break."

Sierra wanted to sit at that lunch counter and visit with Sully all morning, but she had made commitments. She promised to call Beth, for one thing. She met Beth in recovery and asked her to be her sponsor. Beth had five years under her belt but that was about all they had in common. Beth was forty-five, had two teenage sons, *Talk about a reason to drink!*, a mean ex-husband, a large extended family and her parents were elderly but healthy and active. When Sierra finally decided to move to Colorado, she and Beth talked about staying in touch, at least for a while, but Sierra had promised to find a sponsor in her new home.

There was a meeting in Leadville at seven. It was being held in a rec center and when she arrived, she read the marquee at the front door for the room number. There was also a sleeve of pamphlets that listed all the classes and activities for the center. AA, yoga, Pilates, water aerobics and a variety of other things. There were groups and classes for all ages all day long but in the evenings there was a veritable smorgasbord of support—solo parenting, grief group, singles, nicotine anonymous, AA, Al-Anon and Alateen.

She could smell the coffee. One thing about AA, the setting was almost always familiar—the folding chairs, the podium, the big box of doughnuts next to the disposable coffee cups. She was a little early and there were only a few people milling around. One of them was that sourpuss from the bookstore, so she smiled at him again. His expression softened only slightly, but he approached her.

"I don't think we've met," he said. "I'm Moody."

"I'm so sorry," she said. "Didn't you sleep well?"

"My name is Moody," he said, clearly unamused.

Well, that would explain things. His mother named him Moody and he spent the rest of his life living down to it. She put out her hand. "Sierra," she said. "I'm new in town. Well, not this town. I live near Timberlake, which is how I saw you in the bookstore."

"How long have you been around here?" he asked.

"Just a few days, but I found a job at that diner across from the bookstore. My brother and sister-in-law are nearby and I was ready for a change. I lived in Iowa."

"Coffee?" he asked. "Doughnut?"

"I'm about coffee'd out already," she said. "I'll just sit down and wait till the meeting gets started." A few more people were straggling in. "Have you been coming to this meeting long?"

"Long," he said. "Anything I can tell you about it?"

She shrugged. "I'm pretty familiar with the program. I'm nine months sober," she said.

"Good for you!" he said. His expression became more open, but he was stuck with that dour countenance. "I'm happy for you," he added. "You're young. Would you like to meet a few people?"

"Maybe after," she said, noticing still more people entering the room. "Thanks, though. That's nice of you."

She had hoped this might be a small meeting, five or six people. By the time Moody was ready to begin, there were at least thirty. He had his agenda, typed in large print and slipped between protective plastic sleeves—even that seemed almost universal. They had a prayer, recited the steps, called out to newcomers. Sierra jumped up, just to get it out of the way. She still hated this part. "My name is Sierra," she said.

"Hi, Sierra," they said in unison.

"I just moved to the area, looking for a meeting, just meeting people." She explained she was in recovery nine months and they clapped for her. There were a few comments—this meeting was a good one before work, they called themselves The Sunny Side Up.

There were two more newcomers—a woman about fifty, fresh out of rehab, a guy about thirty, here by court order and needing thirty days of signed chits. And then a guy stood up and said his name was Mark. He didn't add that he was an alcoholic but Sierra thought, *We have a winner!* His coloring was pale with splotches, he was trembling, his eyes were red and watering. He was a little stooped—his gut hurt. Chances were good he was just coming off a bender. They were going to corral him right after the meeting, she bet. Nothing more was required of him, just that he listen. And he might bolt, but they were already on to him. Something might've happened to get him to a meeting. His wife might've finally left him, he could've lost his job or spent one too many nights in jail. He didn't look like he'd been in a fight. Just real hungover. As usual, she asked herself if she'd ever looked that bad.

When the meeting was over, people scattered pretty fast. This was, after all, a before-work meeting—convenient. She met a couple of women who welcomed her and told her they hoped she'd join them again and she said she probably would, but she wasn't sure of anything except one thing—she was going to scope out the locations and times of the meetings around her so she wasn't searching for one when she absolutely needed one.

Maybe she'd come again. She liked moody Moody for no apparent reason. He might be grumpy but he seemed steady.

She went to Cal's to explain her new living space and, predictably, he was thrilled to hear she'd be staying at the Crossing.

The next morning she got up extra early knowing Sully would be up, but instead of rushing off to a meeting, she hung around at the breakfast bar until Enid and Frank showed up. After visiting with them for a while, she did a little cleanup in the store, then headed for the garden.

After two hours in the garden she took a nap, read her book for a while, washed some of her clothes and offered to cook Sully's dinner. And she thought, *My God, this is living.* There was no television in her cabin, but Sully offered his if she wanted to watch TV. "Just lock the door when you go home," he said.

"I'm surprised you lock doors around here," she said.

"I forget most of the time. But lock yours. Every now and again we get a bad apple. Last spring Maggie shot a lowlife who'd kidnapped a girl."

"Really?" she asked, astonished and impressed.

"I'll tell you about that sometime when we run out of stories..."

She didn't think they'd ever run out of stories!

Cal and Maggie were around the Crossing a little bit on the weekend, Maggie more than Cal. Cal worked on making a home every day.

Then came Monday morning and her new job began early. The diner didn't open until seven but she was required to be there at six thirty to set up. There was training for her, but she'd waitressed on and off so many times over the years, very little instruction was required. There were several early customers who she learned were mostly locals or business owners and workers from the town and a bit later, a few tourists. It was steady but not what she'd call busy. There was competition off the highway and in surrounding towns—bigger places like Applebee's and Denny's.

And then at eleven who should come in but Moody. Just the sight of him had her beaming as though she loved him. Someday she'd figure out what it was about her and slightly mean men. *Slightly* if she couldn't find a really mean one! She couldn't put this on her brothers or father. Jed Jones might be nuts but he was sweet. Vulnerable. And the boys had always been kind, to women especially.

"Isn't this a surprise," she said to Moody.

"You aren't hard to track down," he said, sitting at the counter. "Coffee?"

"No, thanks," she said. "I'm pretty coffee'd out. Oh! Do *you* want coffee?"

"You're very funny, aren't you?" he asked, not cracking a smile.

"To some people," she said, grabbing a mug from under the counter. She poured him a cup. "Anything to eat? Breakfast? Lunch?"

"Nah. Just the coffee."

She took a breath. "You were tracking me down?"

He took a sip. "No, not really. But then I realized you told me where you worked and I come by here sometimes. I thought I'd let you know—there's a meeting here in town. Seven on Thursday nights at the church. I go sometimes, depending what's going on."

"Is that early meeting your home meeting?" she asked.

"I get up early. I like getting it out of the way."

"Is this a house call?" she asked, teasingly.

"We don't make house calls," he said. "We do reach out sometimes, but if you ask me not to—"

"It's okay," she said. "It's very nice, in fact."

"Then I'll take a chance and ask you if there's anything you need. I've been around here a long time. And I've been in the program a long time."

She'd heard at the meeting. "Thirty years," she said. "That's a long time, all right. Either you were pretty young or you're pretty old."

There was the glimmer of a smile, but it was small and showed no teeth. "Both."

"Either you know the ropes by now or you've been a real tough case."

This time he did show teeth. He even gave a huff of laughter. "Both," he said again. "Think you'll be around awhile?"

"I hope so," she said. "My brother and his wife are expecting. I wouldn't want to miss that. But this was a leap of faith. It's quite a change. A beautiful change, but still..."

"You staying with your brother, then?" he asked.

She shook her head. "My sister-in-law's dad owns a campground just outside of town and he loaned me a cabin. So I have a place of my own but I'm kind of with family at the same time. It's private, but..."

He lifted his eyebrows. "Sully's place?"

"You know Sully?" she asked.

"I think everyone knows Sully. Maggie is your sister-in-law?"

"And you know Maggie?"

"Sierra, I live here. In three weeks you'll know everyone."

"And you go to meetings here? In town?"

He nodded. "I think the word is out on me. I don't talk about anyone else's business. You going to stick to Leadville?"

"I don't know. I haven't thought that far ahead. I did notice they have a meeting for everything in Leadville."

"That's for sure," he agreed. "So, you have a place to stay, know where the meetings are, have family around—that can be good or not, depending. Anything you need right now?"

"Not right now," she said. "I'll be looking for a sponsor, but for right now I still have my last sponsor by phone. We talk all the time."

He took out a pen, grabbed a napkin and wrote his name and cell number on it. "While you're checking things out and meeting people, here's my number. Why don't you use it sometime. Check in with me until you get a new sponsor."

"I don't expect to need anything, Moody, but—"

"Then just check in to say hello," he said. "It's a good idea to have an anchor or two. Floating around without connections can be risky."

"Okay, sure," she said, taking the napkin, folding it in half and slipping it in the pocket of her shorts. "But I'll probably see you around."

"How you doing on the steps?"

"Oh, I ran through the steps. I'm spending a little extra time on number eight. And ten—seems like there's an endless amount of accounting."

He sipped his coffee. "Remembering more or admitting more?" he asked. When she didn't answer immediately, he said, "Maybe we'll have coffee after a meeting sometime. Talk about the steps?"

"I thought that might happen after the last meeting but I guess everyone was either rushing off to work…or maybe busy with that guy who was having a hard time. Mark."

"Mark shows up sometimes. I'm always glad to see him," Moody said. And he said nothing more. It was like a contract. These stories were shared in the meeting but nowhere else. Not everyone played by the rules, but they were expected to, nonetheless.

The bell on the door tinkled and in walked Adonis. Well, except he didn't have that black Greek hair. His hair was brown and his eyes so blue she could see them from the door. Sierra felt her heart catch. That meant he must be a bad idea. But the sheer height of him and the girth of his shoulders was almost shattering. His T-shirt was tight over his chest and arms; there was a firefighter's emblem on one pec. She had to concentrate to keep from sighing. She wondered, not for the first time, if absolute beauty was a requirement to be a firefighter.

His eyes twinkled at her. But he said, "Hey, Moody." And he stretched out his hand toward Moody. "How's the weather?"

"It's nice," he grumbled. "But it's bound to turn. Connie, meet a new waitress. Sierra this is Connie. Connie this is Sierra."

"Conrad," he said. "Connie for short. Nice to meet you."

That big, meaty hand swallowed up her small hand.

And she gulped.

Life is thickly sown with thorns, and I know no other remedy than to pass quickly through them. The longer we dwell on our misfortunes, the greater is their power to harm us.

—Voltaire

Chapter 4

SIERRA HAD AN UNFORTUNATE HISTORY OF being involved with men who were not good for her, but a lot of that could be blamed on alcohol. Or maybe she started out with perfectly good men and destroyed the relationships with alcohol. At this point it was pretty irrelevant since there hadn't been a man in her life in a long time. Nor alcohol. The last one, Derek, had been so toxic and dangerous she not only swore off men, she ran to rehab. No one could get to you in rehab. Just the people you put on your list as approved visitors.

She felt the calluses of Connie's strong, large hand, looked into those blue eyes and told herself, *It doesn't really matter who he is—I'm off men*. But she couldn't deny it—there was a tingle as his hand enveloped hers.

"Nice to meet you. Do you prefer Conrad or Connie?"

"Everyone calls me Connie no matter what I might prefer. I haven't seen you around here before."

"I haven't been here long."

"And what miracle had you choose Timberlake?" he asked, smiling. Smiling like a man who thought he might get laid.

"Do you know Cal and Maggie Jones? I'm Cal's sister."

The big man's smile vanished instantly. Nothing like an older brother to make a man rethink his objectives. Funny how that never went away even with age. Sierra was thirty and Cal thirty-eight. You'd think by now a guy wouldn't be intimidated by a big brother, but it was just as well.

"How do you like it around here so far?" he asked. And there was obvious distance in his gaze. His warm blue eyes cooled way down.

"It's great. Amazing, in fact."

"You can't be staying in that barn," he said.

"You're right, I can't, but not because it's an unfinished house. Because I really don't want to live with my brother. They're newlyweds, for one thing. And I'm crazy about Cal, but he's my brother. I lived with him long enough growing up."

Connie laughed. "I've felt that way about my brother. I'm here for an order. A big Caesar salad. You know about that?"

"Oh, that's you? I'll get it."

She'd been told it would be picked up. It was ready in the kitchen. She put it in a bag and rang it up for him. He left with a casual "See you around."

After a few moments passed Moody said, "Want to have coffee sometime when you're not working? Talk about the program a little bit? Go over steps or something? Take each other's pulse?"

Hers was a little amped up at the moment. She focused on Moody. "I was kind of looking for an older woman."

"I get that. You never know. I might be good in the short term."

"I'll keep that in mind. Thanks."

Sierra was off work at two and was scheduled to work at least two mornings a week, no weekends unless one of the other waitresses asked her to cover for them. The weekends, she was told, were busier in the mornings and the tips better so the waitresses who had been there before she was hired wanted those shifts, particularly the students. Her schedule wasn't the least bit taxing; she enjoyed meeting the locals. And of course most people knew her brother and absolutely everyone knew Sully.

Sierra had plenty of time after work to do things, like stop by Cal's to check on the progress at his place, then get back to the Crossing to see what, if anything, she could do to help Sully. Most of the time all he wanted was a little company for dinner, which he sometimes convinced Sierra to make for them. "Just bear in mind, if it ain't bland and tasteless I can't eat it. I have to stay heart healthy. I won't live any longer, it'll just seem longer."

"You're in good hands," she said. "I'm very healthy." *Now*, she thought. And before two weeks had passed, she had Sully nearly addicted to her stir-fry—just chicken, vegetables, broth and some seasoning. She was allowed soy sauce but he was off salt; his indulgence was one drink before bed and she could not join him, of course. It seemed a reasonable trade to her.

Two weeks, though not very long, had revealed some marvelous changes in the land and in Sierra. First of all, she did contact Moody and they did meet for coffee a couple of times. As she learned more about him, she was glad she'd let him talk her into it. Moody's name was Arthur Moody but no one ever addressed him as anything but Moody, including his wife. He was fifty-eight years old, a biology professor at a private university in Aurora and he was admittedly a late bloomer. "I was busy in my twenties when everyone else was trying to get an education and a start in life. My start came later, in my thirties." She could do the math—he had been sober for thirty years. That meant that until the age of twenty-eight he was busy spiraling down.

She went to that Thursday evening meeting in Timberlake. She found a nice group waiting there—small, but significant. One of them was Frank, Enid's husband. Frank was an old-timer, a vet, a man who earned his stripes the hard way. He might've been surprised to see her because he beamed, putting those snazzy false teeth on display for her.

She did not tell her story yet, even though she was starting to feel at home. But she couldn't help thinking about her story. Every day.

★ ★ ★

"What was it, Sierra?" The therapist encouraged her to be honest. "What finally sent you running to rehab?"

"Well, there was an accident. I wasn't driving but it was my car. He was driving. He took me out of a bar, took my keys and was driving me home. He said I was drunk and he was just taking me home. I think he put something in my wine because, seriously, it wasn't that easy for me to get wasted like that. It was still early. I knew we hit something but I didn't see it happen. He stopped the car and looked and got back in and drove away. He said it was a cyclist and he left him there. Left him. Left him to die.

"He told me he called the police and said he was a witness, that he saw a woman driver hit a man and leave him. I didn't hear him call the police. I don't know if he did. I don't know if he hit a man or a tree branch or a dog. I was in and out. He told me what he said. I said, 'But I wasn't driving!' And he said, 'No one will believe you—you have a history.' And then... And then he convinced me. In a brutal way. In a terrifying way. He said I would never tell anyone anything. Or I'd be sorry.

"So I left my car in the airport parking garage and took a bus to the bus depot. I ran. I went to the farm, the only place I could think of. Eventually I went into rehab, a place he couldn't find me. Or even if he found me, he couldn't get to me."

Spring was upon the land and the afternoons were often warm and sunny. Just being at the Crossing was the best part. Sierra enjoyed watching her sister-in-law grow that little baby inside her and it filled her with warm family feelings. Being a part of Cal's new family was precious to her. Cal was intent on working on his renovation but not so much that he couldn't take a few breaks to see his sister. They often sat atop a picnic table by the lake and talked, or they went for a short hike into the thawing hills that surrounded the Crossing.

Tom Canaday stopped by the Crossing sometimes—maybe for a cup of coffee, maybe a beer after work. His son Jackson came by now and then, sometimes with his dad and sometimes to lend a hand. There were firefighters and search and rescue volunteers and rangers who dropped in on Sully because the drinks were cold and the atmosphere friendly and laid-back.

"This place just keeps getting better looking," one of the firefighters Sierra had not yet met said, eyeing her keenly.

"Did I remember to mention Sierra is Cal's little sister?" Sully asked.

There were a few groans in the group. But when Sierra turned her back someone said, "Hell, I can take Cal."

"Be careful of those smoke eaters," Sully said. "They come in two flavors—real gentlemen where women are concerned, or they're dogs. Players. Sometimes it's hard to tell the difference."

"We're safe," she said. "I'm not interested in either type."

Cal and Maggie didn't question Sierra's assertion that she had no room for dating in her life right now. They had other things on their minds. Not only was picking out slabs of stone for countertops giving them fits, they were tending their bump.

"Do we know what we're having yet?" Sierra asked when she noticed a book of baby names sitting out on the picnic table in their great room.

"Not yet. But soon," Maggie said.

"No, I didn't mean boy or girl," she said with a laugh. "I meant state, city or mountain range!"

The Jones kids were named California, Sedona, Dakota and Sierra—in that order. "Hell no," Maggie said. "We'll be changing that trend."

As the month of April drew near and the weather warmed, the wildflowers came out to play and were resplendent. Columbines, daisies, prairie phlox and coppery mallow grew along the paths and carpeted the hillsides. Hikers had begun to show up at the Crossing. Sierra found that—as Sully had promised—her own hikes worked wonders on her frame of mind. The exercise stimulated her and the sunshine renewed her. Freckles had begun to show up across her nose and on her cheeks. The time alone and all the thinking gave her a sense of inner peace. She felt closer to God and she'd had very little training in religion, except for that relatively short period of time her father had believed he was Christ.

As she came around a curve in the path she looked up to see three men climbing the flat face of the hill on one side of the mountain. She moved closer until she could actually hear them—a little talking, a few grunts, the soft whisper of their climbing shoes sliding along the rock face and wedging in. As she got closer still she realized she knew them—Connie, Rafe and Charlie. She'd seen them in town and they'd been around the Crossing a few times. They were from Timberlake Fire and Rescue. She wondered if they were training or playing; they weren't wearing uniforms and there didn't seem to be any fire trucks nearby. But those boys could certainly do lovely things to shorts and muscle shirts.

She watched the clever shifting of their hips to give them lift; the muscles in their calves and arms were like art. Little buckets hung off their belts in the back and they dipped into them for chalk, the sweat running down their necks and backs. My goodness they were a lovely sight, slithering up that rock face, their shorts molding around their beautiful male butts.

She couldn't help herself, she was thinking about sex. She had so much mental and spiritual work to do she wouldn't risk getting screwed up by falling for some guy. But it had been a bloody long time.

The last man in her life, Crazy Derek, should have cured her of all men the way he'd cured her of drinking.

She sat down on a rock to watch them for a while. She was achingly quiet and still lest she make a noise and one of them fell. She was afraid to even drink from her water bottle. One of them seemed to briefly dangle in midair by his fingertips as his feet found a crevice to toe into, giving him another lift up the rock face. She held her breath through the whole maneuver. That's when she noticed he wasn't wearing a harness. That was Conrad! The other two were all trussed up but he had no anchor. God, she was suddenly terrified. And exhilarated. The freedom of it, moving up a dangerous rock without a net. She couldn't imagine how powerful he must feel, how uninhibited. It must feel like flying without a plane. It was the impossible, yet accomplished with an almost mellow gliding movement.

It didn't seem to take them very long, or maybe it was because she was mesmerized by the steady climb, but soon all three of them disappeared over the top of the rock. She let out her breath and gulped her water.

She was exhausted and decided she'd had enough of a hike. She headed back to the campground. When she got there it was early afternoon, the camp quiet, and Sully was sitting on the porch eating a sandwich. She ambled over and sat with him.

"Good hike?" he asked.

"Beautiful. Isn't it late for your lunch?"

"Aw, I got caught up in cleaning and painting trash cans. They were looking pretty awful."

"There were three guys rock climbing," she said. "That really big, flat rock face that looks like you shouldn't be able to find anything to hang on to, yet they slithered up to the top like lizards. What does it take to do something like that, Sully?"

He swallowed a mouthful. "Insanity, if you ask me."

"I assume you haven't done that?"

"I've done a little climbing, not up a flat rock like that. I've climbed where you can get a good, solid foothold and grip, a decent angle. I'm not afraid of heights, but I'm not real comfortable with falling off a flat rock like that." He shook his head. "They love that rock. Ever been to Yosemite?"

She shook her head.

"They climb El Capitan—it's flatter and way steeper than that. They pound in their spikes and anchors to hold their tents and camp hanging off the side—it's the damnedest thing I've ever seen. Look it up on your computer—look up 'climbing El Capitan.' It'll scare the bejesus out of you."

"Watching them was terrifying and exciting, but I'm not afraid of heights. Cal doesn't much like heights. He has trouble even looking at pictures of scary heights."

Sully grinned. "When you get some pictures or a video, show it to him."

"I wonder if I could learn to do that," she muttered.

"No, you can't," Sully said. "I forbid it."

So that's what a real father sounds like, she thought. A normal father—sane, decisive, controlling.

She went to get her laptop and came back to the porch. Before she opened up and signed on she asked Sully if he had any chores she could do for him.

"Nah, I got nothing much to do," he said. "Where you having dinner later?"

"I'll be around here. Why?"

"I got some salmon, rice and asparagus. If I share it, will you make it for us?"

"I'd be honored. Where'd you find asparagus this time of year?"

"I paid top dollar at that green grocer in Timberlake, that's where. I don't know where it comes from but the stalks are fat and juicy and plump up like steaks on the grill. You like that idea?"

"I love that idea," she said. "I'd love to share your dinner. I'll cook it and wash up the dishes after. What time would you like to eat?"

"Since I'm just getting lunch, is seven too late for you?"

"Just right," she said. "Gives me a little time to play on the computer and maybe read."

It was about four when campers started coming back to the Crossing, washing up after their day of exploring. Then a big Ford truck pulled up and the three rock climbers piled out. They nodded to her and said hello as they passed to go into the store.

Connie came back, holding his bottled water in one hand and an apple in the other. Without asking, he sat at her table. "How you doing?"

"I watched you climbing that steep, flat rock."

"Did you? We call that rock face Big Bad Betty. She's mean as the devil. I didn't see you, but we don't look around much. You have to be pretty focused."

She closed her laptop. "What does it sound like up there?" she asked. "When you're hanging on by your fingertips, what does it sound like?"

He smiled at her. "There's a little wind," he said. "The swooshing of hands and feet as you look for a good hold. Breathing— the sound of my breathing is loud in my head."

"Heart pounding?" She wanted to know.

"No. Just a good, solid rhythm. You have to like it, feel it, be safe in it or your diaphragm will slam into your chest, close it up and bad things happen. No pounding. It's tranquil."

"Does it make you feel powerful?" she asked.

"It makes me feel independent. Self-reliant."

"Free?"

"Yeah, free. But it takes thinking. Planning. I've climbed that rock a lot and I planned ahead. I know where to go. Even when you climb a new rock you plan ahead—look at video, pictures, listen to what climbers say, try it with a harness and ropes first to see the lay of the rock. And even then you have to be flexible. Sometimes you have to improvise. But it feels so good. Every grip and hold has to be just right and when you get it, you know you got it. It's a smart sport. No one can get too much of that feeling."

"You weren't wearing a harness. I didn't see any ropes."

"Free solo," he said. "As climbing challenges go, it's the best."

"And when you get to the top?"

"Eureka. Hallelujah."

"I saw you go over the top and disappear but I didn't hear anything."

He grinned brightly, his eyes twinkling. He had those sweet bedroom eyes sneaking a peek from behind lots of brown lashes. Young girls could buy lashes from him, he had so many. "Then we weren't loud enough," he said.

"Can I learn to do that?"

"Maybe," he said with a shrug. "Takes a lot of upper body strength. There's a wall in a gym in Colorado Springs, a good training wall. There are a lot of climbing gyms in Colorado Springs. A lot of trainers."

"Is it expensive?"

"It doesn't have to be, but you should try a training wall before you do anything else. You might hate it. If you don't hate it, Jackson climbs. I climb. Some of us have extra harnesses and other equipment. But first the wall."

Just as he said this last bit, the other two men came onto the porch. They also sat down. People around here didn't ask if they could join you, they just did.

"I'll show you how," Rafe said. "I'm Rafe. I think we met a couple of weeks ago. And this is Charlie Portman." He peeled a banana, bit off a big chunk and seemed to swallow it whole. "I'll teach you," Rafe said.

"First the gym, Rafe," Connie insisted.

"She's little," Rafe said. "Hardly any weight to pull up. I could take her up on my back."

"It'll go easier and you won't waste anyone's day off teaching you if you just try the gym first to see how it feels. That might be the beginning and end of it right there."

"It just looks so cool," Sierra said.

"Because it is," Rafe said, tipping a beer to his lips. When he did that she noticed his wedding ring.

"Was it a training day for you guys?" she asked.

"Not for Timberlake station," Rafe said. "For Rocky Mountain Volunteer Search and Rescue."

"Sounds like you're good people to know if I get in trouble," she said. "I'll be sure to let you know when I'm ready for a little training."

"He's married," Connie said.

Rafe smiled handsomely. "No problem, Sierra. Lisa knows I'd never be interested in another woman."

She sighed. "Do you have a brother?"

"First the wall," Connie said. "Then *I'll* show her."

That was twice now, Sierra thought. Twice he was warm and friendly, almost flirty, then it shut down and he became distant and a little cold. The first time was when they met and Moody mentioned Cal, so she wondered if Connie didn't like Cal. But that was crazy. Everyone loved Cal. Then, when Rafe offered to teach her climbing, his eyes went cold again. So probably he didn't like *her*.

She didn't have the best instincts, she knew that about herself. She wasn't likely to ask Sully about a single guy, especially a firefighter. Sully had already passed judgment on those guys— half gentlemen, half dogs.

When a little more time passed and more evidence collected, she'd probably just ask Conrad.

The month of April was perfect for Sierra. She went to a gym in Colorado Springs on a couple of her days off and learned how to climb on the wall. Of course she overdid it and all her muscles ached, but it made her feel so smug. Who knew she could do that? She worked a few mornings and went to a few meetings. She had coffee with Moody and learned he had four grown children. She hung out a bit at The Little Colorado Bookstore getting to know Ernie and Bertrice and picking up a few details about her new home.

But the best part of her new life was Sully.

"Tell me about Maggie shooting someone," she begged.

"It was a damn fool thing to do," he said. "Her reasons were right but her follow-through could've used a little more thought. She saw a young girl she recognized as one of our camper kids in a pickup with a couple of low-life characters and could tell she wasn't there by choice, so she tricked the driver into taking a cabin. She told him she'd give him a special deal and turned out he was as stupid as he was bad. Once she had him boxed in she called the police but she wasn't inclined to wait on 'em to get out here, not with that girl in danger. She loaded up my old shotgun and kicked the cabin door in and fired on them." He shook his head. "She could've called me or gone for Cal, but no. Maggie's accustomed to do as she pleases, when she pleases. She had a roll of duct tape in her pocket and had 'em all trussed up before the cops got here."

Sierra was speechless. Awestruck. "What a *badass*!"

"Those old boys were big and nasty. They could have rushed her, walked right through that shot and taken her down."

"But she shot them first."

"Well, one of 'em anyway. The shots brought me and Cal. It would'a been smarter to get us first."

"And the little camper girl?" Sierra asked.

"Scared to death but otherwise unharmed. She was separated from her family on the trail north of Leadville and they grabbed her. I never heard of such a thing happening around here before."

"That's creepy, Sully. It's not safe out there?"

"Up to that moment I'd have said there's no safer place than our trails. I hear there's a lot more Forest Service people out there these days than there used to be, on account of that incident. You got anything to protect yourself with?"

"I have a little can of pepper spray…the kind single women in the city are known to carry…" There were times she considered a handgun but in the end she was afraid to arm herself too much. What if she was incapacitated and it was used against her?

"Might have to fix you up with some real mace, just for my own peace of mind."

"Should I stop hiking alone?"

He shook his head. "You're not very alone. There are hikers out there, more of 'em every day. Just don't get too far away."

The mace appeared a few days later but Sierra was a little more vigilant, knowing that story. She admired Maggie more than ever. That's what Sierra had always thought she was, had always aspired to be—a fighter. A fearless, ninja warrior. And it did seem the trails grew more crowded, especially on the weekends. She assumed summer would be nearly hectic for the wilderness.

Meanwhile, she enjoyed nature more than she ever had before. A herd of elk must have taken up residence on a piece of grazing land nearby because she saw some in the campground in the early, early mornings. And of course there were deer now and then, making her drive to Timberlake very cautious. With her work hours beginning right after dawn, she was bound to see a lot of wildlife, something that made the start of her day very special.

Now that the weather was warmer, she and Sully were taking their morning coffee on the front porch. Since he had the pot on before the crack of dawn and she had to leave for the diner by six fifteen, this became their morning ritual. She found herself rolling out of bed early even on days she didn't have to work at the diner. Sully was reaching a part of her that had long been neglected. She kept very close track of her hours of helping around the store and grounds, proud to note that she was more than deserving of that free cabin. She was at the Crossing afternoons during the week and spent almost all weekend there. She could tell it worked out for Sully, since the campground was busiest then. And she still had time for herself and to check on Cal's progress.

The last weekend in April the campground was over half-full of cheerful, enthusiastic campers. The wildflowers were in full glory, the lake was still icy cold but it didn't scare off boaters or even some floaters. There were lots of kids, some dogs that Beau watched very carefully, but they were either friendly family dogs or they were penned and leashed. Beau didn't mind sharing his territory with the occasional friend; there was a chocolate Lab who Sully said was a regular guest and she liked to swim with Beau. They played havoc on the ducks.

A family appeared with a fifth wheel on Friday afternoon who were new to Sully but he took notice of them right away because the nine-year-old boy behaved a bit oddly. Sully said he might be autistic. He clung close to his mother but seemed to concentrate on his fingers and mutter all the time. There was a little girl, maybe five years old, who had much more energy and attentiveness than her brother, and a golden retriever pup around a year old. The golden was trapped in a kennel that was much too small for her and when she was let out, she was wild and crazy. The man couldn't handle her, had her in a choke collar that he pulled on relentlessly, shouting, "Down! Down! Molly get down! Sit! Sit!" Then he would just chain her to the trailer and she'd strain against her leash.

The mother, Anne, and the kids were exploring and playing by the lake, but the father, Chad, preferred his lounge chair under the camper's canopy. The dog spent far too much time in the too-small kennel and her break time was limited to being chained. She was never taken for a run or a walk. And she had a lot to say, barking and whining. Well, she was confined all the time and didn't get any attention or exercise and she was still a pup, though nearly full grown.

Chad constantly yelled at the dog. He was, in fact, more irritating than the animal. "Molly! Shut up!"

His name was Chad Petersen and he was on Sierra's wrong side right off. He had a big fancy trailer but he clearly wasn't camping for recreation, but for relaxation. He was overly friendly, had a big laugh and a loud voice, was very social with his neighbors and always had a beer in his hand. His wife was the one who took the kids walking to the base of the mountains to pick flowers or the edge of the lake where they could play with other children. It was his wife who put out the dinner and turned the burgers on the grill and fed the dog. It was Anne who picked up the dog droppings.

And when the dog got on Chad's nerves she was stuffed into that too-small kennel. Molly whimpered and whined to be let out.

On Saturday afternoon Sully wandered down to the lake where Anne and the children were. He talked to a few of the women there, including Anne, and when he came back to the store, he reported what he'd learned. "Their boy is autistic, like I figured. He's real antisocial. His dad thought a puppy would help—bring out his personality—even though his wife told him it might have the opposite effect. She's not a service animal, for God's sake. And now that the dog is big and dumb as a puppy, Petersen is frustrated and short-tempered and rather than admit he might've been wrong, he's determined to whip that puppy into shape. I might've editorialized that last part, but ain't it just obvious?"

"That poor little boy," Sierra said.

"Doesn't appear the boy knows what's going on with the dog and his dad."

Sierra stuck her neck out, probably where she shouldn't. She approached Chad as he sat under his canopy. Beau was with her and sniffed Molly, who was on her chain. "If you invite the dog to have a swim in the afternoon when it's sunny or take her for a really long walk up the trail, she'll tire out and be less noisy," she suggested.

"If you'd keep your dog away maybe mine wouldn't bark so much."

"*My* dog?" she asked. "This is the owner's dog. This is Beau and it's Beau's campground. Besides, the dogs like each other. Molly's only barking because she's bored and lonely."

"I'll put her back in the kennel," Chad said, standing from his lawn chair.

"No! No, please don't. Anyone could see that kennel is too small. I just thought you could use a suggestion, that's all. This place is family friendly and that includes pets as long as they're not vicious. She's just playful."

"I'm thinking about drowning her," Chad said. Then he grinned.

"Aw, jeez," Sierra said in disgust. "Come on, Beau."

She went back to the store and located Sully behind the lunch counter.

"Try to stay out of it," he advised before she even said anything.

"They're not okay," Sierra said. "The wife and kids try not to get in his way, they give him a real wide berth, even that little boy. And the dog is barking and straining because she hasn't had any training. And he said he was thinking of drowning her. I hate him."

"Don't waste your hate," Sully said. "Nobody's drowning anything at my campground. And how they conduct themselves is not our business unless they're breaking the law."

"He's one inch from breaking the law, I can smell it on him," she said.

The ruckus of the dog whining or barking and Petersen barking back continued while Sully and Sierra had their dinner on the porch. If a customer appeared one of them or the other jumped up to go inside and wait on them. The few campers who came to the store remarked on the barking dog and the man with the booming voice. "Don't make the mistake of offering him advice," Sierra said. "I did and he threatened to drown the dog."

"Is there anything you can do?" one woman asked. "I think he's more annoying than the dog!"

"There's nothing we can do but ask him to leave and take his dog somewhere else," Sully said. "I hate doing that. I apologize for the noise."

Things seemed to quiet around the campgrounds as the sun was lowering and people were stoking their evening fires but every time a dog barked poor Molly was set to answer. Then would come the noise of her owner. "Shut up, Molly!"

Sierra was tormented by what was clearly animal abuse. The chain, the cage, the choke collar. A kennel, the right size for the dog complete with blanket and chewy toys, was a good training tool, even Sierra knew that, though she hadn't had a dog, not really. There had been dogs on the farm when she was growing up, but that wasn't the same as a pet like Beau. She knew Sully was right, she should just mind her own business.

He knows not his own strength who hath not met adversity.

—SAMUEL JOHNSON

Chapter 5

SIERRA BID SULLY GOOD-NIGHT AT ABOUT EIGHT but she remained on the porch with a hot cup of tea. She took a great amount of comfort in routine—she usually got into bed with her water at her bedside and her book in her lap and read until she slept. But tonight her routine was screwed because she could hear Molly whimpering and her heart was breaking.

She wandered over to the Petersen campsite and saw that Molly was stuffed into her kennel outside while the family was inside. The dog cried and let out the occasional yelp. The bluish flickering that indicated a TV in the camper could be seen in the windows, which meant they probably could not hear Molly.

She was going to kidnap the dog.

No, Sully wouldn't like that. And she was Sully's guest. So... she would stay up until the dog finally went silent, and then she would sleep. In the morning she would report this abuse to someone, she'd figure out who. She would suggest to Mr. Petersen that he give her the dog to take to a no-kill shelter where she would surely find a wonderful forever home. Maybe she would stroke his ego and tell him he was a good man to take on the dog but it was okay if it didn't work out with a pet, just do no harm. That's what she'd do. One way or another she'd separate Molly from the Petersens before they left the campground.

She went to her cabin to get a blanket and pillow and she made herself comfortable in the hammock, just a couple of spaces away from the Petersens' camper and a still very lonely and unhappy Molly.

Despite the sound of the whimpering dog, Sierra drifted off. She was wrapped up like a burrito in her blanket, snug as could be with the breeze rocking her when she heard a yelp. She jerked awake.

"Just shut the hell up!" Chad loudly demanded. There was another yelp. "I said, quiet!" The yelping grew louder.

Sierra bolted off the hammock and ran to the campsite where her worst fears were realized. Petersen held the dog by the chain collar and smacked her on the head again and again.

"Stop!" Sierra screamed. "Stop that!"

"Mind your own goddamn business," he said, hitting the dog again.

It took a second to comprehend that he'd behave so, yell so, when he was literally living outside among a large group of campers. "Stop! I swear to God if you strike that animal again..."

He hit her again. Molly cowered and whimpered.

Sierra lost it. She threw herself at the man's back, launched on him with her arms around his neck and her legs wrapped around his waist. "*You're* the animal!"

"What the hell...?"

"Treating a defenseless animal so cruelly, how do you like it?" she said, tightening her arms around his neck.

The man shook her violently, but she hung on. He tried prying her arms from around his neck, but there was no give in her. "Beast," she muttered. "Animal!"

"Sierra! Let loose of that man!"

At Sully's command, Sierra let go and fell clumsily to the ground, landing on her ass. The fall jolted her for a moment, and then she regained her wits and saw that Anne and her daughter stood in the open door of the camper while Sully stood a few feet away, one hand leaning on a baseball bat.

Petersen huffed a bit to catch his breath. "Good thing you warned her," he said. "I was close to forgetting she was a girl and give her what for."

Sully hefted his bat. "You forget that was a defenseless animal, too?"

"It's my animal!"

"More's the pity. We got some pretty strict cruelty laws in this county and that was plumb cruel. I called the police."

"Well, good for you," he grumbled.

"If you don't want that dog, I got a home for her," Sully said.

"Bugger off, old man."

"Police chief might take her. He's got four goldens already but he's mighty fond of 'em and might fancy another. They sleep with him."

"Take her," Petersen said. "It'll save me the trouble of drowning her."

Sierra got to her feet slowly, brushing off her rear end. The very first thing she noticed was Molly sitting docilely beside her miniature kennel, her head cocked to one side with what looked like a satisfied expression on her face. Sierra quickly went to the dog, took her collar in hand and led her out of the campsite.

Petersen went into his camper, out of sight.

"Come along," Sully said, heading off for his house, not the store, leaving Sierra and Molly to follow. "I bet you were a lot of trouble to raise."

"I was hardly noticeable," Sierra replied.

"There's a lot of bullshit if I ever heard any," he said.

He didn't go inside, but rather to the front porch of his house. He took a seat in one of the rocking chairs, resting the bat on the ground beside him.

"What are we doing?" she asked, standing there.

"Have a seat," he said. "Just keep a hand on the dog till she decides it's okay to lay down and relax."

"Where's Beau?" she asked, because Beau was usually close to Sully.

"I penned him in the bedroom for now. Molly doesn't need the distraction."

Sierra sat down next to Sully. They rocked in the dark and she kept a hand on Molly, gently stroking her. When she'd stop, Molly put her head on Sierra's lap. She was docile as a lamb. "Why are we sitting here?" she finally asked.

"I'm awake," Sully said. "Might as well sit up awhile longer and see if there's anything to see."

"See? See what?"

He sighed. "Just give it a few minutes. Patience, Sierra."

After a few minutes, she quietly asked, "Do you think the police chief will take the dog?"

"I doubt it," he said.

"But you said—"

"Girl, I say a lot of things."

Sierra just fell silent, Molly's head in her lap while she scratched behind the pretty girl's silky ears. She couldn't imagine what they were doing just sitting there but she took comfort in the fact that Molly wouldn't be back in Petersen's care. Then in about fifteen minutes it all began to make sense. Chad Petersen started his big, extended cab truck, backed it up to the fifth wheel, threw the lawn chairs inside the trailer and his family into the truck, disconnected his hookup, reeled in the canopy, attached the trailer to the truck hitch and pulled out.

"What time is it?" she asked.

"Round about ten," Sully said.

"Hey, you knew he'd do that! Didn't you?"

"I had an idea."

"You heard the noise when he was hitting her and it woke you?"

"Sierra, I'm over seventy. I sleep in my drawers. You really think I'm spry enough to get my clothes and my boots on and run on over to the campsite in under five minutes? I knew what was gonna happen and just like you, I waited on it."

"Just like me?"

"Didn't you take up watch from the hammock?"

"Well…yes! You knew that?"

He nodded in the dark. "Didn't really surprise me."

"You think the police will come now?"

"I didn't call 'em," he said. "Didn't want to waste Stan's time. I knew once I called Petersen on it he'd just pull out."

"What does it mean? Does it mean you won't get paid?"

"I wouldn't care, if it came to that, but as it happens I took a nice deposit from his credit card. What it means, I reckon, is you now got yourself a dog."

Sierra was elated for a moment, until she started thinking about how she didn't know quite what to do with a dog. She knew what not to do. She'd never hurt an animal. But she was no expert in training one. It wasn't until Sully stood up to go to bed, finally, that she asked. "Can I borrow some dog food?"

"Just take a bowl with you to your cabin for water and Molly can have breakfast with Beau in the morning. Time she got on a decent schedule."

"Are you going to help me a little bit?"

"If I don't, that dog will starve or run off," he said. "Good night, Sierra."

It should have come as no surprise, Molly had not had a proper grooming in a while. She slept with Sierra, snuggled up close, quiet and content and…smelly. Fortunately, Sierra had the whole day to herself on Sunday and could not only make sure Molly had a thorough shampoo but that the linens in her little cabin were also laundered. "We'll just start over," she confided to her new best friend.

Molly had to learn some manners for dining with Beau at

breakfast—she wanted whatever he was eating, even though it was the same food. It looked like manners could take a while. But Sully coached her to show Molly what to do, then praise her, then praise her again, then let her perform again. "Someone should have tried that approach with me," she muttered. But Molly, for her part, acted as though she knew who had rescued her. She sat still, wagged and smiled up at Sierra in a way that threatened to melt her heart.

Next it was spa day for Molly and she was prettified. Sully had an extra collar and leash and Sierra employed both to try to show her how to walk beside her, and that was going to take forever. Instead, Sully suggested they show her how to come when called. Molly sat beside Beau, Sully hanging on to both dogs while Sierra told them to sit and stay. Then she walked away, turned back, said their names and the command, "Come." Molly very likely did what Beau did, but she did it. And both dogs got a small cookie.

"I have to go to work tomorrow," she said. "How will you manage?"

"Lots of hands around during the day, Sierra. We'll manage. And if you change your mind, there's a great shelter not far from here. They'd treat her right until a home can be found."

"I fought for her," she said. "Let me try. But if it gets too much for you, do you promise to tell me?"

"Not a lot seems like too much anymore," he said. "We all deserve a second chance. And I reckon Beau will help train Molly."

Sierra came home from work with a few new toys for Sierra. She made sure her cabin was puppy safe—nothing left out to get into trouble with. She first walked her, worked with her a little bit, then put her in the cabin with water and two new toys, and left her for only twenty minutes. Then she rewarded her with lots of affection, paid attention to her for twenty minutes, and left her again. That went perfectly well three times.

Then Molly chewed off the handle of her circular brush, which had been sitting atop the bureau. Out of reach.

"Whose reach?" Sully asked.

"Oh God, this is going to take forever!"

"Takes a lot longer to raise a human. Be patient."

The next day she brought home a new brush and two raw-hide chews. The brush went in the drawer and the rawhide came out only when she left the cabin for a while, then it was put away again.

When she came home from work on Thursday afternoon, Frank was sitting on the porch with Molly. Sierra parked behind the cabin and walked over to the store. When she came around the corner Frank told Molly, "There she is, girl." Molly burst out at a dead run and nearly tackled Sierra, jumping on her, licking her face, half barking, half crying as if Sierra had just returned from war. It brought Sierra to her knees. She crooned to the dog, "I'm home, I'm home, I love you, too." And then she let Molly lick her face until she was covered with slobber.

"She scratch you or something?" Frank asked when she came up on the porch.

"No," she said, wiping her wet face. "No one's ever been that happy to see me."

Tom Canaday was seen around Timberlake all the time since he lived in the neighborhood. He was as involved in the kids' school activities as much as his schedule would allow and all the local businesses knew him even if he did travel a bit farther for most of his building supplies to get the best prices. He stopped in the diner now and then, maybe for a cup of coffee or slice of pie. Really, he was a very sociable guy without a lot of time on his hands to be social.

"Hey there, fella," Lola Anderson said. "Haven't seen you in a while."

He sat up at the lunch counter and she automatically poured him a cup of coffee. "I didn't know it was your day," he said.

"I'm working at Home Depot tomorrow and the next day," she said, speaking of her second job. "You have a day off?"

"I've been putting in a lot of time at Cal's barn. I took the day to catch up on a few other things since Cal's spending the day in Denver with Maggie. Her car's in the shop and he drove her in on Wednesday and will bring her back tonight. While they're there, they're looking at tile, carpet and flooring."

"It must be coming along nicely," she said.

"Looking good. And pretty much on schedule. How's school?"

"Slow and steady, but I only take a few credits a semester and I'm taking the summer off from classes. I have a kid starting at community college in the fall—I can't believe that."

"Tell me about it—Jackson's twenty already and Nikki starts in the fall."

"Pretty soon we'll be empty nesters," she said, leaning on the counter.

"Not for a while," Tom said. "I've got younger kids at home. But if we ever get caught up, we should try meeting for a movie or an ice cream or something. Something adult but without kids."

Lola smiled patiently. "I've heard talk like this before," she said.

"I mean it. It's just finding the time, that's all."

Lola shifted her weight to the other leg. "How's Becky?"

"Fine," he said. "Great."

But Becky was neither fine nor great, he thought. And he knew exactly why Lola had brought her up. Tom and Becky had been divorced for years but everyone was of the opinion they were still a couple, that Tom was never going to be finished with that relationship. It was his own fault. He'd been letting Becky come around, visit and stay with him and the kids and people just assumed they were not quite divorced.

That was all changing, but there wasn't a delicate way to explain that. And he liked Lola. He'd known her most of his life. They both grew up around here.

The door to the diner opened and Connie Boyle walked in. He was wearing his navy blue fire department shirt. Now Connie might be a lot younger than Lola, and younger than Tom, for that matter, but Tom didn't miss the way Lola's eyes lit up and how she grinned when she saw him. All the women seemed to have that reaction—he was good-looking, a fire-fighter and single.

"Hey," he said, sitting at the counter beside Tom. "What's up?"

"Not too much. I just grabbed a couple of kids from school, got them home and started on their chores because they both want to go to friends' houses since there's no school tomorrow. I thought I'd take a run out to Sully's and meet the new family member."

"Sierra?" Connie asked. "You haven't met Sierra?"

"Not Sierra—of course I met her, she's been here two months already. And I've been at Cal's most days so I've seen her plenty. It's Molly, the new addition."

"There's another sister?" Connie asked.

"You haven't heard?" Tom asked with a laugh. "I don't usu-ally get the drop on you when a new female comes to town. Molly's a golden retriever pup about a year old. Sierra rescued her from an abusive camper."

"Oh, this should be good," Lola said. "That explains why she charged out of here the other day when I showed up to relieve her. She never said a word."

"Happened about a week ago. Sierra was keeping an eye on the camper because he treated the dog badly. Here's how Sully said it went—the camp quieted down except for the dog, cry-ing and barking from the kennel she was stuffed into, a kennel about big enough for a little cocker spaniel. Sierra didn't even go to her cabin—she hung close by. And when the guy came out of his camper and started beating the dog to shut her up, she challenged him. When he wouldn't stop, she jumped on him. Sully said she hung on him like a tick on his back and he couldn't shake her off. At the end of a scene right out of a bad movie, the camper and his family left and Sierra has herself a completely untrained, abused, young and crazy golden." He sipped his coffee. "Gotta be worth seeing."

"Sierra attacked him?" Connie asked.

"So it's told. No surprise there, I guess."

"No surprise," Lola said. "She might be young and small but she has no shortage of guts. We like that here."

"She might be a little stupid," Connie said. "What if he'd turned on her, knocked her senseless just in self-defense?"

"Sully was waiting up, too. He does that when things don't feel right at the campgrounds. He wanders around with his handy dandy baseball bat, the only weapon he carries. I wonder if he's ever used that thing."

"How'd you hear about this if you haven't seen the dog?" Lola asked.

"I work with Cal every day. Cal keeps tabs on his sister, almost every day. And Maggie is at Sully's on days she's not in Denver. Trust me—there's no shortage of conduits for the news." He drank the last of his coffee and checked his watch. "Time to see if the kids ran out on their chores." He put a dollar on the counter, gave Connie a slap on the back and told Lola he'd see her soon. He walked the two blocks home.

One of these days he should make good on all his promises to take Lola out, but it was awkward. Ever since Becky left eight years ago, he'd been acting like a married man even though his wife lived elsewhere. But like every small town, people noticed when she came around, when she stayed a few nights or a weekend. Once one of the old biddies in town asked his Nikki where her mother slept when she visited. Tom told Nikki to politely say, "None of your business, ma'am." But the truth was, Becky slept with him. Even though he knew Becky had boyfriends, knew she wasn't a faithful wife or a wife at all, knew he was just a fool. He'd told himself they were divorced, it was her choice to date, see men. It was his choice not to date or have girlfriends. He had secretly kept hoping she'd realize she'd been hasty and come back to her family.

But everything had changed last year. Last year when he learned Becky hadn't had boyfriends, not really. No matter how Becky referred to these men, they were customers. She had explained herself as an escort, just a little company, not necessarily an intimate. No matter what she said, Tom knew what she was.

And speak of the devil. When he rounded the curve to his street, whose car was parked in the drive behind his truck but Becky's. She had stopped warning him of her visits, stopped asking if it would be all right. He hadn't had the heart to tell his kids, not even the oldest ones, not for his sake or Becky's, but for theirs. They loved their mother. And why wouldn't they? She was probably the prettiest, sweetest girl in town.

He walked in and found her in the kitchen, rinsing out a coffee cup. She turned toward him, smiled and said, "Tom."

"Where are the kids?"

"They're finishing their chores. I told them I'd take them out for pizza if their chores were done."

"But unfortunately, you've been called away," Tom said. "You can't do this, Becky."

"They miss me. I miss them."

"I know. But you can't pretend nothing has changed. At least I can't."

"I told you, that's over now."

"You do as you please, Becky. But you can't change the past eight years and I can't change the way I feel."

"Nothing was ever different with us. It had nothing to do with us."

He laughed hollowly. "Seriously? Yes, everything changed

with us. How many were there, do you think? A hundred? Two hundred?"

"Not even close. Hardly any," she said.

"Do you know how many women were in my life? From the day you left till now? Zero. Well, there was you—pretending you were working in a doctor's office and going to yoga classes with girlfriends."

She shook her head sadly and tossed her beautiful red hair, hair that was not really red. Her blue eyes teared—she was the only blue-eyed redhead he'd ever known. She affected duplicity with such an air of innocence it still shook him. "I was not pretending."

"I won't let you do to them what you did to me, Becky. You can see them, only here and only if you make plans with me first. And you can't spend the night anymore."

"I'll sleep with the girls..."

"No, Becky, no. Don't force my hand."

"Why are you doing this to me?" she asked, a catch in her voice.

He almost laughed. She was arrested three times for solicitation and thought that having the charges vacated, the third time with the help of Cal Jones, criminal defense attorney, meant it had never happened.

But it had happened.

"I'm not going to talk about this now, with our youngest two kids upstairs. Take them to pizza and then tell them you can't stay. Leave. Or I'll tell them now, tell them why I don't agree to let you spend the night or let them stay with you. I'll tell them. I'm going to have to tell them eventually."

"Even though it's all in the past?"

"Well, I can't be really sure of that, can I? It's in the past until you're arrested again, right?"

"It must be nice to have never made a mistake," she said in a mere whisper.

He gave a huff of laughter. "Oh, I've made plenty and you know that. I just never had to be bailed out for any of them."

His youngest son, Zach, came bounding downstairs. "I'm done," he announced.

"I'm almost done!" his fourteen-year-old daughter, Brenda, called from upstairs.

And I'd like a life, Tom thought. *I'd like a chance to start over even though I waited too long.* He admitted it was his fault. He'd been naive and because he always loved Becky so much, he stayed in denial about the fact that she had moved on. She was no help, coming back again and again, sleeping in their marriage bed, giving the pretense that she was still at least partly into the marriage.

Yes, he had foolishly hoped...

But it had been almost a year since that last arrest and he was cured of all naïveté. He'd finished the grief and torment and feelings of betrayal, and all he wanted now was to have a normal life. If he could just remember what that was.

Lola fed her sons, eighteen-year-old Cole and sixteen-year-old Trace at the diner. Some nights she left them dinner, some nights they went to their grandparents' house, some nights they went out with their dad, Dave, from whom she'd been divorced for ten years. She and Dave got along fine as long as they spent very little time together. Dave was on wife number four and, by now, her sons were done with all the steps and halves. Once every couple of weeks, maybe, Dave would take them out for pizza or a burger and that was about it. He never was any good with support payments but sometimes she could guilt him into buying something the boys needed, like gear for school sports. He was basically a good-natured deadbeat dad and serial marrier—someone she'd never been able to count on.

It was Friday night and prom was coming up—Cole was going with his girlfriend, Jen. Jen was on the prom committee and it was a big deal. Cole worked part-time for the grocer down the street, Trace worked part-time at the grill, mostly busing and cleanup. They were letting him take orders now and then, but he couldn't serve alcohol. He was too young. The boys had good, hard jobs that helped Lola in convincing them to continue their educations so they wouldn't be unpacking vegetables and washing dishes for life.

Just as she was doing for herself, finally getting her degree. She'd worked in nearly every small business around Timberlake and a couple in Leadville since she was sixteen and she hoped to remain in the area as a teacher, even though those jobs were hard to come by. Elementary school was her first choice.

The most important thing to Lola was that she liked her life as a single woman. Ten years postdivorce, she was settled. She was very busy, had plenty of friends, her mom and dad were close by and in good health, her little house was comfortable and easy to take care of and, as far as she was concerned, there was nothing missing.

It was true there was no man in her life. She'd had a few dates over the years, and they were only dates. She'd gone skiing with a recently divorced dentist and they'd had a good time; but there were no sparks. One of her professors took her out a few times; he was considerably older and the relationship had not progressed, which was just as she'd have it. She'd gone out with a firefighter or two but it had been friendly and casual and they still saw each other around town. She was not looking for a lover, didn't really need another friend.

Lola was confident, energetic, funny and smart—she knew this about herself. What she wasn't was pretty. She was overweight, her massive, curly black hair was beginning to thread with gray though she was barely forty and, even though she got enough sleep, she had dark circles under her eyes. She'd never quite figured out how to shape her brows right and she wasn't good with her crazy hair so she kept it short. Short and shapeless but for the loose curls. She only bothered with makeup for special occasions—namely the dentist, the professor and two firefighters.

But she wouldn't mind having a male friend, someone she was really comfortable with. She didn't care about falling in love and had absolutely no illusions about a second marriage. The last time she was in love was Dave, and that had been a disaster. But a kind guy to hang out with, a companion—that would be nice. In fact the one man who intrigued her was Tom Canaday. Unfortunately he was clearly still very screwed up about his divorce and if there was anything Lola wanted less than a man it was a man's baggage.

But what she loved about Tom was that he never complained. His ex-wife had left him with four kids to raise on his own and he shouldered the responsibility, took it on and got it done, was a great parent, remained positive and happy as though he, too, liked his life. She wondered if it was true, what they said, that he'd never really accepted the divorce, that his incredibly beautiful ex-wife still paid regular conjugal visits. Because if that were true, then they had nothing in common, after all.

If you can find a path with no obstacles, it probably

doesn't lead anywhere.

—FRANK A. CLARK

Chapter 6

"WAIT UNTIL YOU SEE THIS," SIERRA TOLD CAL proudly. "Molly, sit!"

Molly sat.

"Amazing," Cal said. "Is she ready for the circus?"

"Shut up. This dog is in recovery. She needs patience and affection and lots of positive reinforcement."

"What has she chewed up lately?"

"She's had a good week," Sully said. "She only chewed up a pair of leather rappelling gloves that were hanging on the bottom hook over there by the door and a pair of my socks that were sticking out of my shoes on the back porch. Oh, and she got a paperback but it was ready for the recycle anyway. That's all we know of. If we x-ray her, we might find a ton of stuff."

"So, Sierra has a new toy," Cal said with a grin.

Sierra didn't care one bit if they made fun of her as long as they were very sweet to Molly. Everyone treated Molly like a precious gift and it was obvious in the dog's behavior that she'd never experienced anything like it before. She was a lovable pest. She leaned against people for a pat, brought people gifts—usually one of her toys but sometimes something she'd stolen—laid her head in their laps and sometimes just sat in front of someone, anyone, and barked until they gave her some attention.

Sierra had a new friend and she thought her adorable. That first week she'd been in a panic that Molly might wander off and get lost, but as it turned out there were two secret weapons at her disposal. First, as Sully pointed out, Molly had that special dog's nose and could find her way back to the campground as long as she hadn't gotten too far away. And second, Beau was only too happy to go get her and bring her back.

Beau was doing as much to train Molly as everyone else. And Molly might be a little bit in love because she hung close to the Lab.

When Conrad showed up on the weekend, Sierra knew word had traveled far and wide.

"So, this the mutt you wrestled for?"

"You watch your mouth!" Sierra said. "I don't think there's anything but golden in her! Do not offend her or she won't like you. She has shown excellent taste so far!"

Connie clicked his teeth, dangled his hand at his side and Molly wagged her tail enthusiastically and went right to him, nudging his hand for a pet.

"She might have a little slut in her," Sierra muttered.

"The best of us do," Connie said, crouching to give the dog a serious scratch.

"Isn't she beautiful?"

"I guess she's kind of good-looking," Connie said.

"She's my first dog," Sierra confessed.

"Seriously? You didn't have dogs growing up?"

"There were dogs on the farm, but they were outside dogs, barn dogs, not dogs that slept on the bed. My grandma would have chased them out with a broom if they got in the house. My brother Dakota kind of claimed one of them and that dog followed him everywhere. It was all we could do to keep him off the school bus."

As she recalled, those times they landed back at the farm when she was very young, they lived in the bus. Her grandparents had a small farmhouse and couldn't really take on six extra people, so through spring, summer and fall, they continued to sleep in the bus, but would eat their meals and shower and use the facilities in the house. In winter they all crammed in the house together. When she was eight and Cal was sixteen, they took up permanent residence at the farm because Grandpa had passed. Space was found, though not much more than they'd had before.

Sierra went to get Molly's leash off the hook in the back of the store. When Molly saw it, she got all excited, the only dog in the history of the world who was free most of the time and got excited by the leash. But she was smart and she knew it meant she was going somewhere. Beau ran to Sierra's side immediately; he liked to go along, but Beau didn't need a leash. "Would you like to join us?" she asked Connie.

"I'll just hang out with Sully for a while," he said. "You and your little friends have fun."

"We certainly will," she said, heading across the yard for one of the trails.

Connie went into the store and found Sully stocking shelves. "Need a hand?" he asked.

"I got it," Sully said. "Grab a cup of coffee."

"Holler when you're ready for boxes from the storeroom. You know I like to show off my big muscles."

"Just seen you show off the one between your ears, son," he said. "Besides, there don't seem to be any pretty young women around at the moment."

"I'll just practice, then."

Connie positioned himself at the lunch counter where he could visit with Enid and be handy when Sully started toting big boxes of supplies out of the back storeroom.

Conrad Boyle was thirty-three and had grown up in and around Timberlake. For a while his family lived in Leadville when they'd found a good rental house there. Then they moved back to Timberlake when Connie was in first grade and his mom and dad had divorced. When his mom remarried, they'd stayed in that house and his stepfather moved in with them.

Connie wouldn't call his growing up years hard, but they were at least inconvenient and at times very difficult. First off, his father and then his stepfather had both been brutish, angry men while his mother was a kind, hardworking, even-tempered woman. To this day, Connie didn't understand why his mother couldn't find better men to marry. And if she couldn't, then why didn't she just live as a single woman?

"You'll understand someday, Connie," his mother, Janie, said.

Right then and there he decided that if he didn't find a good woman, one with whom he had mutual respect and happiness, he wasn't going to do it. He did not ever come to understand, as his mother promised he would. His mother might not be gorgeous but she was certainly attractive, had a nice figure, a pretty smile and a sunny disposition. Both his father and stepfather were verbally abusive and while they did work steady, they did as little around the house as possible, yet their demands seemed constant. *Conrad, you get that garage cleaned yet? Help your mother in the kitchen! I never saw anyone as lazy as you! That's your yard, kid—every Saturday come hell or high water! Why the hell ain't that driveway shoveled? You're a fucking idiot. If I can put food on the table you can at least keep ahead of your chores!*

To add to Connie's misery growing up, he was small. Hard to believe, looking at him now. He was small and he had a girl's name—everyone always called him Connie. Even if he corrected them and said, "It's Conrad," they'd still call him Connie. He felt like a boy named Sue; he had to defend himself a lot. There were guys in his class who had the shadow of a beard in sixth grade, but his growth didn't kick in until he was fifteen. It was like that summer between ninth and tenth grade his feet grew from size seven to eleven. Testosterone descended on him and he shot up. Thank God.

His mother divorced his father when Connie was six and his stepfather when Connie was seventeen, not quite finished with high school. He had a half brother, Bernard, who they called Beaner, ten years younger than Connie, and with that second divorce, his mother got a job in Denver and took seven-year-old Beaner with her.

Connie stayed in Timberlake and moved in with his buddy Rafe's family even though they had five kids. It was where he'd been hanging out whenever he could anyway. Rafe's mother, Margarite Vadas, said she'd always kind of wanted six kids so it was perfect. And at the Vadas home, Connie found the kind of family life he admired and wished he could emulate. Carlos Vadas, a cook and outdoorsman, loved kids. It was a revelation to Connie that just the simple action of enjoying one's family could make home life nearly perfect. It wasn't flawless, it wasn't without its tense or grumpy moments, it certainly wasn't without arguments—just the fights over the bathroom alone could be staggering. But it just wasn't challenging all the time. No one held a grudge and the single most important thing—no one seemed to walk on eggshells or brace themselves for the next blowup. He never once heard Carlos Vadas complain about the work of feeding his family or ridicule his children or call them names.

The Vadas kids, like all kids, could be lazy about their chores and Carlos would say things like, *I think someone wants to go to homecoming and have a new dress, but she doesn't like doing the dishes. I think that's not the way it works, does it?* Or, *I hear someone wants to use his mama's car on the weekend but he isn't so interested in mowing and trimming, do I have that right?* And of course everyone got in trouble sometimes. *No phone, then. Maybe if you have no phone you have no opportunity to make plans that will only get you in trouble.* Or, *You don't like that curfew of midnight? I think you will like eleven better, yes?*

Connie realized he developed an idea of the kind of life he

wanted from the neighbors, it was as simple as that. Carlos and Margarite were not as attractive as his mother and father had been yet were far more affectionate. They were always playing on the same team when it came to the kids. Connie wanted that—a wife he could love and depend on into old age.

He had wanted that until he thought he had it and had lost it in a most miserable and humiliating way. Now he was trying to figure out what kind of life he could have instead.

Connie had stayed on in Timberlake, taking a few college courses, joining the volunteer search team and training until there was an opening in the fire department and he tested right alongside his best friend, Rafe. They were both twenty-five when they were hired and it seemed they were junior firefighters forever. When he was twenty-seven he met Alyssa. She was cutting hair in Timberlake and she was *hot*. She was tall and leggy, big breasted with long, thick dark hair, dark eyes and ruby lips that were full and delicious. Connie was suddenly needing a lot of haircuts. They began to date and Connie fell in love—hard; he'd found the one. He'd bought some land just outside of town, a beautiful acre in the foothills, not even half-paid for. While he and Alyssa talked marriage and children, he began to build her a house. Well, he was having it built, but he took great pride in being involved and helping. It was a small house to start, but it was designed for future add-ons. Within two years they were living in it and planning a wedding.

And then things went south. Alyssa grew moody and distant. He knew something was wrong but she denied it. Yet there were red flags all over the place. She wasn't in the mood for sex, there was whispering into the phone, he caught her crying a couple of times—she blamed everything on her hormones. He decided to do something really nice for her so he took her car and washed it and detailed it to surprise her...but he found a pair of her sexiest panties under the seat. He put them on the kitchen table and asked her just what the hell was going on.

"Where'd those come from?" she'd asked.

"Under the front seat of your car. Care to explain?"

She had claimed they'd been pinching her so she'd slid them off and stuffed them under the seat, out of sight and forgot about them. Then she'd laid into him for taking her car without telling her, and she was furious.

Connie was getting desperate. He was close to asking Carlos for advice when it became unnecessary. He took some personal time from work one afternoon and went home with some flowers for Alyssa and a hope they might straighten some things out, but there in his drive was the car of a fellow firefighter, Christian Derringer. He was a little older than Connie, married with a couple of little kids, and he was a whore. He was a screw-around and didn't have any conscience about it.

Connie found them in the bedroom. He grabbed Chris by the ankles, dragged him through the house and out the front door, hefted him up and tossed his naked ass into the snow. All the way Alyssa was screaming, clutching a sheet to her naked body, raging at Connie.

And right at that moment all of Connie's ideals and preconceived notions collapsed.

"I'm going back to work," he told her. "I'm filing a complaint with the captain and while I'm there, you move out. Be gone when I get home."

"This is my house, too," she yelled. "You can't throw me out!"

"Oh yes, I can," he said. "We're not married. Thank God."

"I'm keeping this house!" she screamed. "At least half of it."

"Sue me," he said.

His captain had talked him out of filing a formal complaint but he did move Chris out of Connie's unit. For a couple of years it was kind of hard to tell whether Connie would pull Chris out of a burning building. They were never going to be able to work together again, but they were still from the same small town. Connie gave him a real wide berth. He sincerely hoped Chris would never be trapped on a ledge somewhere when Connie was on duty.

The drama divided the firehouse. There were those who sided with Connie and thought he'd gone easy on the bastard. "I might've killed them both," Rafe said. Rafe was the gentlest man in Timberlake. And then there was the other team—they were kind of a mishmash. Some thought Connie should've taken out his wrath on Alyssa and not Chris; some thought Chris was just screwing around and it shouldn't be such a melodrama. "Get over it already! You dodged a bullet!" they'd say to Connie, like Alyssa was the only one at fault. And some thought all was fair in love and war.

Chris had invaded Connie's territory and Connie hated him for it. But he took the high road. He gave himself a reasonable period of time, maybe about six months, then decided Alyssa and Chris were in his past, they were dead to him. His secret was he might never be over it, not as long as he could remember what it was like loving her while she was loving him. But as far as others could tell, he had moved on.

Of course Chris stayed married, kept running around on his wife, and Alyssa was still cutting hair in Timberlake. They couldn't help but run into each other and after a year or so Connie told her he wasn't angry anymore.

"Connie, it's the biggest mistake of my life," she'd said with tears in her eyes. "Can't we try again? We weren't married, after all."

And he had said, "No. I can forgive you for what you did but we won't be trying again."

Connie dated quite a bit. Hardly ever the same girl for three dates, always a beautiful girl. He had no trouble getting girls and no interest in being tied down. He half wanted half feared getting that feeling again—that lurch in the heart, that dazed brain, the fuzzy vision and lightness in the head. Rationally, he didn't want to believe his one and only chance was Alyssa who would be so coolly and easily unfaithful. Emotionally, he had no interest in going through that again. Was it even imaginable that he would trust again?

Not likely.

Sierra had to keep reminding Molly to stay with her; she had to keep reminding Beau, for that matter. Beau was a trailblazer— he liked to get out ahead of them and nose around. She wasn't sure what she'd do if Beau cornered an elk buck or a bear. She had the small canister of mace in her vest pocket but she didn't think it would do much good on an angry bear. She had dog treats in the other pocket and her water in her backpack.

She kept telling Molly how good she was, how well she was doing, stopping every so often to work on voice commands. They were starting to experiment with "Down!" She had to add a little incentive, a gentle push on the head until Molly was in the down position. And she couldn't help but fantasize her dog becoming the best trained dog in the universe. Of course Sully only said, "Let her get to be about four years old and you might really have something. Those goldens are the best-natured dogs."

The walks, at least one a day and sometimes two if she didn't have to work at the diner, were good for the dogs. They were both less trouble, calmer. Well, except for bunny chasing. She probably shouldn't have, but she hadn't been able to resist letting Molly join Beau on a little chase. It just filled Molly with such joy. But Molly's chasing days were now done. The problem came when the dogs had actually caught one. Beau, being older and better trained, just loped off to find Sully and present his catch and Beau soft-mouthed his catch so Sully could just release the bunny, usually back behind the garden shed. But Molly had brought Sierra a bunny that had been mortally bitten. "Oh God, what do I do *now*?" Sierra had wailed, horrified.

"Dig a hole," Sully had said. "City girl."

Well, she was the farthest thing from a city girl, but there were parts of this country living that were alien to her. And difficult. But it was still better than the life she had lived before.

Out here, on one of the many paths and trails that led into the mountains, it was easy for Sierra to let her mind wander. Gratitude was almost automatic, something that was a struggle under other circumstances. When she was out here in nature, she could think about how lucky she was to be alive. When she'd been struggling in the city, in rehab, at work, it was too easy for her to feel sorry for herself. Addicts had the market cornered on self-pity. They were experts at it.

She and the dogs were well out in the wilderness on a very good, well-traveled trail when it happened. She stepped in a hole, her ankle twisted and she heard it crinkle almost like tissue paper—*crunch, crunch, crunch.*

"Shit," she said as she landed on her butt. Molly immediately began licking her face. "Not now, Molly," she said. She sat there a minute, trying to assess the damage. It didn't really hurt. But she knew it was probably time to go home so she called Beau, who came trotting back to her.

"Sorry, kids, but I think I might've sprained my ankle. At least."

She hoisted herself up and stepped gingerly on her right foot and pain shot up her leg to her knee. "Whoa," she said. "Damn!"

She took a few careful steps, only able to set her injured foot on her toes. She bit her lip and went slowly and carefully. She was only a half hour out from the campground so if she went slowly, carefully, she could get there. She could probably slide on her butt and it would only take her... Hell, it would take most of the day. She took ten slow steps and the pain brought tears to her eyes. "Holy macaroni," she said to her companions. "Too bad one of you isn't a horse."

Ten minutes and maybe a hundred steps later she sat on a boulder. She rolled down her sock and looked at her ankle. It was already swollen and was turning a very unhealthy color.

She decided she'd just wait a while, someone would be along. There were lots of hikers around. Then she heard thunder. "Perfect," she said.

In five minutes she felt the first drops. As far as she could remember, there hadn't been a cloud in the sky when she set out on her hike. And now there would be no hikers coming along. It was going to be a long, wet afternoon waiting until someone noticed they'd been gone too long.

Connie moved to the front porch with his coffee cup. Personally, he loved the rain. But it was a little inconvenient around a campground. People were driven indoors and most of the time that meant a tent. A couple of campers came jogging across the grounds to the store; they might buy snacks to help them hunker down in their tents or they might decide the porch was a good place to wait it out.

It wasn't long before Sully was on the porch, holding a cup of his own. He just sat down and watched the rain make a mess of the grounds. Surprisingly, it was only the two of them on the porch.

"There's going to be a wet girl and two wet mutts coming along pretty soon," Connie said.

"Yup," Sully agreed. "They won't melt. The dogs'll love it."

"They're gonna track up everything—house, store, everything."

"Yup, I hate that part."

Ten minutes later Connie said, "You'd think she'd be making tracks. Rain and all."

"Hurrying won't make her less wet," Sully said.

Ten minutes later Connie said, "You suppose she holed up under a big tree, waiting for it to pass?"

"Likely," Sully said. "You waiting around for her or something?"

"Nah, I should probably just go. Unless I can lend you a hand?"

"I got nothing to do I can't get done. We're going over to that barn for supper, me and Sierra. I'm closing the store at six thirty."

"I ought to make a run by that barn one of these days, see how it's coming along," Connie said.

"If you can tell, you're a better man than I am. They keep squawking about all the progress they're making and it still looks like a barn under construction to me. I reckon we'll be eating at that indoor picnic table."

Connie laughed at him. "I built my house, you know. I mean, I had some help. I had a general contractor, mostly for looks and for getting inspections. But I did a lot of the work."

"Oh, I know," Sully said. "Can't remember you talking about much else for a couple of years."

"I love that house," he said. He hadn't thought he could do so well and he'd poured himself into it thinking one day he'd be telling his sons he'd built the home they lived in; his wife would tell her friends she picked out every detail from faucets to door handles.

Shortly after the house was done, he threw his woman out for cheating right in his own bed. He bought a new mattress and all new bedding. For the next year Connie had hardly said a word about the house.

The rain eased up to a dribble, ready to stop. "She'll be along now," Connie said.

"You *are* waiting for her," Sully said.

"Well, I wasn't but now I am—she and the two dogs have been missing in the rain for quite a while now and I'll just feel better knowing she got back. That they all got back. That's a nice little dog she got herself."

"Molly isn't little," Sully said. "She's sixty-five pounds at about a year old. She's going to be a nice size. I'm betting eighty pounds, seventy of which will be hair." He whistled. "Between Molly and Beau, we'll keep Hoover in business."

"I'll be getting out of here before the dog washing starts,"

Connie said. And about five minutes later there was the sound of barking. "Here she comes, then."

"Better run for your life," Sully said. "Gonna be messy."

"I'm not going anywhere till I see her," he said. "Bet she looks like a drowned rat. I know it's an easy laugh, but come on."

Then Beau appeared looking like he'd been through combat, mud up to his ears, hair slicked down and soaked. He pranced in front of the porch, barking and Sully stood up from his chair. "Where is she, Beau?" he asked. And Beau answered by barking and prancing. "Holy Jesus," he muttered, going into the store quickly.

Connie followed him, watched as he gathered up bottled water, the first aid kit, rain slicker, some energy bars and dog biscuits as incentive.

"What are you doing?"

"Going to get her," he said.

"No, Sully," Connie said. "I'm going. Will Beau take me?"

"I don't know. I suppose he might—he's back and he's riled and he's soaked to the bone. I don't think he woulda left her. Unless he had to."

"I'm going, Sully."

"Why? Why you?"

"I'm a paramedic, for God's sake. If she's hurt, you think you can carry her? I have a better first aid kit in the truck. I have walkie-talkies. You should stay here in case she comes back and you can radio me. I'll try to get Beau to take me to her."

"He ain't trained in that, you know. But I have sent him off to get Molly when she wanders a little far and he could manage that."

Connie made tracks to his truck. He loaded up his backpack, changed his shoes for boots, put a rappelling rope over one shoulder, put on a harness and grabbed an extra in case. He wasn't sure he'd have to lower himself down a hill or cliff but if he did have to he wasn't going to come back for that stuff. He checked his GPS unit—charged.

Sully was on the porch. "Want me to call the search group?"

"Let's see what Beau gives me first," he said. "I have a feeling he knows what he's talking about." He handed Sully a walkie-talkie. Then he looked at the dog, gave him a pet and said, "Take me to her, Beau."

Many people will walk in and out of your life, but only true friends will leave footprints in your heart.

—ELEANOR ROOSEVELT

Chapter 7

SIERRA SHIVERED AND CHECKED HER WATCH
every two minutes. She had been sitting for over a half hour
and it was cold back in the woods. Beau had abandoned her
and was probably chasing a deer or rolling around in bear poop
somewhere. Her teeth chattered. Molly shivered and Sierra held
her close against her thigh, arm around her, trying to lend heat.

At forty minutes since Beau took off she wondered if she
should start to hobble or crawl or scoot on her butt. She checked
her ankle almost as often as her watch. It was looking more re-
pulsive by the minute—growing red and purple and fat. She
took a drink of her water and then held Molly's chin up and
squirted some in her mouth. Molly looked up at her with very
sad, sympathetic eyes. "I'm sorry," she told her new best friend.
"I put you in a terrible, scary situation. I should have been paying closer attention to the ground." Molly just licked her.

"You are the nicest friend I've ever had," she told Molly. Soak-
ing wet, all her fluff matted down with rain, she didn't seem to
be very big. "Imagine, I could be out here alone, but I feel like
I'll never be alone again now that I found you."

"You're not alone now, either," a voice said. She jumped in
sudden fear and looked up to see Connie and Beau standing on

the trail not too far away. She grabbed her chest, tried to slow her lurching heart. "What's up, Sierra?"

She sat on a rock and lifted her foot toward him. "I fell. I messed up my ankle, I guess. I tried walking on it and I can, but... I looked around for a strong stick or branch I could use like a cane, but no luck."

Connie came forward and shed his backpack, rope and extra harness. He knelt in front of her and lifted her foot, pulling down the sock to look at her ankle. He gently turned it back and forth and she winced. "Crap," he said. "What an ugly mess."

He dug around in his backpack and brought out an Ace bandage.

"Were you going climbing?" she asked, noting the ropes and harness.

"Nope, I was coming after you."

"What's the rope and everything for?"

He met her eyes and once again she was startled by the beautiful robin's egg blue. "I didn't know where I'd find you, Sierra. You could've been at the bottom of a ravine or something." He pulled a walkie-talkie off his belt. "I got her, Sully. She hurt her ankle. I'll bring her back."

"You need transport?" Sully's raspy voice asked into the radio.

"No, I'll transport her."

"How are you going to do that?" Sierra asked. "Are you going to cut down tree branches and build a litter and drag me home?"

"No, I'm going to piggyback you," he said. "The preferred method is the fireman's carry, over the shoulder, but a half hour of that would just about ruin you." He unlaced her hiking boot. "I'm going to wrap this ankle to help get the swelling under control but I'm not taking the boot off—you might not get it back on and it'll be easier to carry while it's on your foot. When we get back to Sully's we'll elevate it, put ice on it and I'll wrap it properly. We might have to go get an X-ray."

"Do you think I broke it?"

"You'll need an X-ray to know that, Sierra. You have water?"

"Yes," she said, holding out her bottle.

He took it and shared it with Beau, who had done a lot of running lately. Then he gave Beau and Molly a couple of treats.

"Did Beau fetch you?" she asked. "I didn't have many options but I thought he might be able to get himself home—he's familiar with the trails out here."

"He did. I think we got ourselves a search animal. Or maybe just a smart animal, I don't know. But he did come for Sully and he brought me to you."

"I couldn't let Molly go. I thought she'd probably follow Beau, but what if she didn't? I couldn't go find her if she got lost."

He finished wrapping up her ankle. "Are you in a lot of pain?"

"Only when I step on it and then, zowie."

He dug around in his backpack and came out with two bottles of water, handing them to her. Then he stuffed the rope and harnesses in his backpack. He took the pack behind the rock she'd been sitting on and hid it behind a bush. He covered it with his rain slicker.

"What are you doing?"

"I don't need the extra weight. I'll come back for it later or tomorrow. You about ready to go home?"

Her teeth chattered and she nodded.

"You'll warm up a little with my body heat," he said. He crouched in front of her. "You're in charge of the water, for me and the dogs. Put it in your backpack and climb on—piggyback."

"Oh, I don't know, Connie. What am I going to do if I break your back?"

He threw her a look over his shoulder that said, "Don't be ridiculous."

"Let's think about this," she said. "You don't have to impress me. I know you're very strong. If I could just lean on you..."

"That'll take too long. Besides, I have to be able to carry

seventy-five pounds up fifteen stories to stay qualified. This will be easier, so let's do it. Come on."

"All right," she said. "It's your funeral."

"That was unnecessary," he said. He hoisted her up, settled her with a couple of bounces. "How's that feel?"

"I feel fine. How do *you* feel?"

"Like we're going for a long walk," he said. "Hang on to Molly's leash. I'm not chasing her. Come on, Beau! Let's do it." And off he went. After ten minutes or so, breathing harder than he had been, he stopped and lowered her to the ground. He was a little raspy. "Little rest. Water please." He shook out his limbs, stretched his back, drank some water, crouched in front of her again.

"Take a little more time," she said.

"I'm ready."

"Really, take a little more—"

"Come on," he said. "I don't want to be doing this all day."

"All right, all right." She climbed on. "Is there anything I can do to make this easier?"

"Tell me a story," he said.

"A *story?*"

"Tell me your story, then. When did you decide to move out here? And from where?"

"A couple of months before I got here. Cal had been after me. He and Maggie wanted me to come. I wasn't sure that was a good idea so I thought about it for a while."

"But you came. From where? And why?"

"You're very nosy," she said. "I was living in Des Moines in a little house with some roommates. My parents live on a farm in the southern part of the state. I'd been through a series of dead-end jobs and I knew I needed to do something different. And I missed Cal. He's my favorite sibling and we were really close growing up."

"What kind of jobs?" he asked.

She sighed. "Seriously bad jobs. I had some college—about three years that took me about six to get because I had to work. I went to school in Michigan and when Cal's wife died and he left the state, I—"

"Wait! His *wife* died?" Connie asked.

"You didn't know that?"

"No, I didn't know that!"

"Three years ago. They were married about eight years, I think. She was a lawyer, too. They were very happy, but she had scleroderma. It's—"

"I know what it is," he said. "It's awful, that's what it is."

"Yeah, the poor woman. My poor brother. After she died and he left Michigan, so did I. About six months later. But he was off on some odyssey to find himself and there was no place for me in that. So, I went back to Iowa, kicked around for a few months near the farm, took a couple of jobs I hated but paid decent and had benefits. Over the last year and a half I waitressed, cleaned airport bathrooms, worked in a couple of nursing homes. The worst job was in a recycle center, separating stuff. Handling garbage, basically. It was awful. My life was going nowhere so coming out here to see if I could make sense of things didn't seem like a bad idea. Cal made sense of his. I think it all came together when he found Maggie."

"Maggie's cool," Connie said. "Didn't you have a guy?"

She laughed. "Oh, Connie. No, there wasn't a guy..."

"Why'd you say it like that? Like it was a dumb question?"

"It wasn't a dumb question," she said. "I don't have a good answer, that's all. I went out with some guys but... Okay, here's the deal—I can't pick 'em. That's all. If I met some guy I liked, odds were excellent he was a loser. There you have it."

"Describe 'loser,'" he said.

"Come on, don't ask me that. You'll just find out how really incompetent I am and I'd rather you think I'm smart and nice."

"I do. Describe loser."

She took a deep breath. "Liars. Cheaters. Guys with bad habits or mean personalities or nasty tempers." *Or psychopathic stalkers,* she thought. That was the real reason she'd left Des Moines suddenly. She thought she saw him there. She wasn't absolutely sure but she saw a guy at a distance, about a block away, who was a dead ringer for Derek Cox. She decided this invitation of Cal's couldn't have come at a better time.

Connie just marched on for a while, silent. Contemplating. "Not one good man?" he finally asked.

"Well, the problem could be me," she said. "I saw Colorado as an opportunity. For self-examination. For renewal. A fresh start."

"Because you'd like to find a good guy," he said.

"I'm not looking for a guy. Definitely don't want to find another loser," she said with a laugh. "Really, I love my life as one person. And now that I have Molly, I feel so connected. Molly is so wonderful. A little naughty and in the most innocent way." The dog looked up at her. "Yes, I'm talking about you. She loves to please. She smiles, she honestly does. When she emerges from puppyhood she'll be the most magnificent dog alive."

Connie grunted.

"Need a rest?" she asked.

"Nah, I'm good. Just seems like since it takes so little to make you happy, you should've found the right guy years ago."

"Maybe I'm finally changing, Connie. Wanna tell me about your girl?"

"My what?"

"Your girl. Don't you have a girl?"

He snorted. "I have a lot of girls."

She laughed. "That figures."

"What do you mean, figures? I go out, okay. I have girls I go out with but I'm not in a relationship."

"Well, that figures…"

He stopped walking and let her slide gently to the ground. "Water," he said.

She pulled a bottle out of her pack and watched as he took a drink, then squirted water in both dogs' mouths. He went through his shaking-out-limbs and stretching maneuvers again, took a few deep breaths, a little more water, then presented his back. "Up you go."

"Are we almost back?" she asked.

"Not far now," he said. And off he went.

A few minutes passed before he said anything. "I had a girl a few years ago. Couple of years ago, I guess. It didn't work out."

Sierra didn't say anything.

"I guess she had a short attention span. She—"

"I don't need to know," Sierra said.

"Someone else came along, got her attention and that was the end of that. Since then I've just been going out for fun. Just friends, you know. There hasn't been anyone serious is all I'm saying."

"Okay, fine, you don't have to explain."

"I know! I'm not explaining. I'm telling you because you told me and that's what people do!"

"Stop it. You're going to get all out of breath."

"I'm fine." He went quiet again. "We might have that in common, you know."

"What?"

"Not being able to pick 'em."

"Then it's probably good we're not picking any right now," she said.

"I never saw it coming," he said.

"Really... I don't need to know this..."

"She cheated. With a guy I knew. A guy I work with."

Sierra groaned.

"So it was pretty ugly," he said. "But that was a couple of years ago. And I don't even think about it anymore."

"I can see that," she said. "Look, I'm sorry that happened to you."

"Yeah. Shit happens."

Thank God the back of the store came into sight. Sully was standing outside the back door, out by the garden. Beau ran to him so she let Molly's leash drop. "Okay, Molly," she said, and her best girl charged for Sully.

When Connie reached Sully, Sierra could see he looked concerned. Worried. "What we got, Connie?"

"A badly sprained ankle, at least. It's going to need an X-ray." He let her slide down to balance on one foot, leaning on him. "You wanna try to get a little cleaned up, Sierra? I'll tote you over to your cabin and if you can clean up and change out of your wet clothes without putting weight on your ankle, you can. Or I can help you. I've seen a lot of naked girls." He grinned.

She made a face. "I'll manage," she said. "I hate for you to go to any more trouble."

"Really, if you walk on it, you could have bigger problems. You shouldn't walk on it."

"I can take her for an X-ray, Connie," Sully said.

"They see me in that urgent care all the time," Connie said. He grinned. "I'm influential there. You just worry about the store and call Cal. You might be late for dinner. She'll probably be on crutches. And you'll have to see about Molly. I think Molly and Beau—they might need a little extra food and water."

Sully picked up Molly's leash and looked down at the two wagging, smiling dogs. "They look ecstatic to me."

"Oh, Sully, I'm sorry—they're filthy. And I bet they stink. Maybe if you call Cal he'll help out," Sierra said.

"I ain't crippled," Sully said. "I been washing dogs since before you were born. Come on you two."

Connie presented his back. "Up you go. Let's get this done." And he carried her off to her cabin. "I'll call the urgent care in town and let them know we're coming. Luckily, they have an X-ray. Can you get along on your own? Hopping and using furniture to hold yourself off that foot?"

"I got it," she said. "Thanks."

Connie felt like an idiot. He had no idea why he'd made so many lame comments to Sierra. He had a lot of girls? Since when? His last serious girl cheated with a guy he worked with? Why not just direct her to the Facebook crap that had been posted at the time? He'd seen a lot of girls naked? Very classy, Connie.

Sierra cleaned up and Connie took her to the urgent care in Timberlake. He had called ahead so the technician took an X-ray and the urgent care doctor said it looked like a bad sprain. He said he'd send the films over to the orthopedic surgeon to see if he found anything more than that. The prescription was a wrap, ice, elevation, stay off it for a couple of weeks. At least.

"I'm a waitress!" Sierra said.

"Not for two to three weeks. You don't want to ignore this, screw it up and limp for the rest of your life. I'll write you an excuse so your boss doesn't fire you. And a prescription for pain meds," the doctor said.

"I'm okay," she said. "I don't need pain meds."

"You might," he said. "I'll give you the prescription and if you need it, you'll have it."

And that was it. Connie stopped by the firehouse to change into some dry, clean clothes he had in his locker and had her back at the Crossing by 7:00 p.m. Cal and Maggie were there. Maggie was setting one of the tables on the front porch; it appeared they'd brought dinner because Sierra had an injury. Cal came out to Connie's truck and plucked Sierra out of the passenger seat and carried her up to the porch.

Connie had wanted to do that. Instead, he followed, carrying her crutches.

"Looks like you're all set," Connie said. "Cal, she got a prescription for pain meds but she didn't want to fill it."

"I'm fine," Sierra said. But by the look on her face, she was barely fine.

"I'd get the pills, just to have them."

"I just need ice and elevation."

"I'll see you later, then."

"Oh no, you don't," Maggie said. "I set a place for you. You're having dinner with us."

"Aw, I'm kind of..." He sniffed in the general direction of his armpit. "I changed but I didn't want to waste time on a shower."

"We're all hardworking people here," Sully said as he came out of the store with a steaming casserole dish for the table. "Besides, my nose has been dead about ten years now. My eyes and ears are struggling to catch up with my nose."

"Sit down, Connie," Maggie said. She was adjusting Sierra's foot up on a chair. "You should get a whiff of me after about six hours inside a skull. It's amazing. Right now," she said, sniffing her sleeve, "I smell like wet dog. And we owe you at least dinner. Maybe dinner and a movie."

"Okay, it's your funeral," Connie said.

"That was unnecessary," Sierra said, smiling at him. "Come on, sit down. After all, you saved my life. We're bonded now."

"He saves lives for a living," Cal said. "Don't give him too much attention."

"You weren't likely to die, Sierra," Connie said. "Just get very wet and make your ankle more swollen." He pulled up a chair, as far away from the group as possible, taking care to sit between Cal and Sully. He wanted to sit by Sierra, but opted instead to sit across from her. He could look right at her.

Cal disappeared and returned with salad and French bread. Sully disappeared and returned with serving spoons and tongs. Everyone sat. Then no one moved.

"What have we got here," Connie asked, suddenly starving.

"Low-sodium vegetarian lasagna and gluten-free French bread," Maggie announced proudly.

"Thrilling," Sully mumbled. "I hope I get to pick a last meal before I croak. Convicted killers get to..."

"It's delicious," Maggie said. "Stop bitching."

"Rejoice," Cal said. "Maggie doesn't cook."

"I cook," she said. "But you cook better and I'm okay with that."

And thus the dinner progressed with stories, jokes, banter, debate. Connie liked the way Cal and Maggie poked at each other, the way Sully poked at everyone and not the least of which was poking at himself. The lasagna was good despite the fact that there wasn't any meat. Connie liked it and it got him talking about his diet. He was a little obsessive about his food and his exercise. He'd always been, since he was fifteen anyway. He avoided processed foods, he told them.

Well, there was that period of time a couple of years ago when he'd been pretty dysfunctional, didn't work out much, ate whatever was handy, got a little flabby and out of shape. People joked about the divorce diet but in Connie's case he'd actually gained fat, had a little floppy belly, couldn't sleep, couldn't concentrate.

He didn't mention that part. He just said he was a little obsessive, having been small when he was a kid.

It was only about eight when he noticed Sierra was getting droopy. He met her eyes across the table. "I bet you're worn-out," he said softly.

"I think so."

He pushed back his chair and stood. "Sierra's saying goodnight and then so am I. Dinner was great, Maggie, but I need a shower. First I'm going to take my rescue back to her cabin, then I'll take off. Oh—someone will have to take her into town tomorrow if the orthopedist wants to see her—she can't drive with that bad ankle. If you need my help, just call."

"I got it," Cal said. "I can take her to her cabin if—"

"I'm good," Connie said. "By now she's almost an appendage."

"I'll bring ice," Cal said.

Connie scooped Sierra off her chair, swung her past the crutches leaning against the wall, clicked his teeth to Molly, told her come on, and took Sierra down the steps and across the yard.

She leaned her head against his chest and he felt warm there. Warm and cozy and pleasant. "You're going to sleep good tonight," he said, resisting the urge to drop a kiss on her head.

"You're going to sleep even better," she said. Then she yawned.

"Listen, about before, all that stuff about my ex, I don't know why I brought that up. It didn't mean that much, you know? It's so over I can hardly remember her face. She's still working in Timberlake and I run into her sometimes but if it wasn't for that I wouldn't even recognize her."

"I thought nothing of it," Sierra said. "But what I told you? About attracting losers? It's real, so stand clear. It's possible that if I like you, it turns you into a loser."

He laughed. "I'm not worried. I'm kind of stuck with who I am."

"Thank you for helping me today," she said.

"No big deal," he said.

"Connie, you carried me on your back for over a mile!"

"Like Cal said, it's what I do. Don't give me too much attention for it." He put her down in front of the little cabin. "You'll be okay now. Your brother is bringing ice. I have to work the next couple of days but if you need something, I can get a few hours of personal time."

"I have Cal. And Sully. And Maggie, too—she doesn't go back to Denver for a few days."

"Well, you're in good hands, then," he said, backing away. "Have a good sleep."

"You, too."

He headed for his truck. He passed Cal, who had an ice pack

and Sierra's crutches. There was very little activity around the grounds; a few campfires here and there. There was a couple down near the lake. They seemed almost wrapped around each other and Connie envied them.

He was suddenly melancholy. He liked Sierra. She'd been up against his back or in his arms for a long time today and it had been perfect. And she, like him, had no confidence real love would ever find her. He understood the feeling.

But damn, he wasn't ready. He might never be ready. He'd been getting by just fine so why now? Why her?

Look out, Connie, he told himself. Looks like you're going down...

Sierra leaned on her door, feeling cold. Molly sat patiently beside her. They both watched Connie walk away and Sierra noted, he did not have a swagger. Nope. Just an even, powerful, confident stride. His back was straight, his legs long, his waist narrow. His arms must be sore, she thought. His back must ache. Even though she wasn't heavy, he'd carried her for so long. And until today she thought his words sometimes had a little bite in them, but today, he was nothing but sweet.

He regretted mentioning the ex and she knew what that meant—he was still stung. He thought they had something in common, that failure to find a good partner. Ha! He had no idea! She hadn't even thought about falling in love! She'd just been looking for a guy and, back in her drinking days, just about any man would do. They usually turned out to be creeps and users and liars, but not unlike she had been. Then that last one, the one she'd let into her life, the one who put her in danger, the one who left her in trouble, that one made her realize she'd been in no shape to have a man in her life. Not until she could stand on her own two feet, use actual clearheaded judgment, would she deserve the kind of man she really wanted. Needed. Could love for real.

At dinner, they told the story of how Maggie was lowered over a cliff to save Jackson Canaday, who had fallen, cracked his skull and lay unconscious on a precipice three hundred feet from the ground. If he came to and rolled around, he'd have fallen the rest of the way and be dead. If Maggie hadn't been lowered down there to drill holes in his skull with an ordinary shop drill, he'd be dead. If the rope that dangled her down to that ledge had given way, she'd be dead. And then Connie and his paramedic team had gone after her, pulling her and the injured Jackson to safety.

He had just looked at his dinner, shy. Modest.

How many times a week was he a superhero, she wondered. How many women had he carried out of a burning house or across the trail for an hour? Because she wanted to be the only one.

She made no sense to herself.

Cal was walking toward her. He smiled as he passed Connie. She took the crutches and let him into her cabin and he waited for her to get in her pajamas—a T-shirt and boxers—then propped her foot up on a pillow and gently covered it with the ice pack. He pulled a couple of pills out of his pocket.

"Motrin," he said. "Maggie checked with the urgent care and you can have two more—won't wig you out or hurt your tummy since you had a nice dinner."

"She called urgent care?"

"Uh-huh. Dr. Maggie is on a first-name basis with every doctor and nurse in town. I know you don't mess around with the other stuff. But don't suffer, Sierra. Call if you need something. Maggie can fix you up, maybe something better than Motrin but nonaddictive. Is your phone charged?"

"All charged. Will you please fill the water bowl for Molly?"

"Sure. Can you think of anything you need?"

She shook her head.

"I'll give you a call tomorrow, maybe around lunchtime. If

you need to go to town, I can take you. You can call the boss at the diner, right?"

"He's going to fire me," she said.

"Tell him you've got a good lawyer."

She gave him a weak smile.

"Oh, you're very tired," Cal said. "I'm going to get out of here." He gave Molly a pat and then watched as the dog got up on the bed beside Sierra, cuddling close. He just smiled and shook his head. "Be sure to call if you need me," he said.

"It's just a sprained ankle, Cal," she reminded him.

"Call for any reason."

"Just go home," she said.

"Listen, stop moping and feeling sorry for yourself. You're going to be fine. And in case you're wondering, Connie is a good guy. He's okay."

She nodded and Cal slipped out the door.

"But I'm not," she said to Molly.

Out of suffering have emerged the strongest souls; the most massive characters are seared with scars.

—Edwin H. Chapin

Chapter 8

CONNIE KNEW IT WAS GOING TO SEEM A LITTLE obvious, but he went out to the Crossing the next three days. His first excuse was he had to pick up that backpack he'd hidden when he went to find Sierra, then he wanted to check on her, maybe give the dogs a little workout so they'd be less restless. Then he said he'd just spend time with her since she couldn't go anywhere. The first day she was down—feeling bad about what her injury meant for other people. Byron, who she couldn't help at the diner; Sully, who she couldn't help at the Crossing; the dogs, who were being neglected by her. The next day she felt better, the swelling was down and after talking with Byron, she was cheerier. With summer so close, school would be out soon and he would have a surplus of waitresses and could cover the mornings. The third day, the campground wasn't very populated and she was feeling better about taking a rest.

"Don't you have to work?" she asked him.

"I've worked two days this week so far and was off one. I just took a couple of hours to come out and check on you," he said. "It's personal time." And he was there every day to see how things were going. If he had a lot of time, he helped out at the store and grounds. If he didn't, he spent an hour or so visiting and then left.

After a week had passed he drove her into town to see her doctor. The doctor told her she could drive as long as she didn't put all her weight on that ankle. That cheered her up considerably.

"You don't have to keep coming out here to check on me," she told him.

"I check on Sully a lot anyway," he said.

"Sully needs checking on?" she asked.

"No more than you," he said. "If you don't want to be friends, say so. I'll make sure to only talk to Sully and the dogs."

She looked at him with a crooked smile. "Friends?"

"We barely know each other, but if you want to consider something more than friends, we can keep that in mind. For later."

"Ha," she laughed. "You're playing me!"

"Don't be ridiculous," he said. "I wouldn't know where to start."

What he was doing was moving really, really slowly so he wouldn't find himself falling for her and then ending up in the same bucket of shit like he had with Alyssa.

Since Sierra was getting around pretty well, he went to the Crossing a couple of times to find she wasn't even there. She'd been running some errands, Sully said. She'd gone to Cal's to check out the barn and to Leadville to poke around.

But when she was there, they'd stake out a piece of sunshine and talk for an hour or so. She asked him when he decided to become a fireman.

"That's a little murky," he said. "I wanted to be a firefighter since I was about four, but I also wanted to be a cowboy, an astronaut and a hobo."

"Hobo?" she asked with an incredulous laugh.

"You know, just a backpack and the open road. But I was a very scrawny kid. I just didn't grow for a long time and I got sick a lot—winter colds and stuff. I got teased a lot, picked on a lot. My dad was the worst—he picked on everybody. So, I wanted to be someone big and strong and someone everyone looked up to."

"And here you are," she said. "Everybody loves Connie."

"Nah," he said.

"Oh, they do, but never mind that. So, you were scrawny and picked on and then...?"

"Then finally I grew. Not a moment too soon, that's for sure. But I hit fifteen and bam! Instant hormones. My mother said I grew six inches in one year and I don't know about that, but my feet were awful big. I played sports, worked out a lot, and in my senior year I thought, yeah—I think I'll be a firefighter. But you can't do that at seventeen and it takes a lot of preparation. I worked all over the place, mostly physical jobs—I worked as a furniture mover, a trucker, ranch hand, you name it. I took a few college courses. Rafe and I did almost everything together—we got jobs together, went to school together, applied to the fire department together. And that's it, really. The history of Connie Boyle."

"That's a work history. What about the other stuff. Did you go to prom?"

"Yeah, I went to prom. I was a football player, it was practically the law. Didn't you?"

She shook her head. "My situation was a little different than yours. But let's get back to you. How are things with you and your dad now?"

That one made him a little uncomfortable. He looked away for a moment. Then he met her eyes. "My dad was a dick. He was mean to my mother and me. My mom divorced him when I was six and even as a little kid, I was not sorry to see him go, even though my mom cried all the time for months. Then she did something I will never understand. She married another dick. Another mean, snotty, verbally abusive asshole. Why would she do that? She said I'd understand someday but I do not understand and hope I never do."

"Sadly, I get it. People do it all the time. Not on purpose. I don't know why we do it, but some of us are magnets to mean assholes. Luckily for you, when women are picking out their husband they should look at how that guy treats his mother, not how he was treated by his father. But I guess at some point all family relationships matter."

"Did you have good family relationships?" he asked her.

"I did, actually. But there were…extenuating circumstances. Like the fact that my dad has struggled with mental illness his whole adult life. That's a little hard to work around."

"I guess so," he said emphatically. "Wanna go out to dinner? Maybe Colorado Springs?"

"No," she said, laughing.

"Too soon?"

"Way," she said.

"Okay. Wanna go down by the lake?"

"Okay," she said, starting to get up.

"Stay put," he said. "I'm going to get a beer—I'm not working tonight. You want something?"

"Diet Coke?"

"You got it."

He went inside and bought a beer and a Diet Coke. He argued a little with Sully about paying for it since it was for Sierra, but in the end Sully grudgingly took his money. He put the beer in one pocket, the Coke in the other, went back outside and scooped her up off her chair and carried her to the picnic table by the lake. She squealed and got the dogs barking and running circles around them.

"What are you doing?" she laughed.

"You like it when I carry you. And then you're really nice to me."

"I'm always nice to you!"

"You're nicer when I carry you. I have a devious plan. I'm going to be nice and friendly and you're going to like me."

"I already like you, Connie."

"A lot," he said. "You're going to like me a lot."

"Sully warned me to look out for the firefighters. They're either real gentlemen with the women or they're dogs."

He stopped walking for a moment. He couldn't help that a little scowl showed up on his face. "He's right. And I know who's who."

Sierra knew Connie wasn't a dog. Not only did he have a fan club around Timberlake and the Crossing, she could tell by his behavior. And while she hated to admit it to herself and absolutely wouldn't admit it to anyone else, she was enjoying his attention. She was not grateful for the sprained ankle, but one of the perks was Connie. It might've taken months for them to get friendly much less have these cozy talks.

Since she was able to drive, she met Moody for coffee at the diner. She was getting to know him better. The personal side of his story made him more real to her. She asked him if he still struggled with wanting a drink.

"While I was in rehab thirty years ago, my wife moved out of our house. I agreed with her decision—our marriage was a troubled mess. I was a drunk and she was a harpy. We had a lot of work to do. Oh, she came to family week at rehab—she was willing to do the work but I'd worn her out and we decided it was best if she moved out for a while. So she did. When I knew she was gone I called a sober friend and asked him to go to the house and get rid of all the liquor before I went home because I felt so vulnerable without my harpy codependent wife to watch my every move. I told him I had bottles stashed everywhere. I told him to please get rid of all of it. When I went home, he had. And I spent the entire night tearing the house apart looking for the secret bottles he might've missed. Not so I could drink, but because it made me afraid, having them lurking there. I ransacked the house to find them and get rid of them. I never did find one." He shook his head. "I was at a lot of meetings on that. But you know why? Really, why? Because no one is conscious of the absence or presence of alcohol the way alcoholics are. We count people's drinks. We wonder how anyone can leave half a drink on the table. Other people don't worry about it. Other people can be done and walk away."

"That hypervigilance is very tiring," she said. "I'm working on minding my own damn business. I don't want to wonder when someone looks at me if they know."

"Well, sometimes they do know. Or guess. What other people think of me is none of my business. Some people guard their anonymity like it's a precious jewel that will blow up if they breech it while others go on talk shows with it. What you do with yours is up to you. Just don't handle anybody else's."

"Course not," she said. "When do I start to feel normal?" she asked.

"When did you last feel normal?"

She had never felt normal in her entire life. She bit her lower lip. "This could be problematic," she said.

"Do you know what prayer I believe God hears the most? The very most?" Moody asked. "'Dear God, why can't I be like everyone else?'"

"Do you feel normal?"

He didn't answer right away and remained silent while their coffee was refilled. Moody took a minute to make adjustments with cream and sugar. He stared at his cup a minute. "There have been days I've felt like the job I have ahead for the day is equal to emptying the ocean of water using a fork. And on stranger days I thought everything was right with the world and God was in his heaven. What if this is the new normal?"

"What if?" she echoed. "What's your most frequent prayer? To not drink?"

"Nah. I'm not going to drink, but I'm vigilant lest I forget. My favorite prayer is, 'Dear God. I'll pedal if You'll steer.'"

"I like that," she said. "I like that very much."

"It's yours. It wasn't copyrighted."

Two weeks passed with Sierra on crutches, her ankle feeling better all the time, the bruising going from purple to a yellowish blue with a hint of green. She was diligent about keeping it elevated as much as possible, staying on her crutches when walking, but she was in only the slightest discomfort—unless she accidentally put weight on it.

Sierra decided to look around a Colorado Springs mall since she had the time. She'd been to the city before when she went to a rock climbing gym but that was the extent of her exploration. She even located a meeting over there and if there was time, she might attend after shopping. But what she was really interested in was spending a couple of hours checking out the clothing stores, the only bookstore in the mall and maybe doing a little people watching.

It had been a long time since she'd been in a department store. She looked through some clothes and actually bought a pair of shorts, but that's where she stopped because trying them on had been more trouble than it was worth. She spent an hour in the bookstore, which was heaven. She bought a copy of *Wuthering Heights* because she was weak—it was one of her staple reads and it didn't feel right not having it with her. As almost an afterthought, she bought something for Cal. Well, for Cal and Maggie—a little unisex onesie that said Auntie's Favorite on it. Sedona's kids would never know! And that was about all she could really carry while on crutches. In fact, mall walking on crutches was about all the exercise she could take and she headed in the direction of the exit.

And then she saw him. Was it him? She was looking at a man's back, but it sure looked like him—the devil Derek Cox, the man who had changed her life in every way. It was the same thick brown hair, curling at the collar of his powder blue shirt. The same type of shirt he wore a lot because it emphasized his physique, which was impressive. It was tight fitting, the sleeves too tight at the biceps...

That was a year ago, her mind argued. And aren't there lots of shirts like that? Don't a lot of men wear them because they love their muscles? She'd thought about that every time she saw that—couldn't they find a slightly larger shirt with sleeves that didn't pinch? Of course they could.

That belt looked like his belt—she was a little too familiar with that belt. The shoes, she'd been with him when he bought them—Tommy Bahama—just ordinary loafers but they cost a fortune. She barely knew him then. It was the day of their one and only official date and she'd been impressed. How many people could have that hair, that shirt, that belt, those shoes?

The man was with a woman. A girl, really. His hand was gently guiding her at the small of her back and she had long blond hair.

I had long blond hair then, Sierra remembered.

The girl was laughing, happy to be with him. Would she be happy tomorrow?

Sierra worked those crutches hard, following him because as much as she didn't want him to know she was there, she needed to know if it was really him. She moved over to the side of the mall walkway, closer to the storefronts in case she had to dart inside to avoid him. She tried to stay a little bit out of sight.

That gait, the way he walked—it had to be him. His heels lifted a little more than necessary with each step—the swagger. His confidence showed in his walk. He was headed for the same exit she would use, but she followed anyway. She kept what she thought was a safe distance—he didn't know she was in Colorado. And why would he be looking for her at this late date?

The man reached the exit door and he turned toward his companion. Derek, the bastard, didn't have a nose that big! Did he? She was frozen. Her eyes were probably huge. She didn't know if it was him or not.

He turned to look over his shoulder, typical. She remembered thinking that was odd about him, always looking behind himself like that, careful to see if anyone was following him, looking at him, looking for him. She thought it was odd until he committed a crime, then she got it.

Before she could study the face more closely, she turned her face away, looking down, her brown hair making a canopy over her profile, concealing her. She waited a few long seconds. She slowly turned, peeking through the strands of her hair.

Gone.

She had to wait a bit before she could dare follow. Maybe it was him. Just in case it was him, he must not see her. He would come right to her, smiling as though they were friends, long-lost friends. He would talk fast, smile broadly, maneuver her away from help or escape, mesmerize her and manipulate her, try to make her think he's okay, not just okay but good for her. By the time she got to the exit doors, there was no sign of them. She watched the parking lot from inside the glass doors. She didn't recognize any people or vehicles.

"Maybe I've just lost my mind," she said to herself.

That's when she realized she'd dropped her packages somewhere. They were gone. She went back the way she'd come— no sign of them. A mall security guard directed her to the lost and found. There were no packages turned in, of course, but they took her name and cell number.

She decided to leave. She sat in the pumpkin for a while, devastated over the loss of a book, a pair of shorts and a onesie. Her throat burned.

Or maybe it was over almost seeing the most dangerous man she'd ever known...

It was the first thaw of spring in Michigan. It was fifty-five degrees that afternoon and she went to her favorite pub to enjoy drinks on the patio with her peeps. The new guy picked her out immediately and they were together all evening. He was so handsome, all the girls were interested, but he chose her. She wouldn't let him come home with her but she did give him her number and she was pathetically thrilled when he called her the very next morning. He showed up at her office building where she worked in accounting for an independent insurance carrier. Her boss was annoyed but then her boss, a middle-aged woman with a stick up her butt, was never happy anyway. Derek wanted to know if he could take her to lunch. Of course he could!

It was much later that she wondered how he had found her. Picked her out like that. Had she told him where she worked? She must have. How else could he have found her? She brushed off the curiosity because who knew what she'd tell someone when she'd been a little lit up with mojitos. Mojitos, a spring drink.

He met her after work. He got sulky when she wouldn't let him spend the night so she tried to make it up to him by being extra sweet and it worked—he went back into Prince Charming mode. Called and texted all the time.

He was fascinating—he dropped out of law school to enlist. Since one of her brothers was a lawyer and the other a captain in the Army, they had something to talk about. He told her how he went to Afghanistan and ended up being trained in special ops as an undercover officer. When he got out of the military, he worked under civilian contract as a…well…the civilian version of a spy, flying all over the world for special projects with a team of specialists. He had grown up in an interesting family—his father was a race car driver. Not one of the famous ones, but he'd made a good living and the family followed races all over. His mother sang backup in a country band—a pretty famous one. His grandfather, a chemist, actually invented the pregnancy test. He had trained malamutes for a while—bomb-sniffing malamutes.

At first she teased him about being Forrest Gump. Then she

began to wonder how a guy barely thirty-five had time to accomplish all that. Then she stopped believing him. But it seemed like the other people in her crowd ate it up.

From that first night, he was never far away. He called, he dropped by her office, he took her to lunch, he took her out in the evening. It wasn't long before he got into her panties and…it was awful. He had trouble getting and maintaining an erection and he grew angrier and angrier until she told him to leave. He refused and they fought until, miraculously, it rose. Then he was on a mission—he wanted to do it every which way. He wasn't ejaculating. It wasn't until she began to say enough is enough and pushed at him that he finally had success.

Then he wouldn't leave. He left her to lie there beside him, wondering what the hell had happened. In the morning she kicked him out so she could get ready for work and decided she wasn't going to be seeing him again.

Of course he pursued her immediately, so she told him over the phone. She wasn't interested in a relationship, especially one that included fighting. He twisted that to make it sound like a guy had a little trouble and wasn't a stud on their first night together and that was it? "No," she insisted. "I don't want a relationship right now, especially one with fighting." She wanted space; no more surprise visits, no more calls, no more texting. She wanted him to move on. She stopped answering calls and texts but he was waiting in parking lots and outside work and he was everywhere. She told some of her friends he wouldn't leave her alone, so he stood back six feet, put his palms up, smiled eerily and didn't exactly do anything, but he was creepy and frightening. He always knew where she was. She'd make plans to go to a different bar or club and guess who would show up? She'd walk around a corner and he was there. A few times she actually bumped into him, splat!

One of her friends said she'd had a creep like that once and you had to be firm and direct. She was as clear as she could be when she said, "Go away and leave me alone! I don't want to date you or anything!"

So he worked the crowd she hung out with, she was always aware of him and she started needing an escort home. She went to the police to talk to someone about him. He was stalking her; she feared he meant her harm.

He didn't have a record. "Stay out of bars," the officer told her. She asked if she could have a restraining order.

"Has he done anything?" the officer asked.

"Besides bother me constantly, watch me, follow me, creep me out? Does he have to do something to hurt me?"

"Yes, or at least threaten you," the officer said. "Ignore him. Call the police if he does anything harmful or threatening."

He began to ingratiate himself to other people in the bars, making them laugh, doing favors, buying drinks, giving them things—he had everything, money, drugs, whatever. People thought he was a little strange but harmless.

She didn't know why he wanted her. She thought maybe he only wanted to hurt her. If she didn't go to her usual haunts, he would still find her wherever she went, try to talk to her, ask her if she wanted a ride, could he take her out for a decent dinner. "I'm a little concerned about you, Sierra," he said. "You're living dangerously."

That's when she became stupider. When she should have stayed away from alcohol to remain vigilant and safe, for some reason she just drank more. But she tried to stay around people. She had a roommate, Bobbie Jo, but they weren't really friends, just two women who needed a roommate to share costs. They got along fine, though Bobbie Jo wasn't around much, off doing her own thing. She had a boyfriend and they were either in bed together or out or at his place.

One night she had a little too much to drink. Not exactly a red-letter day—that happened to her now and then. That night she wasn't sure what had done it—it seemed like it had only been a glass or maybe a glass and a half of wine but man, she was having trouble staying on her feet. Next thing she knew, she was in the car, her car, a six-year-old Honda sedan. And she was dizzy and felt sick. Her head was spinning, her stomach flipping, her vision blurred.

And the car was moving. She struggled to focus, to see what was happening and, oh God, it was him! Driving her car. Derek was laughing and talking to her and telling her they were going to have some fun. He was speeding, she thought. She didn't know why they were in her car. He was turning to look at her while he was driving, saying things that made no sense, like "It's your turn now," and "Let's see if you can get out of this one."

She couldn't understand what was happening. There was a thump and the car skidded to a stop. He got out of the car, got back in and just started driving again. She knew something bad had happened. "You hit something. Did you hit something?" she asked. And he laughed and said, "No, you hit something. Someone. But don't worry—he won't last long."

She started to scream. His hand came out and struck her in the face so hard her neck snapped and everything went black. She was just coming to again when he pulled her car into the small detached garage beside the sixty-year-old two-bedroom house she shared with Bobbie Jo. And when she struggled against her seat belt she saw that her roommate's car was gone…and Derek was pulling down the garage door. She was trapped. With a madman.

"You'll never forget me now," he said.

She couldn't keep doing this.

Most of the way back to Timberlake, she tried out Moody's prayer, promising to pedal if God would steer. Seeping through the murky mess of her brain, through the fear and paranoia, she found herself driving toward Cal. It was approaching dinnertime and she realized Maggie was in Denver. She made a deal with herself—if Cal wasn't home or if there were people around, she would take that as a sign that she shouldn't talk to him about this.

But if he was alone, she would tell him now. She had run from Michigan to get away from Derek, she had run from Iowa when she thought she saw him near where she was living. Where was she going to run next if that really was him in Colorado Springs? She had to find a better plan. She had to tell someone.

She pulled up to the barn and saw that only Cal's truck was parked outside. The front door of the barn stood open and she could hear the Shop-Vac at work. She sat in the pumpkin for a little while, contemplating. If it was Derek Cox in Colorado Springs, she was at risk and would need help. If there was anything she'd learned in the last ten months it was that it was dangerous to try to handle serious problems alone. There was no one she trusted more than Cal.

He saw her standing in the doorway and shut off the vacuum cleaner.

"Hey, you're getting around pretty well there," he said, smiling.

"I have to talk to you about something. Something very serious. It's the hardest thing I've ever done, I think. Telling you this."

"Sit down, relax, just say whatever you have to say. You know I'm on your side."

"I know. Back in Michigan, back before I went home to the farm in Iowa, I ran into some trouble. And no one could help me."

"Go ahead," he said. "Something to drink?"

"Arsenic?"

He chuckled and went to the refrigerator, getting two sodas for them. "Sit," he said. "Take your time."

"I have to get home to Molly soon…"

"Just do it, Sierra. Tell me what you came to tell me. I think you know you can trust me."

She toyed with the tab on the can, taking a couple of deep breaths. "It might seem impossible to believe."

"Come on now, Sierra. You're stalling."

She told him everything, from the first time Derek targeted her, hit on her, to the night that ended in her garage. Her brother's face grew pale, then crimson. She thought his hand was shaking as he lifted his soda can to his lips. His lawyer's poker face wasn't working so well as he listened to her.

"What I couldn't make sense of at the time… I'd been at a bar. A bar I went to sometimes, where I knew people. I wasn't with anyone, but the bartender and waitress knew me. He must have drugged me, slipped something in my glass of wine. Then took my keys and got behind the wheel of my car. I couldn't focus, I was sick. Believe it or not, that didn't happen to me a lot. I didn't get sick, didn't have blackouts, I just got really stupid, unsteady, made bad choices and had a terrible hangover the next day. This was different. He must have drugged me."

"He left you in the garage?"

She looked down at the table where they sat. "After he beat me and raped me," she said quietly. She couldn't look at her brother. She hated that she had shame when she hadn't done anything wrong. "He left me there, walked out, closed the garage door and just walked away. I never saw him again. Well, I thought I saw him a number of times but I'm not sure if it's a mirage made up of my fear or if he really found me."

"What did you do that night?"

"Just what you're not supposed to do—I showered. I tried to treat the cuts and bruises. But then I realized what he'd done and went to a clinic. They did a rape kit but I wouldn't talk to the police. They took some pictures. I know I should have gone to the police but I was just too afraid. Of him. I'd been to the police before—they weren't helpful. I'd asked them for a restraining order…"

"They couldn't give you a restraining order because he annoyed you or scared you—there had to be a crime or a threat, an obvious threat."

"The clinic said they'd be keeping that rape kit for a while, gave me the name of some counselors, a crisis center. They gave me some phone numbers, did some cultures and blood panel, wrote me a prescription for a morning after pill, which I wasn't going to need—I was on birth control. But they said I could call in with my patient number and get the test results and, if needed, get treated for any sexually transmitted disease."

"What did you do?"

"I went home. I decided I had to get out of town. I was all done there. I thought at the very least he'd drug me, beat me and rape me again. I was afraid he'd kill me or something. And I was afraid he'd hit someone out on the road—my memory was spotty but I remember something happened and I don't know where we were. Seems like we weren't in the neighborhood. I don't think we were on the highway. There was a dent and a really long scrape in the fender. I thought about checking with the police to find out if anything happened. Instead, I packed a duffel, drove to the airport, to long-term parking, and left the car. I took a bus to Iowa. I owed money on that car and I abandoned it. I didn't say goodbye to anyone and I turned off the phone, afraid of who might call me."

"Did you tell anyone about Iowa? Does he know about our parents? And that they're in Iowa?" Cal asked.

She shook her head. "I didn't talk about our parents. Not a lot to brag about there, huh? Once I told my roommate I wanted to go to California." She smiled sheepishly. "I did want to. And here I am."

Sierra called Sully to say she had stopped to see Cal, then stayed about an hour. She finished her story and her cola and left to see about her dog before it got much later. Sully was holding dinner to have with her. Letting her leave, letting her crutch her way out into the dusk was hard for Cal—she seemed so small, so alone. He held her for a long time before she pried herself away.

He had asked her if the event of thinking she saw this dangerous man from her past made her want to drink and she had said, "Just the opposite. That was another life and I have no desire to go back. But I think I will go to a meeting tomorrow morning. It never hurts and it usually reaffirms everything I know to be real."

He was so proud of her. Scared for her.

"But thinking I saw him made me realize, what if it was him? If not now, someday? I could disappear for real without anyone knowing the details. I had to tell you. I had to tell someone."

After she left he went for a beer for himself—boy, did he need it.

Cal wasn't sure if Sierra had ever paid any attention to it or not, but he had been one of the hottest criminal defense attorneys in Michigan. He was doing a little lawyering here in Colorado, but nothing too high profile. He was still licensed to practice in Michigan if it came to that, if she needed a defense. He wouldn't defend her, of course. But he knew the best of the best and he could always sit second chair.

Meanwhile, he could get information. Sierra wasn't sure she wanted to know, but it probably wouldn't hurt. Not only was his old detective available by phone, he was no slouch when it came to investigation. He could find out if there was an accident, any police investigation, if this Derek Cox had any kind of criminal record, if he was wanted for anything. He could find out if anyone was looking for him. Or for Sierra. He didn't even have to ask her the make, model and license number of that Honda she'd abandoned—he could find it. If anything came up, if she needed him, he would be ready.

And then there was the issue—if there had been a broken law, they would have to face it or worry about the consequences of obstruction.

She told him that she got a job with the county sorting through refuse in the recycle plant in Iowa. She borrowed Mom's truck to go to work and stopped for groceries or whatever they needed on the way home. After a couple of months, maybe three, she came home from work and her mother told her some man had come around asking about her, asking if she was there. Marissa, who had been dodging "official looking" people her entire life to keep her schizophrenic husband safe, had said, "She's in Michigan, isn't she? I don't know when we last saw her."

"Good old Marissa," Sierra had laughed when she told Cal. "Luckily my benefits with the county kicked in so I looked at rehab, found one facility in Des Moines that would take my insurance."

She didn't go into rehab to get sober, she went to hide out. One thing she knew, having had so many friends pass that way, everyone made a list of who they'd be willing to talk to and no one else could get through. No information was given out about patients except to police officers with warrants. So, she'd talk to Marissa only, she said. And she'd ask if anyone had been looking for her. Then, when the heat was off, maybe she would go to California. The state, not the brother. Funny how things worked out. Cal wanted her and she thought she was as safe with him as anywhere.

She'd been pretty sure she'd find out in rehab that she wasn't a real alcoholic, but just an active young woman who liked to party. "Imagine my surprise," she said to Cal, "when I found out I'm a drunk and the choices for me are booze or death. I didn't even drink every day! I thought real alcoholics were much more ambitious."

"You must have done some heavy drinking," he suggested.

"Oh, there were times," she said. "But guess what else I learned? From a woman in rehab who had been stalked. There might've been a device in my phone to track me. That might've been how Derek could always find me. I got rid of the old phone, so I'll never be able to find out, but it would make sense. To this day I don't know if he left me on the floor of my garage and walked away, done with me, or if he followed me to Iowa. Then to Colorado. Was that him who talked to Marissa? Or was that some law enforcement person because my car was in an accident?"

"I'll look into it," Cal told her. "I'll find out if there was an accident and I won't have to mention your name to do it. But that might fall into the category of stuff you'd rather not know. It could be a very difficult situation."

"Cal, I'd feel terrible if something happened, but I didn't do it. I know I didn't do it. He reminded me the whole time he was assaulting me that there was no proof he'd even driven my car. I might've been drugged, but I heard that. It was his intention from the start, if anything happened, I would be the guilty one."

"You're not afraid of jail?" he asked. "You didn't hide out in rehab because you're afraid of possible jail?"

She looked at him, her eyes so large and liquid. "Wasn't I clear? I didn't do anything wrong. I'm not afraid of going to jail. I'm afraid of *him*. There's just one thing that haunts me. Why? Why would he do that?"

As Cal remembered that, he took several swallows of his beer. But it didn't help. He leaned his elbows on his knees, gripped the beer in two hands, looked at the floor and wept. His baby sister, his beautiful baby sister, tied with a belt, brutally raped and beaten.

Terrified.

"Talk about scared straight," she had said.

Adopt the pace of nature: her secret is patience.

—RALPH WALDO EMERSON

Chapter 9

SIERRA ATTENDED A COUPLE OF MEETINGS AND they helped. She wasn't sure exactly how, but she always came away with a feeling of peace and comfort as if her decision was reaffirmed. It hadn't always been that way. In the early days she fought it hard, got all stirred up and anxious, but eventually she looked forward to a good meeting, knowing something would be said or done that would set her right.

She stopped at the Leadville bookstore and bought a copy of *Wuthering Heights*, more determined than ever to have it now.

One day she took Molly with her to a meeting, but she wiggled so much they had to leave. "You'll never pass that one off as a service animal," Moody said.

"No kidding," Sierra agreed.

When Sierra and Molly were alone together, the dog was calm and quiet and so sweet. One thing that troubled Sierra was that there were times, though rare, when she lifted her hand to pet Molly and Molly flinched a little. Ducked. And Sierra was sure she knew what that meant.

When it was Sierra, Sully and Beau around her, Molly was quiet and only a little playful, trying to nudge Beau into some frolicking or leaning up against Sully to beg a pet. Molly was a cuddle bug. She now had her own blanket that Sierra spread on the bed to keep all those golden hairs off the comforter and it became hers, so that wherever the blanket was spread, whether on the porch or the backseat of the pumpkin, Molly thought of it as her place.

Of course Molly was young and still got in trouble. She got into Sully's garden and ravaged some vegetables, digging up to her shoulders before Sully caught her. Luckily there weren't many fatalities and she hadn't gotten Sully's prized tomatoes. She ate a few more socks, kept jumping in the lake and coming out all full of mud and weeds, and barked too much when she was left alone. "She has separation anxiety," Sierra told Sully.

Sierra and Molly took comfort in each other. They were both in need of a friend, a safe harbor, a confidante. Sometimes Sierra told Molly secrets and Molly listened attentively, showing Sierra those sad, deep eyes, indicating she understood and sympathized.

Sierra and Molly were in the hammock together, Molly's head in the crook of Sierra's arm, gently swaying, when Connie snuck up on them.

"Are you reading to that dog?" he asked.

Sierra and Molly both jumped in surprise and Sierra closed her book while Molly started wiggling and struggling to get out of the hammock. But Connie just started petting her behind the ears and settled her.

"She likes it when I read to her," Sierra said.

"Do you, Molly?" he asked the dog. But the traitor dog just leaned into Connie's big, loving hands and moaned in ecstasy. "What are you reading to her?"

"*Wuthering Heights,*" she said. "Bet you don't even know what that is!"

Connie sighed. "Okay, so it wasn't my imagination—you're cranky. You've been moody all week and I'm done having fun with this. Is something wrong? You have PMS or something? You mad at me?"

"No," she said, a little meekly. "No to all of that, but yes, I've been a little on the quiet side because I've been thinking. About you, as a matter of fact."

He grinned like he'd just won something. "Is that so? Can't get me off your mind?"

"Not exactly," she said, making a face. "If you can be serious, I'll confide in you. If you're going to screw around, I have nothing more to say."

He walked around to the front of the hammock and squeezed onto it, pulling all sixty-five pounds of Molly onto his lap. He leaned back, settled in and said, "Stop being so bitchy, Sierra. I didn't do anything wrong. And you know it."

She sighed. She knew it, he was right. She took a breath. "If we're going to be friends, there are a couple of things you should know. For starters, I'm not like the other girls you've dated."

He shrugged. "We might put that in the plus column."

"The Jones kids have always known we were different. I was born in a bus, for God's sake. Well, not officially—officially I was born in a clinic. Being the fourth child, I guess I was in a hurry and Marissa, my mother, hated to leave my father for even a little while—he could go off the deep end if she wasn't around. So when she was about to drop me, she went into the free clinic and…well, I didn't grow up the way most people do."

"I think none of us did," he said.

"And also…well, I'm an alcoholic."

"Oh?" he asked. "I've never even seen you drink."

"I'm recovering. Just recently made a year of sobriety. That's it," she said. "You should know that."

"Why?"

"It's a significant part of who I am."

"I don't understand," he said. "How's that likely to affect our friendship?" And then he added in an undertone, "Such as it is."

"I go to AA meetings and I don't drink alcohol. For a long time I didn't even use mouthwash that had any alcohol content."

He sat forward in the hammock a little and Molly instantly

put her head on his chest so he could pet her. "Hey, is that why you wouldn't take the pain meds?"

"That's exactly why," she said. "But it worked out that I was just fine with the anti-inflammatories and ice. But see—I'm not just your average girl. I had a complicated childhood and as it turns out, I have a complicated adulthood."

"Okay," he said. "Is this worrying you?"

"What?"

"Telling me this stuff?"

"Yes. No. I mean, think about it—we don't have much in common."

He scratched Molly behind the ears, and she snuggled closer. Molly moaned almost seductively.

"And if my dog likes you better than me, you are banned!"

He couldn't help but laugh at her. "Is this why you've been so cranky? Because you thought we should have this heart-to-heart?"

"I thought you should know some of the more private and personal stuff about me before you get in too deep. And it's just not easy to do, okay?"

"So you were almost born in a bus, you don't drink or take pain pills, you go to AA meetings and you're very particular about who your dog loves best. Feel better now?" he asked.

"Not very," she said.

"Are we going to get in too deep?" he asked hopefully.

"You really don't get it, do you? I'm not like you!"

"Why would I want someone like me? Oh—hey—does it bother you if someone has a drink around you? Like should I be careful not to drink a beer because it might—you know—make you drool with longing or something?"

She rolled her eyes. "It only bothers me to be around people who are getting toasted and obnoxious. Sully has his bedtime drink at night and I have tea and we're very compatible. In fact, he's the best friend I've had in a long while."

"You have good taste," Connie said. "Sully is good people. So, now can we go on a date?"

"What for?" she asked.

"For something to do," he said, turning Molly a bit so he could scratch her tummy.

Sierra started to scratch her tummy, too, and Molly stretched her neck and back legs, offering more of herself to be massaged. "I feel like you're not taking this seriously," Sierra said. "I'm an alcoholic with a very untidy history who has had troubled relationships and you're just a guy who wants a date with the wrong girl. Think. Use your head."

His hand stopped moving and she looked up. Those blue eyes were boring into her. "Thank you for telling me. It's brave of you to tell me personal and private things. But here's what I'd like. I'd like to go do some fun stuff so we're having a good time while we get to know each other better. I like what I know about you so far and you like what you know about me because you act like it and because it put you in a terrible mood worrying about telling me personal stuff. I figure that's because it's important to you that I like you. And I do, so let's not worry about that anymore. And after we have some time together and you believe that I like you for yourself, your totally unlike-anybody-else self, who was almost born in a bus and can't get near liquor, then maybe we'll get closer and make out like teenagers. That would be good."

She was quiet for a minute. "Oh, that was smooth, Conrad."

"I guess I'm not like the other guys you know because I'm not real smooth with the girls," he said.

"Sully said you've always got a girl," she informed him.

"That's not true at all. I mean, I go out with girls sometimes. Okay, I go out with girls a lot. But they're not, you know, relationships."

"Do you have sex with them?"

"I haven't had sex in so long I forget which armpit it's under."

She burst out laughing in spite of herself. "That could be your problem…"

"I'd like to have it with you, though," he said.

She looked at him in wonder. "Do you always say exactly what's on your mind?"

"I told you. You should know that by now—I'm pretty much an open book. No good moves. But here's what we have in common. We both had some bad experiences with the opposite sex, even though I don't know what kind yours were. But you told me—you can't pick 'em. Me either, apparently. I figure that's a really good place to start."

"Is that so?"

"Yes. We're two people who really like each other but are a little unsure about things like getting involved. Because we've had some bad luck. So here's how I think it should go. We'll hang out some more, kiss some, maybe hold on to each other for a while and get all worked up and decide, what's wrong with taking it a little further? It'll be soft and sweet and we'll get wrapped around each other till we can't breathe. If it was winter and if we were in the truck—that little car of yours is out of the question—we'd steam up the windows big-time. It would be better if we were somewhere private, lying down, though. So then we'll do it. If we do it, it will be so good we'll talk about it for years because we were two people who thought we might not ever match up but we did. What do you think of that?"

She was speechless. She couldn't believe her ears. "Did you make that up all by yourself?" she finally asked.

"All by myself," he said.

"And you think we'd be good together?"

"Epic," he said, smiling.

"No," she said.

"It was worth a try," he said. Then he laughed and kissed the dog on her head. "Molly wants me, that's obvious." He put his big hand on Sierra's head and ruffled her hair as if she were a kid. "How's the ankle feeling?"

"Good, as a matter of fact. This week I get to put a little weight on it and if I have no problems, I can go back to work."

He put his hand on her thigh. "Listen, I should've asked before, is there anything you need—like a loan or something? It must be kind of hard being out of work for so long. I'm sure you don't get comped at the diner, especially it not being a work-related injury."

"A loan?" she repeated. "Really?"

"I didn't even think of it until now," he said. "You've got expenses and probably doctor bills and you're out of work. I have some savings and no worries if it takes you a while on the repayment."

Again, she couldn't find her voice. "Connie, you keep blindsiding me. A loan? No, I'm okay. I have some savings, too. And I'm still helping Sully, though not as much as I was—but I can sit behind that counter and ring up sales all day and night. And if I run into trouble, there's always Cal."

"I thought of that, but he's got that house. I built a house—it can really be a pocket suck."

"You built a house?"

"Uh-huh. The one I live in. Just outside of town. I put money down on some land when I was just a kid—I was twenty-two. I'm still paying on it. It'll be paid for when I'm forty-two. And the house—when I'm a hundred and ninety."

"Must be some house," she said.

"It's a pretty simple house, but I'm a firefighter. We do all right, but we're not rolling in dough, though some of 'em act like they are. Thing is, it wouldn't put me out to help if you need it."

"Conrad Boyle, I think you must be about the nicest guy I've ever met."

He grinned at her. "See, you're coming around. That's good."

"Don't get any ideas."

"Sierra, I've had ideas since about the minute I met you. I figure it's only a matter of time."

"Is that why you offered me a loan?"

He made a face. "Of course not. I thought you might need a hand, that's all. That's how you treat friends, Sierra. Don't be a pill."

"I do like you, Connie. That's why I wanted to be honest with you. I've had a lot of problems over the past few years—most of which I made myself. I'm going to be working my way out of them for a long time. I think you could do better than me."

"That's very nice of you to warn me, Sierra. Now let me make up my own mind about stuff like that. And you make up yours. What you see is what you get."

And there's really nothing better than that, she found herself thinking.

He was completely serious and she knew it. Connie Boyle wanted to be her boyfriend. And frankly, she didn't know when she'd had an offer so good. He was completely unfazed by her confessions and seemed to like her just the same. He was, in fact, the first normal guy she'd been attracted to since she was about fourteen.

Over the next couple of weeks, just in the course of conversation, she learned something else about him that should have been obvious from the beginning. He'd been a firefighter for seven years. And a paramedic and a search and rescue volunteer almost as long. It was in his nature to help, to serve. But also— he'd seen some stuff. Some ugly stuff.

"It's a little town, but we have a big highway, some vast rural land, huge mountains and a lot of people passing through. The police handle the crime but we usually get the mop-up—after a crash or suicide or even homicide, except we haven't had one of those in a long time. If you think just because it's a small and friendly place that nothing interesting happens, think again. All people have complicated lives, get in trouble, have problems and emergencies. We're a busy little fire department."

He had a medic's knowledge and perspective. His stories were daring and fascinating. One of their search and rescue guys fell out of a helicopter and was killed—they spent hours looking for his body. It was a freak accident—the guy with the best balance and safety record in the state somehow slid right out of the chopper. Then there was the time some dipshit blew up a house because of an unsettled debt and blew up himself in the process; he was cut in half, his upper body up in a tree three hundred yards from his lower body. An old man died alone while eating a bowl of spaghetti and it was a while before someone realized he might be sick or dead. Hikers and campers were continually lost; farmers and ranchers had mishaps with heavy equipment. They rescued a seventeen-year-old from a grain silo—usually a death sentence but they got him out. They even tracked a fugitive once—that was dicey. He was wanted, they worried about the complications of actually catching him, though he was supposed to be unarmed. "Someone just decided to cut our losses and punched him in the face. Knocked him out cold. No one can remember who did it. But he's behind bars again."

"No one can remember who did it? Did it ever occur to you to check the knuckles in the firehouse?"

With a twinkle in his eye he said, "I guess not."

Sierra lived for stories of his work and she realized her first impression of him was correct—he was a pretty simple man with some shining qualities. He was honest and loyal, and he was incredibly gentle, especially with Molly. Yet there was no doubting his profound strength. She began to think of him as her gentle giant.

One day he showed up around lunchtime and asked her if she could go for a short hike. She told him that might be pushing her luck on her ankle and he said, "I thought we'd go piggyback and take the dogs. Just a half mile. Maybe less."

"Why?"

"I haven't had my workout today and…well, it's a good way

to stay in shape and get close to you. Let's go. Just a half mile, come on."

It was his plot from the beginning, to get her up against his body like that, and they talked while he hiked. Then he put her down to rest and pulled her around to his front, put his hands on her waist and said, "Come on, Sierra. Quit stalling."

She put her arms around his neck and met his lips softly. Then she pulled him tighter and went in for the kill, kissing that sweet mouth of his like a starving woman. She moved over his mouth with passion, letting him tongue her lips apart as he lifted her off her feet. The spectacular kiss didn't stop until Molly barked. He broke away from her lips, but didn't set her back on her feet.

"Hello," he said.

"You planned that."

"Very well, it seems."

"It was just a kiss," she told him.

"One of the best I've had," he said. "Hit me again."

She did. Because the best part of him was that he was playful. And she was a little hooked on it.

She hadn't been kissed in such a long time and kissed so thoroughly—maybe never. What would Moody say? But no—she was not telling Moody or anyone. She was just going to enjoy Connie while she could, before any new disasters befell her.

He put her on her feet. "Told you," he said. "Good idea."

"Well," she said, breathless. "That's where the ideas stop. I'm not going any further with you."

"Water please," he said. She handed him a bottle and he took a long drink, then shared with the dogs. "Ahh," he said. "Take your time, Sierra. I'm stronger than I look. I can wait you out. But I bet pretty soon we're going to do it."

"I don't know about that," she said. "But a word of advice—that armpit thing you've got ideas about? Forget it."

And he roared with laughter.

★ ★ ★

Tom Canaday took a potted geranium to Lola's house. Except for the time ten years ago or so that he did a little remodel work for her on the house, he hadn't been there. He'd been aware of the place, though. It sat on the high part of town and Lola had lived in it with her kids since the boys were babies. They were still pretty young when she divorced and she stayed on.

From the talks they'd had in the diner or when he went to Home Depot where she also worked, he knew that she'd done many of the repairs and upgrades in the house herself. In fact, one of the reasons she loved working at Home Depot was her love of remodeling. The employee discount came in handy. Every time he'd driven by he admired the look of the place as only a man who'd done most of the building and remodeling of his own could.

It was Sunday afternoon, his kids had all scattered and knew they had to be home by five for dinner. He hadn't mentioned to Lola that he'd be dropping by and he expected either no one would be home or everyone would be and he'd be interrupting family time, two teenage boys bouncing off the walls.

His hands trembled. He couldn't remember the last time he'd done something like this. Never, he thought. Never, because he'd married Becky when he was just a kid and had never in his adult life courted a woman. He rang the bell, but all was silent inside. He waited, but there was no sound, no movement.

Just as well. He put the potted plant on the table between two wicker chairs on the porch and headed down the steps. There was no card or anything. Sometime next week he'd tell her he was the one who left it.

"Tom?"

He jumped in surprise. Lola came around the corner of the house. She wore rolled-up jeans, an oversize man's shirt with the sleeves rolled up, sneakers and gardening gloves. Her dark hair was pulled back and covered with a straw hat.

"You scared me!" he said.

"Did you ring the bell?"

He nodded. "I brought you a plant," he said.

"You did? Why?"

He shrugged, feeling kind of dumb. "There were a couple of them on sale at the garden store so I got one for myself and one for you. I should've called. But, I... Ah, I can't stay anyway."

"Of course you can stay," she said, coming up on the porch. "This is lovely, thank you. And perfect. I love geraniums." She pulled off her gloves. "Let's have a glass of lemonade, shall we?"

"Aren't you busy?"

"Not really. The boys are fishing with my dad and won't be home till sunset. I was in the garden—I have some nice vegetables coming in. I'll go in and get us some drinks. Is the porch okay? The weather's so nice, I hate to waste it inside."

"The porch is great," he said. And then he breathed a giant sigh of relief, which she caught because she laughed.

"I'll be right back," she said.

He waited patiently. He felt like a thirteen-year-old boy when all he wanted in the world was for once in his life to be a little slick with a lady. And so he laughed to himself—who was he kidding? He'd never been like that. In fact, he didn't really want to be. He sure hadn't bought a red geranium in an attempt to sweep Lola off her feet.

"It might not be as sweet as you like it," she said as she was coming out the door with a tray and something under her arm. She held the tray with two glasses and a plate in one hand and with the other, snapped open a small serving table. She put it in front of them, set down the tray and took the chair opposite him. "You really have good timing—I was about ready for a break." She handed him a glass. "I think this is the first time you've been to my house."

"I did some work in the kitchen for you about ten years ago or so," he said.

"That's right, now I remember. That was a long time ago," she said with a laugh. She took a drink from her glass. "This is a nice surprise. Thank you for the plant."

"I should've called," he said again.

"Why'd you come over?" she asked. "I mean, this has never happened before."

"I don't know," he said. "Wait, I don't know why I said that. I do know why. We always have nice conversations when I stop at Home Depot or the diner for coffee, but it's always busy. Half the time we can't finish a sentence because someone needs you for something. Or else someone else wants to be in the conversation. And I started thinking, maybe I should really take you out to a movie, but then we wouldn't get to talk, either. I thought it would be nice to have a conversation sometime without you being at work." He sipped the lemonade. "This is good. Um, we're both divorced. I know a lot of women and then again, not very many."

"Now that makes very little sense," she said.

"I don't have any real close friends, that's all. When I think about who I'm comfortable with, the people who come to mind are Sully, Maggie, Cal, a few of the guys around town. And you. I've been divorced a long time now."

"But, really?" she asked. "Really divorced? Because from what little I know, you and Becky were together regularly..."

"That was my mistake," he said.

She waited.

"I was treating it like a time-out when it was not a time-out— it was a divorce. I would be so far ahead if I'd treated it like one."

"That's a little vague."

"Sorry. I didn't realize there were other men in her life. I was naive. I wish I'd known and I wish I'd moved on a long time ago."

"What do you want, Tom?" she asked.

He looked at her. He realized he loved looking at her. "Oh

God, Lola, I don't want anything! I mean, I have no expectations, I don't. But we're a lot alike. We're single, we've been
working at least two jobs, raising our kids on our own, no
spouses, no significant others. I mean, you never said..."

"I've dated, but—"

"We both get help from our parents sometimes. And I have
a brother who's always there for me and you have a sister, but...
I don't want anything," he said again. "I just know I feel comfortable with you and it's nice to have a woman friend. Maggie's
a friend but we don't ever have long conversations or anything,
we don't talk about our lives. You and I—we talk about our
lives. Our families, our folks, our kids, how aggravating it can
be sometimes when there's no other parent in the house to back
us up. We talk about this carpool nonsense, getting the kids
everywhere they have to go. I don't have anyone else in my life
like you. It's...it's comfortable. I finally broke away from that
dead marriage and realized you're the only person of the opposite sex I enjoy spending time with."

"That's very nice, Tom, but I've worked very hard to have
an independent life, the kind I actually like. I'm not interested
in dating. I don't want a boyfriend. I get along just fine without a lover."

That made him smile. "That's good. I don't think I'm a candi-
date for any of those jobs. Could we just be friends?"

"We've been friends for years!"

"I know! Don't you think it's a little weird the only time we
ever talk is when you're at work?"

"It's where I am!"

"And you're also here. So, Lola, how's school going?"

She sighed as if she found this clumsy. "I'm taking a little time
off. Summer, you know—though I could pick up some classes
if I wanted to. But with the kids around more..."

"How long before you get your degree? Elementary ed, isn't it?"

"That's right," she said. "I think it's practical. I love kids, I'm actually very good with them. When it was time to choose a major, it was the best I could do. I should have a career, right? Something to take me into retirement. Something to spend my next twenty years on so I have a pension of some kind."

"I guess so."

"Have you ever thought about that?"

"About teaching school?" he said. He laughed. "After all the years of homework I've invested in, I probably could. If I spend about twenty more years doing seasonal work for the county, I'll qualify for a pension. My work schedule is pretty crazy, so many different jobs, but it works for me with four kids to chase around."

"You like it, though?" she asked.

"Oh, I love it. I do a little of everything. I do chores for Sully in summer, I do a lot of building, mostly interiors. I plow, I pick up trash, mow fields, paint houses, do roadwork—you name it. Every day can be a new job and believe it or not, I like 'em all. Even the garbage pickup. Right now I'm almost full-time at Cal's house—foreman on his project, which means I do some of the work myself, some we hire subs, some we work with the subs. I have to keep some days open for the county and for my friends."

"How do you keep track of it all?"

"We have a very detailed calendar. Not only do I have to keep track of jobs, the kids have to know where I am and I have to know where they are. If everyone keeps an eye on the calendar, it somehow works. I haven't misplaced a kid yet, though I've come close."

"How often do you have to get family to help?" she asked. "Because that's the hard part for me. My mom and dad aren't as young as they were and they still work, too."

"I think I get help from my mom or dad or my brother almost every week. When we have to be two places at once, usually. I'd be lost without them. But I try hard as I can to give back. And so do the kids if I motivate them. As in—I promise not to hate them. Or ground them. Or confiscate phones. You know, there are two things those phones do for me that are priceless—they let the kids stay in touch so I always know where they are. And they're great contraband for confiscation." He laughed. "Those kids will do anything to keep their phones."

"I know—I have the same situation. You know how I'd really love to spend my time till retirement? If money were no object?"

"How?"

"Flipping houses," she said, grinning.

"As in—flipping houses?"

"As in, buying fixer-uppers, remodeling, selling them. Not only do I get a discount at Home Depot, you can't imagine the stuff I've learned there."

"I've done that twice," he said. "Took way too much time, but if I could do it full-time, it could make money. I lost money on the first one but I learned a lot and doubled my money on the second one."

"Have you ever thought about doing it again?" she asked brightly.

"Lola, I'm thinking about ways to make money all the time. Those kids aren't going to stop eating up money until they qualify for Social Security."

They talked about his remodel of his big house, his remodel jobs elsewhere; she talked about some of the work she'd done on her old house and how much she'd enjoyed the work. She had to hire help for some things but she was hands-on for most of it. She did her own landscaping and her garden was plentiful. Tom didn't have time for much of a garden. Just keeping the yard looking decent was a big enough job and he had a big house on a small lot.

They talked about the stress of managing college tuition for the kids, how difficult it could be having an ex-spouse who wasn't exactly on a visitation or support payment schedule, the guilt of needing to rely on family support.

And then it was four o'clock. Tom realized he'd been on her porch more than two hours, checking texts from kids now and then. "I better get going. I insisted everyone be home before five—we're going to my folks for dinner."

"And I have a chicken to burn for our dinner. I remodeled the bathroom almost totally by myself but I'm dangerous in the kitchen. Good cooks have to have time to putter and I'm always on the move."

"I know what you mean." He stood up. "You know when you asked me what I want?"

"Yeah?"

"This," he said. "I wanted this. Thanks. It's the best two hours I've had in a long time."

"Well, go ahead and buy me another geranium sometime."

A man cannot be comfortable without his own approval.

—Mark Twain

Chapter 10

CONRAD HAD BEEN FEELING PRETTY GOOD about himself. He supposed the secret was out—he liked Sierra. If he wasn't at the diner to see her, he was out at the Crossing. He'd spent a little time in the hammock with her, helped her in the garden—they'd started harvesting the first crop. He talked her into helping him work out by climbing onto his back while he hiked awhile. His reward was usually several amazing kisses.

She was completely off the crutches now but by the end of a long day her ankle was sore and she might favor it a little. No hiking yet, but Conrad didn't mind carrying all the weight. Literally.

He was walking down the street from the firehouse to the grocery to pick up a couple of things for lunch when he was called from behind. "Connie?"

He turned to see exactly who he knew he'd see—Alyssa.

It always shook him a little bit when he saw her. She was still so gorgeous. She was statuesque and exotic with her dark hair, dark eyes. There was a time, when they were a couple, that he couldn't believe a woman as beautiful as Alyssa was with him.

But then, she hadn't really been with him, had she?

When he'd caught her and Chris in bed, she'd been defiant. Angry and remorseless. He had been stunned by what he thought was her stark indifference to their relationship but he would learn soon after that ugly day, Alyssa thought she was making a trade, that she'd leave Conrad's house only to move in with her new lover, Chris.

But Christian Derringer was not going to leave his wife. And young Mrs. Derringer was not going to throw out her husband. The look of rage and rebellion turned to regret and shame as Alyssa begged Connie for forgiveness. But no, he was not ever going through something like that again. All he'd had to do was think back over her strange behavior, her panties under the car seat, her whispering into the phone, and he had quickly realized she'd been unfaithful for a long time before he realized it.

As he looked at her now, standing on the sidewalk, twisting her hands in front of her, her eyes wet with tears, she didn't look so powerful. So bold. She looked so sad. She was five-ten. For a woman of her stature to appear vulnerable was momentarily jarring. She must have seen him walk by the beauty shop; she was still wearing her smock.

"What is it, Alyssa?" he asked.

"It's my mother," she said, one large tear spilling over. "Connie, it's my mom—she's so sick. She's dying."

"What?" he asked. "What do you mean?"

"She was sick and they ran a lot of tests and she just got sicker and sicker and we were so worried but by the time they narrowed it down to pancreatic cancer, it had grown and metastasized." She bit a knuckle as another great tear escaped and rolled down her cheek. "What will I do without her? I can't get by without her."

Conrad was filled with sympathy. He was still very close to his mother; he saw her regularly and talked to her at least every other day. And he liked Alyssa's mother. He had even stayed in touch with her after he and Alyssa broke up, for a while anyway.

He put a hand around her shoulder and drew her to him. She leaned against him and cried and although one of his arms dangled at his side, he held her there for a moment. "You're going to have to be very strong, Alyssa. You don't want Rachel to have the added burden of worrying about you."

"She's my best friend," she whispered.

"Have the doctors said how long they'd give her?"

"Just a matter of weeks, maybe less, probably not more."

"You have Clay," Connie said. "He's a good brother, a good son. How's your dad?"

"Broken," she said, leaning against him again. She looked up at him with her tearstained face. "Will you visit her before... you know, before it's over?"

"Have you arranged for hospice care?"

"Yes," she said, wiping off her cheeks. "They're starting visits the end of this week. I'm living at home again, to be with her."

"You won't regret that," he said. "But you're working?"

"It's the only thing that takes my mind off it for a while. My clients have been wonderful. So supportive. And I cut my hours. Connie, will you visit?"

"Sure. Of course. Meanwhile, tell your mom I'm so sorry to hear the news. I'll stop by one of these days, okay?"

"That would help. Thanks. My mom loves you, you know."

"She's a good woman. This is awful."

"Can we just go get a cup of coffee or a soda or..."

He shook his head. "It's not a good time," he said.

"It's never a good time," she complained with a sniff. She wiped a hand under her nose. "Even now."

"Alyssa, I'm sorry you're hurting and this news is awful for me, too—I'm crazy about your mom, about your family. I'll pay her a visit."

"How about me? Can't you be a friend to me?"

They'd been over this a few times; he'd been honest with her. He wasn't interested in getting back together, he didn't want to be friends. What they were was exes. That was all. He wasn't mad anymore. In fact, he felt terrible for her right now. It was true—she was really close to her mother. Her mother got her through most of the sticky or difficult times of her life.

"I'm seeing someone, Alyssa. I doubt she'd appreciate that."

"Who?"

"Never mind. Listen, I'll call your house right away. I'll visit your mom as soon as I can. I have to get some stuff at the store—lunch. The guys are waiting."

She dropped her gaze. "Sure. Okay. Thanks." Her eyes still on the ground, she turned and went back down the sidewalk to the beauty shop.

He watched her go and looked around. There were at least a dozen pairs of eyes on him. Some of them he knew—Lola from the diner, Jeff from the grocery outside straightening up the sidewalk baskets, Bertrice from the bookstore down the street. But there were others he didn't know and to them, he supposed, he was a guy who just made a girl cry.

He didn't care. He wanted to grab his lunch groceries and get back to the firehouse. He wanted to call his mom, see how she was doing today. He'd just talked to her yesterday but it would feel good to talk to her again.

Sierra could see the street from behind the lunch counter. She saw Conrad walk past. She smiled when she saw him; she almost always smiled at just the sight of him. He had that strong but leisurely gait. That was the thing about Connie—he was sure-footed in all things. His hands were in the pockets of his navy blue work trousers, that blue T-shirt snug on his broad shoulders. He could carry the weight of the world on those shoulders and often did.

She moved down to the end of the counter and watched him pass. She saw a woman step out of the beauty shop and call to him. He stopped and turned and they walked toward each other.

Of course—the ex. She felt pretty dim-witted—how had she failed to put two and two together like that. He'd mentioned she worked in town and they ran into each other now and then. She was a hairdresser, and she was beautiful. At least from where Sierra stood, she appeared stunning. Tall, leggy, long ebony hair, sophisticated.

Then he embraced her. He reached for her, pulled her close, held her for a long time before they parted a bit, talked a little bit longer, then separated and went on their way—he went left, she went right.

What had he said? They ran into each other sometimes. No, he said if they didn't run into each other he wouldn't even recognize her. Oh, but he recognized her. He had held her close.

Lola came into the diner. "Hey there, how's it going?" she asked. She didn't wait for an answer but went back to the kitchen area to stow her big purse and grab her apron. She was back at the sink giving her hands a scrub when Sierra joined her.

"Did you see Conrad with that girl? Across the street?"

"That's Alyssa. They used to be engaged or something."

"Are they good friends now?"

Lola shrugged. "I wouldn't know anything about that."

"They seemed to get along very well for...for 'used to be'..."

Lola smiled. "Who doesn't get along with Connie? He's such a sweetheart."

"They hugged. It looked kind of...romantic?"

"Oh," she said in a sympathetic tone. "You're interested in Connie?"

"No," Sierra said. "I mean, sure...but not the way you're thinking. I just wouldn't want to get in the way of anything. I mean, it's not just that I wouldn't want to complicate things for him, I wouldn't want to end up the silly one who gets let down. Know what I mean?"

"You should just ask him about it, then," Lola said.

As though that was easily done. How do you do that? Do you say, "I saw you hugging this beautiful girl right on the street and I don't want to be getting involved with you if you have something else going on?" But she had told him she wasn't going to get involved, so what was she saying, then? That she was ready to get involved?

Of course she was, but she had intended on keeping that to herself until she was sure. Sure of him, sure of herself.

She mulled over every possibility for another hour, and then she texted Moody and asked if he was free anytime today for a cup of coffee. Moody texted back that he was at the bookstore and would wait for her there. After she finished her shift and clocked out, she went to the bookstore. There was one student at the back table and he had his earbuds in, listening to music while he studied. Moody was in the chair he loved most, a big book of maps spread across his knees. She said hello to Ernie, the store owner, who appeared to be absorbed in some paperwork at the checkout counter.

"What are you involved in there?" she asked Moody.

"Abandoned mines," he said. "I love abandoned mines. I have dark fantasies of falling into them or digging people out of them. Do you have any idea how many abandoned mines there are in Colorado?"

She leaned a hip against a shelf. "No idea whatsoever."

"Would twenty-three thousand surprise you?"

She actually stood straighter. "Jeez. I'd better watch my step."

"You want to talk about something?"

"I want advice on something. I've been kind of seeing someone. Nothing serious, but still... I'm a little emotionally involved, I guess. And I don't want to get hurt or get in the way or...or get in trouble. So here's the thing..." She tried her best to explain about Conrad, who had become her friend and lately, her kissing friend. It was getting a little warm, she said. Tempting. And then she saw—

"Aw, Jesus, is this a girl problem? A romance problem? I hate these things. I'm no good at this! I've been married to Mrs. Moody since I was nine years old, approximately."

"I have a program," she said. "You're my sponsor."

"Here's what I know. You shouldn't start a new relationship for about a year after sobriety—you're still too green, too fragile. But you're a year sober, right? Right! Then if you get in one, it has to be a relationship in balance with your program or it'll end up too rocky. If you get involved with another alcoholic, they might understand your program, and they might have all the same shortcomings and character flaws—it can be supportive or it can be a sinking ship. That's all I know. I hate romance."

"Oh great. Lucky Mrs. Moody."

"She shares your pain," Moody said. "Just ask him. Honesty and directness usually works when all else fails. And use your instincts."

"They might be a little faulty," she said.

"That excuse isn't going to work much longer," he admonished. "Your instincts are pretty good, far as I can tell. You got out of that hostel when it turned drunk, you rescued the dog, you're good friends with Sully, and I don't know what Conrad has going on but I always liked him and felt like he was a straight shooter. Ask him."

"What would I say?"

"Say something like, 'You've been kissing me and I saw you hug a girl. Want to explain?' It would sound something like that. Then you have to judge it. Decide if you believe it."

"Huh," she said. "I was looking for something more along the lines of a guarantee."

"Oh, were you? You came to the wrong place, sister."

"I knew I needed a woman for a sponsor..."

"That might come yet," he said. "Walk on across the street to that firehouse and find him. Those boys only work now and then. Most of the time they're doing firehouse chores—he can break away to talk to you. Then maybe you can settle down and get it off your mind."

"I'm not exactly upset," she argued.

"Aren't you? All I'm saying is—get it out of your gut before it festers." He looked back at his big book and ran his finger along some lines on the map. "More than twenty abandoned mines right in here…"

"Moody, you are a wealth of wisdom."

"I know it," he said.

Even though she wasn't sure she agreed with his advice, she did walk across the street and found that Connie wasn't there. But Rafe was there. He said Connie took a little personal time at the end of the day. "He's probably headed home or out to the Crossing to see you. Doesn't he come to see you almost every day?"

In fact, he did, she said. She wondered if today might be different for some reason. So she went back to the Crossing. But Connie wasn't there. She never paid much attention to his comings and goings and now, having seen that embrace on the street, she had herself all screwed up. She vacillated between thinking he'd been just playing her, trying to make a conquest, to thinking, *what if something's wrong and I never even asked for his phone number?*

"I have his phone number," Sully said. "Did he say he was stopping by today?"

"He never says. And I never asked."

"Call him, then," Sully said. He went into the little store kitchen and came back with a phone number scrawled on a sticky note. "As much time as Connie spends hanging around here, I don't reckon he'd mind a phone call from you. In fact, it'll probably light him up like a Christmas tree. Go ahead, make the boy's day."

Her call went directly to voice mail and her visions worsened. His phone was turned off because he was with someone. What did she expect, since she was so reluctant? All baggage aside, he was still a man and he probably wanted to be with a woman sometimes. She used to understand that, but then certain events changed her thinking—the struggle to stay even, sober and level. She had stopped going from high to low, from emotionally dead to emotionally wild. She had begun to worship the lack of chaos.

Her life had been so chaotic back in the drinking days, jumping from one crisis to the next. And at the moment, she was feeling unsteady, as if all that messy uncertainty was creeping back. In the end it was only the need to reclaim order in her mind and her heart that moved her to do what she did.

"Do you know where Conrad lives?"

"Course I do," Sully said. "Want a little map?"

"I think I'd like to drop in on him, make sure everything is all right, make sure I haven't done anything to..." To what? Drive him into the arms of another woman?

"I don't know what's got you riled up and I don't think I want to know," Sully said. He drew her a simple map on the back of a small paper bag. "Go see him and get whatever it is taken care of."

"Do you think he'd be upset by me just dropping in on him?"

"Well, he drops in on me all the time, so that would be kind of narrow-minded, wouldn't it?"

"I'll take Molly with me. She loves to go in the car."

Sierra set out on what was to be a short and beautiful drive just north of Timberlake. The summer sun was about to start setting, the hillsides were lush, the late afternoon warm and a little sultry from the humidity. The roads weren't very well marked but she only had to make a few turns and Sully had gotten the distances between them very accurate. She found herself in a rural neighborhood—the houses spaced by a couple of acres. And at the drive to Connie's house there was a sign. Boyle.

She drove toward it; it was a sweet house. It was a small ranch with a garage and a circular drive in front. There was a very small porch at the front door and a couple of potted plants by the steps. There was a bay window, the shutters open; there didn't appear to be any lights on in the house. It wasn't dark because the sun was just beginning to sink in the west, but it looked as though no one was home. That gave Sierra unspoken permission to just sit and take in the house. The house told the story of a man who had crafted his own living space; a man who took pride in his home. Yet this was just a young, single man; a physical and darling man who lived life on the edge.

Did he want a place to come home to that would embrace him?

The lawn was well cared for and the house was brick with wood trim. Like many Colorado houses, there was a screen door to let the cool spring and summer air flow through. She imagined there might be a kitchen window over the sink that would be open to let the breeze escape. There were some flowers planted along the edge of the front walk and a freestanding brick mailbox that matched the brick of the house. Details were obviously labored over—brown brick with matching garden border and brick circular drive, flawless white window trim that appeared meticulously maintained, edging along the drive. The house was surrounded by trees, many of them aspen, their silver leaves twinkling in the breeze.

Molly came up into the front seat, sitting next to Sierra. They looked at Connie's house together. To Sierra, a house represented so much. Stability, safety, family. It symbolized something she thought she might never have, something she'd always longed for. She came here for the nearest thing to family she could have—Cal and Maggie. And she hit the jackpot—she got Sully and the Crossing, too. And, she reluctantly admitted, throw in Moody, Frank and Enid. And Molly. If this was all she ever got, she could be content.

Looking at that humble yet rich home, she found herself happy for Conrad. She leaned back in the seat and her hand wandered to Molly's head, petting. Obviously Connie was not at home. Or maybe he was asleep. Asleep next to a beautiful brunette?

Nah—there was no other car there. There would be no cause to hide a visitor's car in the garage. She had her windows down and enjoyed the cool early-evening breeze while gazing at the fruits of Connie's labors. And fantasizing what it would be like to have a real home.

She heard an engine and turned in her seat to see Connie pull his big truck up to the garage. He got out and came immediately over to the pumpkin. Sierra opened her door to get out and Molly instantly escaped but she ran right to Connie, jumping on him.

"Hey there, hey," he said to the dog, massaging her behind the ears, calming her.

Sierra shook her head with a small laugh—Molly loved Conrad. Molly was such a tramp—she gave herself to the big man. And after a bit of canine foreplay, Molly sat like a good girl, looking up at him adoringly. The little traitor.

"Sierra, what are you doing here?"

"I just wanted to make sure everything was okay," she said. "I went to the firehouse to see you and you had gone. You weren't at the Crossing today and I called you and there was no answer."

"I was at the Crossing," he said. "I just came from there. Sully said he'd told you how to get to my house. I came right away. I thought I might pass you on the road."

"You were at the Crossing...?"

"I'm there all the time. Or haven't you noticed?"

"I realized I was taking that for granted because the first time you weren't there, I didn't even have your phone number so I could call and see if everything was all right."

"Sierra, everyone has my phone number!"

"Yeah, except me. So Sully gave me the number and it went right to voice mail."

He yanked it out of his pocket and looked at it. "Oh, I had my ringer off. But you didn't leave a message?" he asked. "Or a text? What's going on with us? Why can't we have a normal relationship?"

"I don't know," she said tiredly. "It's probably me. I told you— I'm no good at this."

He laid his hands on her shoulders and looked down into her eyes. "Why were you looking for me?" he asked.

"Why'd you have your phone off?"

"I went to see my mom," he said. "I wasn't planning to but I saw I could steal a couple of hours from work at the end of the day so I called her. She was free at four when she got off work. I drove to Denver to see her. I hadn't seen her in a while. I talk to her all the time but I haven't seen her in a month or maybe two. We just spent about an hour together, that's all. I must've forgot to turn my ringer back on."

"Your mom?" she asked.

"Yeah, she's great. I'll take you to meet her one of these days. If you want to."

Sierra laughed at herself, feeling foolish. "Oh, Connie," she said.

He rubbed the knuckle of his index finger down her cheek. "So, you were looking for me? You've never done that before. Should I take that as a good sign?"

"You have no idea what I thought," she said with some embarrassment.

"Oh? What did you think?"

"I saw you with that woman," she said. "I guess I jumped to conclusions..."

"What woman?" he asked, his brow furrowed.

"Lola said that was your ex-girlfriend. You were hugging her. You must be on very good terms with her."

"Huh?" he asked. "Oh, you mean Alyssa? No," he said, shaking his head. "I wouldn't say we're on very good terms. I mean, I behave when I see her. We were horrible to each other right after we broke up, but like I told you, that was a while ago—

over two years at least. But today? She wanted to tell me something—her mom, who I always liked a lot, has cancer and she's in the final stages. Alyssa has always been close with her mom and she was all messed up about it, which I guess anyone would be. It was terrible news and I felt sorry for her."

"Oh," she said. "Oh, I'm sorry…"

"She asked me if I'd visit her and I said, sure I would."

"You will?"

"Yeah," he said. "It's the decent thing to do. Like I said, she's a very nice lady. But it had the worst effect on me, hearing that. I went back to work and couldn't stop thinking about my mom. My mom has not had an easy life. She's had two lousy, abusive husbands, never had an extra dollar to spend, but she was always there for me. You know? Always pulling for me, having long talks with me about every stupid, pissant problem I thought I had. She's always doing a little extra for me—like making my favorite dinner if she knew it had been a big day. My brother, too—she made so many sacrifices for both of us. A lot of the time it was just me and my mom. She's about the same age as Alyssa's mom—not even sixty years old. Just the thought of her suddenly getting sick and dying—it just hit me. I should do more for my mom. I should at least let her know how much I appreciate her because you never know. Right?"

"Did you tell your mom why you wanted to see her?" Sierra asked.

"Not till I got there, but she figured out real fast that I don't drop everything and drive to Denver unless I have something on my mind. Something I couldn't figure out on my own. But why'd I have to do this at rush hour? I hate traffic."

"Oh, Connie, I'm just not used to a man like you," she said, touching his cheek.

"I hope that's not a bad thing," he said.

"Are you feeling better now?" she asked.

"Yes. I'm not sorry you were worried, though. Thought I

was going to make another run at Alyssa, did you?" he asked with an evil grin.

"For a minute, I did," she said with a laugh. "She's very beautiful."

"So are you," he said.

"I'm a little woodland creature compared to her," she said. "A gopher next to a gazelle..."

"You're very beautiful compared to her, not that any comparisons ever crossed my mind. Sierra, get this straight—Alyssa doesn't tempt me. Not in the smallest way. How can I say this without sounding like an ass? I'm glad she screwed it up because now I can see it wasn't right." He shook his head. "I don't even think of her as a friend."

"But she wants to get back together with you, doesn't she?"

"I don't know. She did before but I shut that down. And if she still does—it's not my problem. It's not possible."

She just looked at his beautiful face for a moment. Molly nosed her hand, looking for a little attention. "You went to see your mom. And I thought you were with another girl."

"I'm flattered, but I'm really not that guy. So—since you're here, wanna come inside?"

"Yes," she said. "Can Molly come, too?"

"All your family is welcome," he said.

If I loved you less,

I might be able to talk about it more.

—JANE AUSTEN

Chapter 11

CONNIE SCOOPED HER UP, CALLED TO MOLLY, AND carried Sierra over the threshold and into his house. He stopped just inside the closed door. "I guess you can tell, I wasn't expecting company."

His clean laundry was dumped on the couch for folding, two pairs of running shoes and a pair of boots sat on the floor where they'd been kicked off. There was a small dinette in the breakfast nook and each one of the four chairs held up a jacket or down vest. Molly was off, nosing around the place, probably looking for something to chew on.

"It has that lived-in look," she said.

"I don't spend much time here," he said. "Especially lately."

He leaned toward her until their lips were almost touching and with a gentle tongue, outlined her lips. Her arms around his neck tightened just slightly. "I wanted you in my house," he said softly. "I want you in my bed."

"I don't know if I can," she said. "My last time was—" She didn't finish but she did cast her eyes downward.

Connie kissed her, softly at first, then with more pressure, yet tenderly. He pulled her lower lip between his, sucking it into his mouth. "I have an idea," he said. "Why don't you not think about the last time? In fact, don't think about any other time, ever. And we'll go very slow. Very, very slow, so slow you'll ask me to go a little faster. But I won't. I'm just going to take my sweet time and you're going to be in charge. I have a feeling it's going to be good. I mean, epic." Then he buried his lips in her neck, kissing and sucking.

"Oh God," she whispered.

"It's bound to happen one of these days," he said. "If it doesn't happen now, let's at least play around a little."

She couldn't help herself. She giggled.

"Seriously, I have to touch you," he said. "I'm not going to rush you."

"Okay," she said weakly. "I'm a little nervous."

He gave her lips a little peck. "Me, too."

He carried her into the bedroom where the bed was made. "Amazing," she said. "A bomb went off in your living room, but you made the bed?"

"I like it that way."

"Have you been planning this?" she asked as he put her down.

"Every day," he said. He toed off his shoes and got on the bed beside her, pulling her into his arms.

"Oh-oh," Sierra said just as Molly jumped onto the bed.

"Not this time, Molly," he said. "Down."

The silly dog did exactly as Conrad instructed.

"You're going to have to show me how you did that," Sierra said.

"Later," he said, covering her lips with his. His hands moved from her back to her butt to her hips to her thighs and back again. He untucked her shirt and slid his big hands underneath, moaning into her mouth as he massaged her back, her belly, her breasts. Her body immediately strained against his in a movement so natural it almost took her by surprise. He lifted her shirt over her head, got rid of her bra and immediately transferred his kisses to her breasts, favoring one then the other, gently taking a nipple into her mouth.

"Okay," she whispered. "Okay, good idea..."

"Told you," he said, unzipping her shorts. He took so long in starting to slide them over her hips that she got in his way and did it herself, bringing a throaty laugh from him. He filled his big hands with her round butt, pulling her against him. He was hard as a rock and ready. And very big.

"Oh boy," she whispered.

She felt him through his pants and then almost in a panic, had to get her hand on him just to be sure he was human. She unbuttoned his pants and, not taking nearly the time or care he had, shoved them out of the way. He kicked them off and rolled away just enough to get rid of his shirt. Then he pulled her against his chest and hummed.

And here we are, she thought. *Right where I want to be, pressed up against the most beautiful man, his large hands both stimulating and comforting.* She was safe. She was protected. She lifted a leg onto his hip.

"I need a condom," he said.

"Please."

"I don't want to let go," he said. "They're in the drawer. Your side."

"I don't want to let go, either," she said.

He rose over her and looked into her eyes. He smoothed back her hair. "You're making it very hard to go slow," he said.

"I'm having a hard time with that myself," she said. "Please. Suit up."

He leaned over her, reached for the drawer and located the condoms. He got one out of the wrapper as quickly as possible and rolled it on. Pushing her onto her back, he touched her from her shoulder to her thighs, slowly, in even strokes. Then he let his fingers slide gently between her legs, first giving that small erogenous knob a little attention, then deeper, finding her more than ready. Then he was looking into her eyes again. "Sierra, I think you want more."

"Oh boy, do I..."

"I think I have to have a taste," he said. "My mouth is watering."

"Not too much," she said. "I'm not going to be able to wait for you if you do too much of that."

He laughed, his blue eyes twinkling. "I don't care if you wait for me. You think I'll have trouble catching up?"

He kissed his way down her body, taking his time at her breasts, licking and stroking, his finger busy in her soft center all the while. Somehow without removing his hand from her tender parts, his tongue was there. His tongue was in her while his finger worked her.

"Oh God," she said. And then she lost it. There was an explosion that lifted her off the bed and caused her insides to tighten and pulse. She was awash in spasms so he just went at her harder until she pressed her thighs so hard against his head, she wondered how he could breathe. It was an almost unbearably long orgasm that eventually slowed and her breath was coming hard and fast.

Connie slowly worked his way up her body to her lips.

"Oops," she whispered.

"That was nice," he said, giving her a series of short kisses.

"That was better than nice," she said. She could feel him pulsing against her belly and she immediately had a hunger to have him fill her. Reaching her hand between their bodies, she began to stroke him. "Come on," she said, spreading her legs under him. "Come on. I don't want to wait anymore."

"You didn't wait," he said, tonguing her lips apart.

"I don't want to wait again," she said. "I want you."

He was completely still for a moment. "I like the sound of that," he said.

She held him in her hand and guided him until he made a slow, deep entry, then held her still for a moment. He pinched his eyes closed and seemed to luxuriate in the moment. He finally moved, his hand under her butt, his lips on hers. He lifted her to him as he took a few slow, deep strokes. Then he dived into her. Her heels dug into the bed as she pushed back against him.

And it happened again. Her orgasm came fast and hard and he pulsed inside her, making it yet stronger and tighter. They clenched together for a long time, their bodies slick and feverish.

"Whoa," Connie said.

"Holy shit," Sierra said.

"Epic," he whispered, kissing her.

Then a sound came from the floor and they both looked to see Molly on her back, having what looked like a wrestling match with one of Connie's socks in her mouth. Molly was apparently oblivious to everything but the sock, just as Conrad and Sierra had been oblivious.

"Oh, I'm so sorry," Sierra said.

"You're kidding me, right? I'll buy her a case of socks." He rolled onto his side, bringing her with him. "I want to tell you a couple of things."

"Listen, I'm not ready to—"

"You don't have to be ready for anything, Sierra. I just want you to know a couple of things for your peace of mind. I'm a simple guy and that happened between us because you're important to me. When someone's important to me, they're safe with me. I won't ever lie to you, I won't be with other women and I won't hurt you. At least I'll try to never hurt you. You can trust me, Sierra. You can count on me. But I'm not taking hostages. If anything about this, about us, doesn't feel right or good, all you have to do is tell me."

Inexplicably, she felt her eyes tear. She hadn't cried in so long, she thought she had dried up forever. "Do you have any idea how sweet you are?" she asked in a soft voice.

"I'm just an ordinary guy, Sierra. I like my life just fine. I like it better with you but that's my issue, not yours. You tell me what you need and I'll do my best. Okay?"

She shook her head. "I won't lie to you, either."

"Thank you for this," he said, pulling her close. "I think I was a lot more ready than you were, so thank you."

"Conrad, you are very welcome." She shifted her hips a little. "Very welcome."

Sierra hadn't slept with a man she truly cared about in so long, she couldn't remember when. Maybe never. No, that wasn't right. She'd had a few relationships that lasted awhile—maybe three or four months. They were troubled, of course, because she was troubled. Unstable and difficult and all over the emotional map.

She hadn't slept with a man like Connie, a sweet and kind man who just happened to be a blockbuster in bed. She curled up beside him, her head on his arm, soothed by his callused hand gently stroking her.

The bed dipped as Molly tried to take her place between them, but Connie said, "No, you have to get on one side or another. Right over here. Eee! Jesus, that nose is cold!" Sierra giggled. "You think it's funny?" Connie said. "I was goosed!" She giggled more.

Sometime in the night she heard his phone ring and her paranoia kicked into gear even though she was the one naked and sated beside him. Some woman, she thought, making a booty call?

"No, Sully, she's not lost in the woods. No, Molly isn't lost, either. Good night, then."

"Sully?" she asked.

"He woke up and saw your car wasn't back yet. He couldn't resist. He's pretending he was concerned but I think we both know—he's nosy."

In the very early morning when the sky was just beginning to lighten she was awakened by Molly barking and Connie yelling. She ran, stark bare-ass naked, to the back of the house to look out the kitchen window where she saw Connie clad in only boxers, holding on to Molly and shouting at six or seven elk to get out of his yard. The elk didn't appear to be the least bit concerned with either Molly or Connie and it made her laugh.

She dashed for the bedroom to wrap the sheet around herself when they came back inside. She looked at the clock; it was only five thirty, but that wasn't too early for Molly.

"I should probably get going," she said. "It's time for Molly's breakfast."

He grabbed her around the waist, whirled her around and, lifting her slightly, kissed her. "Your dog woke me up to go outside. Say thank you properly." And then he buried his lips in her neck and growled.

For once in her life, Sierra chose not to kick good fortune in the teeth. She put her arms around his neck and let go of the sheet. It was caught between them and dragged, which of course made Molly think it was playtime. She bit at the sheet, pulled it, chewed it and wouldn't let go. But Conrad was not discouraged. He reached into his bedside table, grabbed a condom and then grabbed Sierra, pulling her into the bathroom and closing the door on Molly. He was not the least bit distracted or dissuaded by the barking, whining and scratching at the door. He made sure Sierra was completely satisfied before he satisfied himself.

"Oh my God, who taught you how to make love?" she asked him.

"No one taught me," he said. "That's ridiculous. Nature taught me."

"Nature didn't show you how to back a woman up to a bathroom counter and melt her bones like that."

"Isn't it amazing what you can figure out when you have to?" He gave her a kiss. "Do you want a shower before you go? Breakfast? We could improvise for Molly..."

"I'll take you up on that shower...alone. Then I'll get Molly home for breakfast and I'll have my coffee with Sully."

"I hate to let go of you," he said.

"The dog will starve if you don't."

"Can I be serious for a second?" he asked.

She felt a moment of dread. She wasn't ready for him to get too serious. "Sure," she said.

"I think it was almost the best night of my life," he said.

She smiled at him. "You're just saying that because my dog goosed you," she teased.

"I'm saying it because it was. Can we talk later today?"

She nodded. "Of course. Are you working?"

"I'm helping out with a bunch of camp kids at the firehouse—just a few hours. I'll come to the Crossing later. Is that okay?"

"You've been doing that almost since we met, Connie," she said.

"Oh, that's right."

She took a breath. "It was one of the best nights ever for me, too," she finally said.

He slapped her on the ass. "I don't know how it could be. The dog didn't goose you."

There was another thing for which Sierra was grateful, if a little nervous at the same time. She had someone to come home to. Sully was waiting for her. Molly's dish was full and Beau hadn't touched it, though he'd eaten his own.

"Well, good morning, ladies," Sully said. "And did we have a nice evening?"

"I spent the night," she said. "Big deal."

"Coffee?" he asked while pouring a cup for her.

"I'm thirty years old," she said. "Old enough to make adult decisions for myself."

"Did I say anything?" he asked.

"You're judging me," she said.

"If I were judging you, which I am not, my judgment would be that you chose a good man to pal around with. I've known

Connie since he was about seven. How about an omelet? With bacon?"

"Are you supposed to have bacon?" she asked.

"I'm making it for you. You probably need sustenance."

"So, how long are you going to have fun with this?" she asked.

"I don't know," Sully said. "I have a lot of stamina. Just ask your brother."

She was planning to see Cal that afternoon but talking to him about Conrad was the last thing she wanted to do. "It occurs to me I have a shortage of women in my life. And a surplus of very bossy men. As it happens, I was thinking of going over to Cal's to see how the barn's coming along, but I wasn't planning to discuss my personal, um, business."

"Then you better wipe that glow off your cheeks. Your personal business is shining all over your face."

"I'll have an omelet," she said. "Extra bacon, please."

Sierra worked around the Crossing in the morning and after lunch she went to see her brother. Molly went with her, of course.

Cal and Tom had made tremendous progress on the downstairs—the kitchen was complete and most of the flooring was installed. The laundry room and mudroom were finished, complete with cabinetry. Cal had had the cabinets made and brought to the house to install them all, an operation that took three days, but it gave the barn a classy, complete look. Except there was no furniture, but for that picnic table, which at the moment was covered with catalogs and fabric samples. "We're getting started on the furnishings, some of it will take nearly a couple of months."

"I hope the baby doesn't come early for your sake," Sierra said.

He tilted his head and peered at her. "Did you get a little sun today?"

"Probably," she said. "I helped Sully this morning, since I didn't have to work. I'm going to help him this week as much as possible—the Fourth of July is coming up and the campground is full from Wednesday till Tuesday."

Cal looked at her more closely. "Could that be...whisker burn?"

"California!"

"It's whisker burn," he said, grinning at her. "I'll be damned. I thought Connie was going to have to work at it all summer."

"We're very good friends," she said.

"Sierra, don't get your back up. I don't care if you have a boyfriend. In fact, that makes me happy. After what you've been through—"

"He doesn't know," she hastened to inform him.

"And that's okay, too," Cal said. "I haven't even told Maggie. I probably will, eventually. Or you will. But it broke my heart. Just like it broke yours. And I want you to have a chance to heal."

"He's not my boyfriend," she said. "He's my good friend."

"I don't care, Sierra. As long as you feel good about it, whatever it is. I don't know Conrad that well but Maggie does. And Maggie loves him."

After they talked awhile longer, after Cal pointed out every seam in the floor, every door frame and hinge, every fancy cabinet with slide-out shelves and special drawers with dividers, they hugged and said goodbye. Sierra held the door of the pumpkin open for Molly to jump in the backseat. She looked at her rosy cheeks in the rearview mirror and said to Molly, "It's okay if we have a boyfriend as long as he's a good boyfriend." And Molly smiled.

Connie was at the store when she got back to the Crossing. He was loading some trash into the back of his truck for Sully.

"What's going on?" she asked him.

"I was just hanging out, waiting for you to come back, and I told Sully I'd take this to the dump on my way home. How's the barn look?"

"It's starting to look great. They've been at work on it for eight months and it looks like they're going to make it. Are you hanging around for a little while?"

"Sure. Want to come home with me? Have dinner?"

"I'm sure you'll sympathize, but I'm a little tired…"

He grinned proudly. "You have plans?"

She shook her head. "Just dinner with Sully. I bet you could stay if you want to."

"I'll just have something cold to drink, then get to the dump. If you change your mind, you have my number. I'm staying home tonight. Other than tired, you doing okay today?"

"Excellent," she said. "I'm taking a little teasing from Mr. Sullivan. Are you?"

"He hasn't said a word. What could he say to get to me? I won the lottery. I'm the luckiest man alive."

"And how were the camp kids today?" she asked him.

"It was so much fun," he said. He put a hand at her back and turned her toward the store and pushed her gently in that direction. "They were all over the rig, screwing around with the hoses, trying on the hats and one kid even got his hands on turnouts and boots. We gave 'em lunch, talked to them about fire safety, about campfires and wildfires, and I'm pretty sure we have fourteen wannabe firefighters, seven of 'em girls."

"How old were these kids?"

"Camp kids—they were ages eight to eleven. I always forget how much energy they have. Then to make sure they wouldn't slow down, we made ice cream sundaes. They're going to wiggle all night. Till they pass out."

"Do you always volunteer to deal with the kids?"

"Only if it's convenient, but most of the other guys have kids. Maybe they get enough of 'em at home. I like the kids. Unless they're brats. I have a hard time with the brats."

"But you love kids," she said.

"I love kids, but mostly good kids."

They helped themselves to cold drinks and sat on the porch. Within a couple of minutes Sully was with them and had a lot of questions about Cal's progress on the barn so Sierra described everything right down to the hardwood floors that weren't really wood but porcelain that looked like wood. "And according to Cal, it doesn't require any maintenance like the wood does."

After a couple of cold drinks, Sully was ready to make dinner and convinced Sierra to help and Connie to stay. They worked together to grill fish and vegetables, a staple to their diets. And when dinner and dishes were done, Connie was ready to go. "Walk me to my truck," he said to Sierra. He kissed her goodbye, deeply, letting her know with his lips and embrace how much he'd like more. But he told her to sleep well.

Sierra and Sully hung out together until the sun was nearly down. The grounds were quiet, the dogs peaceful, Sully had his nightcap and Sierra her tea and Sully said good-night.

"Just in case you're inclined to worry, I think I'm going to take Molly out for the rest of the evening. I'll be fine."

"The rest of the evening or night?" he asked.

"Whatever feels right at the time. I'll have my phone if you need me."

"I've gotten by over seventy years without you. Enjoy yourself."

She drove with the windows down, Molly hanging her head out and letting the wind billow her lips. She'd felt a smile inside of herself all day long. She couldn't help it, she felt strangely renewed. She'd enjoyed physical love that felt clean and pure; sex without a price or consequence with a man who made no demands and respected her speed, or the lack. He respected her space and her body and he didn't push her. He was honorable. He had integrity. She had forgotten such men existed. Indeed, in her world, they'd been very rare and they'd never been hers.

She wasn't sure why but Connie cared about her. And she was falling for him.

Molly was barking the second she got out of the car. Sierra ran the short distance to the front door, but it opened before she could knock. She threw her arms around Connie's neck and kissed him.

"Is this a booty call?" he asked, smiling.

She nodded. "You don't have company or anything, do you?"

"I left you less than two hours ago. You think I have a booty call speed dial?"

"You don't?"

"Sierra, this is my first booty call. Am I going to like it?"

"I can almost guarantee it," she said.

Sierra slept so soundly, she never heard a sound. When she rolled over in the early morning, Molly was sleeping where Connie had been. She said, "Well, good morning." And Molly burped in her face. "Nice," Sierra said. "What have you done with my boyfriend?"

Molly stretched.

Connie had whispered late last night that he'd be going to work early in the morning and said she should sleep; he'd be quiet. Sierra was typically an early riser and had fully expected to stir when he left the bed, but instead she slept deeply. She thought he said he'd be leaving at six. She looked at the bed-side clock—seven. She'd missed morning coffee with Sully by a couple of hours.

She slid out of bed and grabbed her T-shirt off the floor. She headed for the kitchen but paused for a second. Connie's house wasn't big like Cal's but it was an open plan—living room, kitchen, breakfast bar, dining area, all together. And it was im-maculate. No more clothes hanging over chairs or tossed on the furniture. The kitchen shone; the carpet had vacuum tracks. There was a note on the counter.

I hope you slept in. There's coffee ready—just flip the switch. Molly was fed and has been outside. Call me when you're up. Love, C.

She looked down at her dog. "You've been fed?" Molly wagged. She saw that by the door there were two dog bowls—one with water in it. The other empty.

She went back to the bedroom to grab her phone. She called him. "Conrad, when did you do all this?"

"Ah, you're up. All what?"

"The spotless house, the dog dishes, dog food…?"

"I had a little time yesterday before I met the camp kids. And I got the dishes and food on my way to work. Just in case…"

"Just in case Molly spent the night again?" she asked.

"Always prepared," he said. Then in a lowered voice he said, "She didn't even goose me last night. But it was a great night anyway. Hey, there's cereal and milk and fruit and eggs…"

"I'm going to get out to the Crossing. I promised to help Sully this weekend."

"I'm on for twenty-four hours. I might be pretty tied up. And if I can steal a little personal time, I have that errand…that sad errand…"

"I don't know what you mean," she said.

"I promised to look in on Alyssa's mother. I'm only planning to do that once and I should do it before I'm too late. Not for Alyssa. Because I always liked Rachel. She's a good woman."

"Of course," Sierra said. "I'll talk to you when you have time."

"I'll call you, if that's okay."

"Sure. And, Connie—thank you for the dog food. And everything."

"I'm really glad you came over," he said in a hushed voice. "I could get used to that."

"Don't get used to it," she warned. "Let's not set up a lot of expectations."

"Whatever you say, Sierra."

"I could get used to it, too," she said. "I just don't want to put a hex on it. I have rotten luck with men, you know."

"So you say. But I can't stop smiling. If that's rotten luck, bring it on."

Be willing to have it so; acceptance of what

has happened is the first step to overcoming the

consequences of any misfortune.

—WILLIAM JAMES

Chapter 12

CONNIE BOYLE WAS IN LOVE. HE'D BEEN IN LOVE before, of course. But now, feeling the way he felt for Sierra, he was sure he'd just been going through the motions with Alyssa. Just following the steps—he started out thinking Alyssa was hot, that she turned him on and made him happy in bed and most other places, so they moved in together and began building the house and the idea of a family.

It was different with Sierra. She was different. She just wasn't like other women. For one thing, she wasn't the type who had been looking for a happily-ever-after and she was certainly the first woman like that he'd ever known. Including his mother!

"It's probably my program," she'd tried to explain. "It's just about today for me—just this one day. Sometimes it's very hard work, remembering to live in the moment, and other times it's such a relief, such a blessing—there's not very much pressure in it when I don't have to try to live up to any grandiose expectations."

"No big plans for the future, then?" he had asked.

"I'm trying to be careful about that. It's such a dream come true just to feel secure today. Can we be good with that?"

"As long as I can be with you, I'm good," he'd said. And he meant it. He wasn't sure how long he could keep it to himself that he loved her. But, he believed he'd know the right time and place to tell her.

She was brilliant. It perplexed him that she didn't have her degree after about six years of college. She explained that she always had to keep an almost full-time job to afford college, even though she had some scholarships along the way. And, she admitted, she partied too much. But she had studied so much on so many different subjects. She knew all about the solar system; she could explain nuclear fusion in a way he could understand. She'd found her niche in mathematics and for a while toyed with the notion of an advanced degree and teaching at the college level. But then she'd taken a fancy to philosophy. "Not that unusual," she said. "Albert Einstein was a physicist and philosopher. Some of his writings probably influenced me."

And like all the Jones children, she had a great appreciation for literature. He loved it when she told him about the stories she'd read, infused with the emotion she'd felt while reading them. In fact, he couldn't believe the variety of things they talked about—books, religion, philosophy, politics, wars, even medicine. Connie knew quite a bit about medical intervention, being a paramedic. "If I was smart enough, I wouldn't mind being a doctor," he had told her.

"Hmm. Are you sure you're not smart enough?"

"I'm pretty convinced, yeah," he had said.

He and Alyssa had only talked about what their future would look like, how many kids they'd have, where they'd go for entertainment, their friends, work. It felt like they talked all the time but he was figuring out now they'd only talked about their schedules and plans. Oh, and there was gossip. Gossip had been pretty important to Alyssa. Who knew she'd become the subject?

"Don't you have any gossip?" Connie had asked Sierra.

"Well, Cal's mother-in-law is coming around a lot these days, helping Maggie with decorating things, shopping for her, because Maggie hates that stuff but she wants her house to be beautiful. And she drives Cal nuts. But she drives Maggie more nuts. It's kind of fun to watch."

"You don't seem to like to talk trash too much," he'd observed.

She had shrugged and said, "I don't really have any dirt on anyone. And besides, I'm the trash that used to get talked about a lot. I'm willing to leave that behind and swear off gossip."

So was Connie. For a while after Alyssa he had to quit Facebook and Twitter, there were so many disparaging and destructive opinions about him, her, the state of their relationship and their breakup. Even though he was the victim, the cheated upon, people were not shy with their opinions about what he must be lacking for his girl and his friend to hook up behind his back.

He couldn't imagine ever being bored or irritated again in his life as long as Sierra was around. And she might shy away from proclamations of love and longing, but there was no disguising the healthy flush of her cheeks, her quick laughter, the soft way she unfolded when she was in his arms. He loved her with the greatest of care and the most practiced of skill, and she told him so. She was no docile lover herself—she met him more than halfway, driving him out of his mind with lust and drenching him in satisfaction. The deepest most penetrating satisfaction he'd ever felt. She brought out the best in him; he'd never made finer love in his life. And when they had those long, deep, intellectual discussions about things he knew so little about, he felt smart. Better than smart, he felt wise.

They hardly ever made real plans. Once he'd asked her if she'd like to go to an outdoor jazz concert in Aurora. Dogs were welcome if they could behave. Sierra had been the one to suggest they invite Maggie and Cal. The four of them packed a cooler, brought lawn chairs and plenty of dog treats. Molly was very well behaved and they all had a wonderful time. And though he often asked her if she wanted to come to his house, she usually just surprised him. A couple of times he'd knocked on her cabin door at night and had been admitted. Despite their lack of plans, they ended up sleeping together every night that Connie wasn't at the fire station.

He was a simple man with simple needs. He enjoyed hard work and was filled with pride that he could serve as a firefighter and paramedic. He wanted a worthy woman to shower with love and he wanted to be a good woman's strong arm. He believed he wanted the same things Sierra wanted—security, love, stability, trust. He wasn't a man of mystery and Sierra didn't seem to be a woman of mystery—she was incredibly straightforward and almost achingly honest. She might not want to admit how much she cared for him, but she had trouble disguising it.

There was only one thing that gave him pause. "I have some loose ends from my checkered past to tidy up, Connie. You'll have to be patient with me." she'd told him.

"Tell me if I can help," he had said.

"I'm afraid it's up to me."

"I hope you can resolve whatever it is and I'll wait as long as it takes. Just know I'm on your side, no matter what. You can trust me."

Cal was watching the summer pass by the size of Maggie's belly. By the end of July she was over seven months along with a little girl who was due to arrive in October. She'd taken to wearing constriction stockings while driving and working to keep the swelling in her ankles manageable. "Cankles," she called them because there was no real definition between her calves and her ankles. Her back was bothering her and she was starting to have some heartburn. But aside from the generally accepted discomforts of pregnancy, she was feeling fine and in excellent humor. Except for the house and her mother.

Those two things were driving her crazy. Apparently the master bath was way more important to her than Cal ever supposed. The tub that had been installed was way too big, the base built around the tub was huge, leaving the space in the master bath small enough that they might have to shimmy around each other en route to the enormous walk-in closet or the shower.

"We'll be crowded," she said.

"Much too large," Maggie's mother, Phoebe, agreed.

"It'll be fine," Cal said. "When it's done, you'll love it."

"It's a fucking monument," Maggie said. "I want it out!"

"Who are you and what have you done to my wife?" Cal asked.

And that was nothing to the fits the bathroom countertop was giving her. Or the quartz he'd chosen for the hearth. "What were you going for here?" she asked him. "Brutally ugly or just nauseating?"

"Hey, I tried, all right? I didn't want to bother you."

"Stop trying and ask me!"

Because of these developments, Sully was not getting much of Maggie's help around the Crossing. Maggie was spending all her days off working with Phoebe and Phoebe's decorator trying to either improve or replace some of Cal's installations.

"I might be a little cranky," Maggie admitted. "I want a whole house when the baby comes. And it's my own fault—I didn't get involved enough. Plus, I want this baby to have a name when she gets here."

"How about Portland," he said, joking.

"I told you, no geographical references."

"What's wrong with Aurora?"

"No Disney princesses! You have too much history there."

"Not with Aurora," he said with a grin. Cal had had a brief and enjoyable career with the big theme park where he got involved with one of the princesses, off duty of course, but was fired because of it. He still maintained it was both unfair and quite pleasing. "I should have sued them. You can't fire people for engaging in adult activities on their own time."

"We've been married almost a year," Maggie said. "Isn't it time you at least tell me which princess?"

"Never. If I told you, you'd never get that image out of your head. Too risky."

Cal thought he had the perfect marriage but had lately stumbled on a few minor flaws while turning the barn into a house with Maggie. "I hate chaos," he said. "I was getting along fine with Tom."

"I work in regular chaos," Maggie reminded him. "I'm a born crisis manager."

"Can you manage Phoebe, then? She drives me crazy."

"I tried to warn you," Maggie said. "But, like it or not, she's getting things done. Things I hate doing—like shopping."

It was true. Phoebe, with her decorator Janet, gathered up things from dishes to rugs to paintings and brought them to the barn for Maggie's approval. And if Cal was extremely diplomatic, he could weigh in. Not only did Cal find Phoebe irritating, the way Janet placated her and trotted after her like a faithful pup made him want to shake her.

Then Jaycee Kent, the OB and Maggie's best friend said, "I think you might be doing too much, your blood pressure is up a little and I don't want it to get higher. You need longer rest periods, shorter surgeries—you can't stand in an operating room for nine hours anymore. You have to lie down and put your feet up a few times a day, cut out the salt, no heavy lifting and lower the stress."

Cal agreed, Maggie had too much on her plate. She was fretting over the house, helping Sully every free minute she had and working in Denver three days a week.

Maggie agreed to cut her work hours slightly—she was seeing patients in the office more often, passing off the more complicated surgeries to one of her partners and she was no longer taking emergency room on call.

Cal talked to his sister. "You've been helping Sully a lot at the Crossing. I don't want to overload you, too, but is there any more time in your schedule so you can spell Maggie out there? We can work out pay, of course. Sully doesn't like to admit it but he needs help, especially in summer when he's full of camp-ers. He's no kid."

"Really, he does very well, but it's been so busy," Sierra said. "I can cut back on my hours at the diner. The high school girls are begging for more time. Let me see what I can do."

"Just be sure you have plenty of time for your own life," he said. "You have important stuff, too."

Sierra laughed. "I work with friendly people a few hours a week, the Crossing is not only outdoor work and exercise, it's fun and Sully is my new best friend. He looks out for me. Every-one looks out for me. I even have a nice boyfriend. Cal, my life has never been this good."

"Really?" he asked, shocked and yet wondering why he was shocked.

"More time at the Crossing for the summer won't hurt me even a little bit. And I think Molly would love it."

"And Connie would like it," Cal said.

"Connie is a busy guy. He has way more commitments than I have. He works a couple of twenty-four-hour shifts a week, goes out on search and rescue detail, trains, and then whenever there are fund-raisers or kids at the firehouse, he's first in line. I like that about him."

"Right now all I want to do is take a little pressure off Mag-gie so she doesn't have to be such a bitch."

"Cal!" she scolded in a laugh.

"Well, she's very pregnant, her blood pressure is up, her mother is hanging around too much and I can tell she's afraid of the house—afraid if she doesn't throw herself into it and make good choices it's going to look like Sully's place."

"Yeah, you don't need to spend much to get that look," Si-erra said.

"Not that I have a problem with that," Cal added, smiling. "So. You and Connie? Is this the real deal?"

"You know I can't answer that," she said. "For both of us, for right now, it's real enough. He's still coming off a bad relationship and I'm coming off something…something worse. By the way…"

"I haven't heard anything yet. Okay, I haven't pushed on it too hard. Want me to push harder?"

"I don't know," she said. "I suppose you should. But I don't want to be in jail when the baby comes."

He reached out and smoothed her hair back behind her ear. "I'm pretty sure you're not going to jail. You didn't do anything besides fail to investigate. It could've been a tree branch. Or an animal."

"'Pretty sure' isn't good enough," she said quietly. "If something bad happened…"

What Cal didn't admit was that he had been stalling. He took a cursory look at the public records, just enough to establish there had been no fatal accidents on or around the date she provided. When a victim dies days or even weeks after the incident, it's upgraded to fatal. He was relieved enough to stop there, for the time being anyway. He didn't want Sierra to need him while Maggie needed him. There was no easy way to balance that.

"Don't worry. We'll be okay. I have to say, Sierra, I was a little nervous about you coming here and now I'm glad you did. It's been wonderful for us."

"Wonderful for me, too," she said.

Having at least two jobs, new friends, a dog and a boyfriend took a lot of time. Delightful time. She still made time for meetings here and there but she wasn't seeing Moody for coffee quite as often. He was diligent in his role as a sponsor, acting like he wanted to keep the job.

"I think it's time for a catch-up," he said when he called her.

"There's an open meeting in Leadville with a good speaker— I've heard her before. Let's have dinner in Leadville at five, then go to the seven o'clock meeting. Want to meet at the café where they have the heavenly hamburger? Bring your notebook."

She was devotedly reading her big book, going to at least two meetings a week, when at one time while she was in rehab it was at least two meetings a day. She was writing in her journal and in her notebook, but there were times lately she just didn't feel like it. There were times she wanted to forget that this was still a priority. Of course she didn't dare, and even if she did dare, Moody would sternly remind her that her only chance was a green memory.

She went to the café early and, with a cup of coffee on the side, she opened up her notebook and did a little review. She wasn't just a girl who partied too much. She got in trouble when she was drinking and had done some shameful things, things that for her recovery, she shouldn't forget. With as many mishaps and misdeeds as she'd had, she was going to be on step eight for a long time.

Alex D.—I'm sorry about the car. Sorry I took it without permission just because I wanted a ride. Sorry about the fender, too. And your sunglasses, which I sold.

Joel W.—I told your wife you were screwing around on her. I was drunk, of course, but I was also malicious. She didn't deserve you! Of course, I didn't deserve you even more but in my twisted mind, I thought I did.

I sexted and sexted and sexted. I hate that I did that. I could never do that without being drunk. Not to mention all the drunk dialing...

I can't wait to throw away this notebook.

"Love to see someone hard at work," Moody said, sliding into the booth across from her. She loved his aging hippie look; his gray hair pulled into a ponytail, his bushy gray eyebrows were a little crazy. He was wearing his T-shirt with the peace symbol on it. "You got room for the rest of your transgressions or should I buy you a new notebook?"

"This should do it," she said. "Luckily, I have many memory failures."

"That does come in handy. Did you order dinner?"

"Not yet," she said. "But I'm ready for a hamburger. A big greasy burger. I don't eat stuff like that with Sully. We're minding his heart. Let's order."

"You read my mind. And a chocolate shake?"

"Shouldn't you be watching your cholesterol?"

"Don't be taking my temperature here," he said.

The waitress, having seen him join Sierra, was at their table at once.

"You want a review of my transgressions?" Sierra asked after they'd placed their order.

"I'm sure it's fascinating," Moody said. "But what I'd rather hear about is what you've been doing with yourself these days. Word has it you cut back on your hours at the diner. And the word is also out—you're Connie's girl now."

"You told me to bring my notebook," she said.

"I thought it would remind you—you have a notebook and it needs attention. So—what's up?"

"My pregnant sister-in-law can't help out at the Crossing as much—her ankles are swollen and her house is almost done," she said. "I'm so happy to be doing that. Makes me feel better about that little cabin, which I love. I didn't think I needed a place of my own, but I was wrong. I've been rootless for such a long time and I like having walls again. Walls I'm not sharing with anyone. It makes me feel grounded in a way. And I realized that when Cal said he needed me—it was pure joy. Sully calls me family, being Cal's sister. My concept of family is a little screwed up."

"How is it with your brother?" he asked.

"Very good. He's very protective," she said. "I kind of hung my addictions on him by telling him that everyone left me and I turned to booze. It appears he may have taken the bait." Then she smiled.

"That's a nice sister," he said. "Do you plan on letting him off the hook or are you going to add him to the list of people you've wronged?"

"It would have to be both now, wouldn't it?" she said. She had wronged Cal by blaming him for a problem that was entirely her own and yes, she fully intended to make sure he understood that even though it came as a result of her childhood, her disease belonged to her.

"That's very mature," Moody said.

She never knew when he was being funny, sarcastic or genuine. She frowned.

"Wanting a drink?"

She shook her head. "Not today," she said. "I know I might tomorrow but I don't today."

"What I wonder is—do you feel isolated out there? In your new home? Because you haven't called me lately."

"Oh, Moody, I'm sorry. I should have been more honest with you. It's true, Cal, Maggie and Sully need me, but what time is left I'm spending with Connie. Every day. Most nights. It's been very nice. He's such a dream man."

"I like Connie," he said. "Can't say I know him well, but he seems okay."

"He's okay," she assured him. "I haven't given him a lot of specifics, but I have told him that I'm in recovery." She bit her lower lip. "I kind of hate for him to know the whole story. I think he gets it, that I'm an alcoholic, but he's not much of a drinker himself. He really has no idea..."

'I don't know how important he is to you," Moody said. "But—"

"We're only as sick as our secrets," she finished for him. "I've tried not to think about it too much, as if I could keep it casual, but he's important to me."

"You have over a year of sobriety now," Moody said. "You'll always be on thin ice but the good news is, with hard work, it's going to get thicker. You've done a lot of good work. It's okay to take a little pride in that."

"Do you?" she asked.

"I do," he admitted. "Cautiously. Honestly. Humbly. My new normal?"

After burgers and a little talking about more mundane subjects, they went off to the meeting. It was crowded; it was an open meeting, which meant you didn't have to be in recovery—or hoping for recovery—to attend. People she knew from the closed meetings were there with friends or family. There were the curious who weren't of a mind to commit. The speaker for the evening was a beautiful woman with a big laugh, an obvious sense of style and an amazing dimpled smile. She was in her midthirties, had clear eyes, straight teeth, a rosy complexion and thick, healthy mahogany hair. She wore jeans, boots and a leather jacket that was to die for. People were greeting her, introducing themselves, anxious to meet her like she was a celebrity. Apparently she was well-known on this meeting circuit. When it was finally time to begin, they started with a prayer, took care of some business, read over the steps and the speaker was introduced. She took the podium.

"Hi. My name is Neely and I'm an alcoholic."

"Hi, Neely," the room responded as one.

"I had my first drink when I was four years old. My parents had friends over a lot. There were always half-filled beer bottles and glasses around and I went through the family room and kitchen, sipping at the leftovers. The first time I remember being seriously buzzed, I was about ten. And thus began my drinking career. I've been sober for nine years now."

No one gasped. No one groaned. No one whispered. They'd all heard this kind of story before. It wasn't even shocking.

The new normal, indeed.

This woman, Neely, was so confident, so captivating, such an engaging speaker, the kind that could make a person almost feel lucky to have this scourge of alcoholism because of all the wisdom brought by the growth. Neely was so sophisticated, so smart. Sierra felt a stirring of envy. She'd given her testimony several times, but nothing like this. This was a performance. When Neely was done she was instantly surrounded by people, praising her.

She was something of a star.

Sierra got to thinking. She'd known Connie since March. August was only days away. They'd been intimate since about the end of June. She knew him better than she'd known a man in maybe her whole life. It seemed like all the relationships before Connie had been shallow or dysfunctional or abusive or all of the above.

In several of their long conversations Connie had described himself as an ordinary man with simple needs. He was far from ordinary. He was a first responder, a hero, a decisive man of action. He said all he'd ever wanted since he was a kid was to live and work in this part of the Colorado mountains. He wanted to help people, he wanted to be a family man. "I get enough adventure at work," he had said. "I'm not looking for a lot of craziness. Just a few good friends, a quiet and stable home and you know, comfort. Oh, and good food. Good food is important."

Connie was a keeper. She was afraid to make any kind of statement about that, even to herself. But one thing she knew— if he found her lacking in some important ways and decided they couldn't be together, it was going to sting. She'd rather not worry about that, anticipate it, fear it.

The problem was Connie wanted children. He hadn't come right out and said that was important to him, but what else was included in a home life, in a family?

She knocked on his door purposefully. When he opened the door he instantly grabbed her with a lusty growl, lifting her off her feet and burying his mouth in her neck. "Connie! Connie! Put me down!"

"Why?" he asked, not putting her down.

"I want to talk! Can we please talk?"

He still didn't put her down. "Are you going to break up with me?"

"No, I just want to talk about something. Something personal."

"Again?" he asked. He reluctantly put her down on her feet. "Where's Molly?"

Sierra gave a whistle and the dog came running. "She was watering the bushes."

"That's good. If you dump me now we might have custody issues."

"Why would I dump you? You're almost perfect."

"Almost?" he asked, teasing her.

"You have a really bad big-toe callus. It scratches sometimes." She looked past him. "Are you cooking?"

"I'm making cookies. We have more camp kids tomorrow." He leaned down and kissed her neck. "You wanna talk, huh?"

"Yes," she said, closing the door behind her. Molly ran straight to her water dish, always filled for her.

"Maybe we should do it first, so I can concentrate," he said.

"Maybe we should get this over with so I can feel better. It's very scary, revealing myself a little at a time like this, always worrying that you're going to have overload and say, 'that's it— too much.'"

That made him smile. "You worry about that?"

"Of course! You know I'm happy. I know you're happy. Let's sit at the table." She walked past him and pulled out a chair. "Wow, those cookies smell good."

"I was going to bring you some tonight if you didn't come over. Do you want some now?"

"No, right now I want to tell you a couple of things. Then you can think about what I've told you and decide if you really want to be in this...this...whatever this is. Relationship."

He crossed his big arms over his chest. "We talk for hours, do it like bunnies, laugh our butts off, tell each other stories, bare our souls—it's a relationship, Sierra. You are going to have to come to terms with that."

"Well, that's a fact. So, I told you—I'm an alcoholic. One of my steps is to list all the people I wronged because of my drinking and the list became very long because I was clearly out of control. I might not have admitted it at the time, but I was. I did some bad things."

"I think you want to tell me what bad things so I can say, 'okay—that's in the past,' then we can get on with things."

"You think it's just a big funny thing and it's not. I had a real taste for one-night stands. I had no judgment—married men were not off-limits. I was impulsive and reckless. I borrowed a car without permission once—thank God it was only once— and hit a pole in a parking lot. I dented the bumper. I'd get two drinks in me and say any damn thing that came into my head."

"Kind of like I do, but without alcohol assistance?"

"When you do it, it's kind of cute," she said. "I already made amends for a lot of my transgressions—all the drunk dialing, sexting, rumor spreading, character assassination, and I'm truly sorry and embarrassed. And you know I'm not ready to look too far into the future yet, but before we go any further, I have to tell you something important." She paused and took a deep breath. "I can't have children."

His face took on a very pained expression. "Oh, Sierra, I'm sorry." He reached across the table to take her hand. "What was it? Congenital? Something happened?"

"No. No. Nothing like that. Well, something like that, actually. There are the hereditary issues—my schizophrenic father. Then add addiction to that. Any child of mine would have the cards stacked against it. Both those conditions tend to run in families. I've decided I won't be having children."

He was quiet for a moment. "That must have been such a hard decision for you," he finally said, his voice soothing.

"It was the obvious choice," she said. "But I know how much you love kids."

"I do like kids," he said. "Did you think telling me this was going to change how I feel about you?"

"I'm not going to change my mind," she said.

He just looked at her for a long time. "Come here, Sierra," he said, pulling on her hand. "Come on, come here." He pulled on her until she got up from the table and came around to his side. He pushed back from the table and pulled her down to his lap. "Listen, we're both going to bring some baggage to this, to us. Why don't we just take it one day at a time, huh?"

"Are you kidding me?" she asked with a laugh.

"Oh, I get it—you alcoholics think you're the only ones who thought of that strategy," he said. "It's gotten us both through some of the hard stuff we've had to deal with. You're not the only one with some burdens, okay? So, you've decided it's better if you don't have children. I get it. I'm not going to try to change your mind."

"I know you want a family," she said. "Before we spend one more day—"

"Sierra, up until I met you I wasn't sure I'd ever even have another girlfriend. The last one kind of wrecked me and I'll be the first to admit, I wasn't exactly open to the idea. But then I met you. At first you scared me. You're pretty confident. That's a good thing, but it scares the boys."

"Me? I have so little confidence!"

"Okay, then you have determination. You act like you don't need anybody."

"It's true. I *act* like that," she said. "It's kind of a defense mechanism."

He smiled at her, his hand casually rubbing her thigh. "It's a good one. Scared me for a while. But then I got to know you. I think you're a good person who came through some hard times. I think the important part there is that you came through, not that you had hard times. I know you can't change people and I wouldn't try, but people change themselves all the time. When they want to. Sierra, I don't care if you had troubles in the past—"

"I *was* trouble, Connie..."

"Okay, you did some things you had to apologize for. Good on you that you apologized. And I guess you learned a few things. I'm not going to give you up just because you used to be a bad girl. What matters is what kind of girl you are now. And now you're almost perfect. You don't even have a nasty callus on your big toe." He smiled at her.

"You can't have the kind of life you want with someone like me..."

"I can have *exactly* the kind of life I want with someone like you," he said. "I know it makes you nervous to think about promises and commitments to the future so we don't have to go there. I know you'll completely wig out if I tell you I love you."

"You can't be sure of something like that! It's too soon! You don't know me yet, not really! When you get to know me, you'll—"

"I'll let you say it first, okay? Just relax, I'm not going to hurt you, trick you, back you into a corner, try to change you or smother you. I'm going to be with you just the way you are. I like the way you are." He gave her a small kiss. "It doesn't hurt that you think I'm perfect. Except for the toe."

"I like you so much I don't want you to get stuck with a bad girlfriend," she said.

"Then never leave me," he said. "Just one thing. Don't worry that you're going to scare me away by telling me all you've been through. Or all the bad things you did." He leaned his forehead against her forehead. "Sexting, huh?"

"Oh God," she said, closing her eyes.

"Are you still doing that?" he asked. "Under the right circumstances?"

"No! Of course not!"

"That's kind of too bad," he said with an evil grin.

She laughed.

"Here's what we should do. We should go in the bedroom, do boom-boom for a while, then come back out here and have ice cream with warm chocolate chip cookies. Then, if we want to, we can have more boom-boom."

"And the fact that I will never have children?" she pushed.

"If you are worried about your genetics, there are an awful lot of kids in this world without parents. You never know what the future really holds."

"Boom-boom?" she repeated with a laugh. "You're kind of a sex maniac, you know that."

"So are you," he said. "Want me to carry you?"

"Yes," she said.

Our greatest glory is not in never falling, but in rising

every time we fall.

—Confucius

Chapter 13

ONE EVENING WHEN CONNIE WAS TIED UP AT THE firehouse, Sierra decided to attend a meeting in Leadville. She was running a little late but people were still grabbing up coffee and cookies—sugar had traditionally been the alcoholic's friend. When she looked around the church basement for a comfortable spot, she saw a familiar face and headed that way. Neely was sitting in the second row.

"You're still around?" she asked, taking the chair beside Neely.

"I am. I'm sorry, you're…?"

"Sierra," she said, putting out her hand. "I heard you speak a week or two ago and I thought you were doing some traveling. Speaking at meetings. Going to conferences, roundups and that sort of thing."

"I've been doing a lot of that, yes. Steering committee, women's conference committee, lots of AA work. Now it's time for a little personal work. And I like this place."

"It's a good place," Sierra agreed.

"I wonder," Neely said, looking a bit contemplative. "Do you have time for pie and coffee afterward?"

"Sure I do," she said.

From that moment, Sierra was concentrating more on Neely than on the speaker. Will spoke first and she'd heard him before; she loved listening to him, as a matter of fact. Sober twenty years and so steady, but so aware of his roots in addiction and what it had cost. Then Sophie, sober six years and one of the lucky ones—sobriety had saved her and her family before any irreparable damage. Then Jennifer, sixty years old and sober two years, still struggling mightily, hanging on by the skin of her teeth. Every day and sometimes every hour was a miserable battle for her, but she used all the tools available, many meetings, more than one sponsor, a treatment facility, counseling, family support...

But Sierra was thinking about Neely, filled with admiration and a little awe. Neely was so beautiful and confident. She was taller than Sierra; about five-eight and fit. Her hair was thick, rich brown, shoulder length and swayed when she nodded her head. She was smart—just her presentation at that open meeting was so impressive—emotional and funny and wise, like the poster girl for recovery. She was older than Sierra and had found her sobriety at a younger age—Sierra admired and envied her. She had a kind of reverence for her. Neely was the kind of person she'd fantasized having as a sponsor, not Moody. And before she even really knew Neely, she was immediately thinking of that possibility.

And speak of the devil, Moody was there. This was not his usual meeting—he tended to like the early-morning meeting. He sat in his usual place—third row, far left seat, like he was ready to make a break for it. Sierra didn't want to talk to Moody tonight because she didn't want him to horn in on their pie and coffee, which Sierra was already hoping would actually turn into a meal. She wasn't hungry, but she didn't want her date with Neely to go by too fast.

Still, she did the right thing and checked in with Moody, saying hello. And then, because duplicity was a definite enemy to sobriety, she told Moody she was going out for coffee with Neely. And he had said, "Good for you."

"I'm so glad to get out of there," Neely said as they were leaving. "How would you like to meet at that Denny's by the highway? Is that too far away for you?"

"No, perfect," Sierra said, though it was in the opposite direction of the Crossing.

Glad to get out of there? Neely was like a cheerleader for AA, super involved, traveling on a speaking circuit, visiting open meetings, sitting on boards... Even Moody, who was moody, never said he was glad a meeting was over.

They went in their own cars and she couldn't help but notice Neely had a really nice late-model Lexus. When they were seated in a booth in the restaurant, Neely ordered coffee for both of them.

Sierra couldn't even remember when she last had a girlfriend. At least she had Connie these days, the best friend she'd ever had. But there was something about a girlfriend that hit all the right buttons. Connie was great and she was completely grateful for him, but there were girl things he would never get. Like cramps, to name just one.

She'd managed to hook up with all the wrong people since she was about fourteen. And once she'd gotten into AA and met people like herself, she'd gotten close to a few but it always felt a little forced. She wanted to feel some chemistry, a strong connection, someone she could really hang on to for ballast. It had felt close a couple of times, but not exciting enough.

"What did you mean you couldn't wait to get out of there?" Sierra asked.

"Oh, I don't know," Neely said, stirring sugar into her coffee. "I know how important it is for me but there are times I've just heard enough and would rather be doing something else." Then she flashed her gorgeous movie-star smile. "Like this!"

"Like this," Sierra echoed.

"How long have you lived here, Sierra?"

"Oh, not very long. I got here in March so it's been...five

months. I'm from Iowa. My folks live on a farm in Iowa, but my older brother is here and I wanted to be near family, but not on a farm in Iowa."

"I've lived in Vail for the past few years, but I'm originally from Connecticut," Neely said. "I just love it here. Plus, I wanted to get away from the whole family. They're all pretty bad for me. I'm thinking of moving, but not out of Colorado. There was a relationship I had to end. A destructive relationship."

"Do we all have destructive relationships?" Sierra heard herself ask.

"At least one! I attract them like magnets. Don't you?"

She shook her head. "I haven't been involved with anyone in a long time," Sierra said, and then she wondered why she didn't mention Connie. "If you don't mind me asking, what do you do for work?"

"Nothing at the moment, but I'm looking to start a small business. I'm not ready to talk about it yet, but that's why I'm scouting around a little bit. Looking for just the right place."

"What kind of business?" Sierra instantly asked.

Neely grinned beautifully. "Did it go right over your head that I'm not talking about it yet?"

"Sorry," she said. "I guess it did."

"Let's just say a specialty shop and I'll tell you more when things start to fall into place. See, my crazy family did one nice thing for me—they left me a little nest egg. If I'm smart, and I am smart, I can turn it into a larger nest egg and take care of myself without ever relying on anyone again."

"That would be so nice," Sierra said.

"So, who do you rely on?" Neely asked.

"Well, no one, really," she said. And then she wondered why she had said that. She relied on lots of people, she just wasn't financially supported by them at the moment, but only because she didn't need much to live on. "But I have a lot of nice people nearby if I ever run into trouble. My brother and sister-in-law, my sister-in-law's dad, people I've met around town and…well, I've been seeing a very nice guy. He's a paramedic and firefighter."

"Oh, sounds hot! I got involved with a guy right after rehab, just a few months sober, and all we did was drive each other crazy until I left him. Then I did it again and again and again. I'm recovering and running from another one right now. I'm still tempted by the wrong people," Neely said. "I'm starting to think that the only men who are safe for me are the ones I'm not attracted to."

She'd picked herself a young businessman, she explained. A broker of commodities, a respectable guy who had sophisticated friends, and they drank and used worse than the lowlifes she'd known before. There was a radiologist—didn't drink at all, and what a supreme asshole. Then she tried a simple blue-collar guy, a mechanic, who was such a demanding, controlling freak she wondered if she'd ever get away. A schoolteacher, a librarian, "And get this! A minister! I think he was the worst of all!"

"And through all that you didn't drink?" Sierra asked, kind of astonished.

"Nine years. Come on, didn't I have enough problems?" And then she laughed.

Sierra was captivated. She told Neely things she hadn't told anyone in quite a while, things she hadn't told Moody, a lot of them straight out of her notebook. Neely identified, understood, added her own stuff and even though Sierra had experienced that before, there was something about Neely that was so engaging, she felt like a spark ignited inside her. It was, she realized, that female chemistry in friendship that was almost like falling in love. Her nerves of feeling unworthy had shifted to the excitement of being *chosen*. They laughed until tears rolled down their cheeks, they whispered, trading in secrets, they made promises to each other to do this again and again. Neely did something that Sierra recognized but didn't want to acknowledge—a kind of leap to intimacy. "We should take a little road trip up to Montana for a few days," she said. She was ready to go on a trip with Sierra? They barely knew each other! And, "Or, how about Santa Fe? It's wonderful this time of year. And I could stand to look at their shops, for business reasons, of course." And she laughed.

"Well, that sounds great, but my brother is counting on me and I have a dog. Molly. She's such a baby when I leave her."

"A dog?" Neely said as if appalled. "Does she shed?"

"Oh yes. Sully, the owner of the place I'm staying, says she's ninty percent hair."

Neely curled her lip. "I'm not much of a dog person."

"You like cats?" Sierra asked.

"I like goldfish," she said, grinning naughtily. "As long as someone else is feeding them and cleaning the bowl.

Sierra was aware that was about the fourth red flag that she was choosing to ignore. She had been reluctant to mention her boyfriend when he was very important to her. She pretended not to rely on anyone when she did—every day. Neely invited her on a trip, though they'd only met once for pie and coffee. Neely didn't much care for dogs...

Most women were experienced in negotiating friendships, but Sierra knew she was not. In a way she had been left behind. For her early years she was confined to her family, isolated from the world at large as much as possible. For her teen years on the farm, and by the time her sister and brothers left, she'd discovered booze, taking her out of her reality quite often. While other girls had their bonded friendships, Sierra had not. At least not friendships that were very important. She'd never had a close girlfriend. She wondered if that meant she'd missed a fundamental step in her emotional growth.

Sierra looked at her watch. They'd been there for two and a half hours. "Oh brother, I have to go. I left my dog with Sully and he likes to turn in early." Then she bit her lip and rather timidly asked, "Do you think you'll be around awhile?"

"Probably. Let's exchange numbers. Unless you don't feel comfortable..."

"No, I like that idea!" she said enthusiastically.

They plugged their numbers into each other's phones, said farewell for now and all the way back to the Crossing Sierra was filled with hope and fantasies of a bond, having a real girlfriend, being a part of something with someone she understood and who understood her. Connie accepted her and for that she was grateful but it would be nice to be friends with someone who got her. She fantasized doing normal or at least almost normal things—hiking, meeting for dinner, maybe going to one of those boring AA social events together. She told herself just because Neely didn't like dogs didn't mean they couldn't be good friends.

She bragged to Connie. "I met the coolest woman at the last meeting and we went out for coffee. She's so classy, so funny and smart and we hit it off. Do you know how long it's been since I've had a close girlfriend? Almost never."

"Aren't you and Maggie close?" he asked.

"We're getting closer, but Maggie doesn't really understand me the way Neely does. Neely has been through it all. And she's so much fun."

"Good for you, babe."

When Sierra didn't hear from Neely for three days she called her.

"Hey, Neely, how's it going?"

"Who is this?"

"It's Sierra! Just thought I'd check on you and see how you're getting by."

"Oh. Yeah. Pretty busy. Can I call you back?"

"Sure..."

There was a faint beeping on Sierra's cell phone as Neely signed off. She might've been in the middle of something important, Sierra thought. Or maybe she'd been at a meeting somewhere.

But when Neely didn't call back, Sierra sulked. She grieved a loss she hadn't even had. Then she abandoned her dreams of having a best girlfriend. When she explained this to Connie, he just frowned. "Kind of sounds like she wasn't very genuine," he said.

"Know what bothered me most of all?" Sierra asked. "She doesn't like animals. Her lip curled when I told her about Molly. And I *still* wanted to be her friend."

"Maybe she's allergic," Connie said.

"She's not," Sierra said, even though she didn't know that for sure.

When Tom asked Cal if he could bring a friend by the barn to have a look at what they were doing, the answer was simple. "Of course, Tom! You're as invested in this remodel as I am!"

He was not expecting Tom to bring a woman. Cal was introduced to Lola and found himself squinting at her, trying to remember where he'd seen her before.

"Home Depot," she supplied. "We've seen each other there, though I don't think we've officially met."

"Sorry, Cal, I should have told you it was Lola. I didn't even think of it."

"That's no problem. So—we're a couple of months of finishing work away from being done here, but we're living here. As long as I keep the work site clean. The upstairs master and bath are nearly finished. We're close down here. Maggie's ordering stuff. Don't even ask me what stuff..."

"Hi, Lola," Maggie said, coming down the stairs, her belly leading the way. "I didn't know Tom was bringing you out here."

"We discovered we have a shared interest in remodeling," Lola said. "I've put a lot of work into that old house I live in and it's looking pretty good."

"It's better than good," Tom said. "It looks as good as my house. Maybe better."

"When Tom started telling me about this barn remodel, I

couldn't wait to see it. Thanks for letting me have a peek. We were talking about remodeling and found out it's kind of a passion with both of us. Tom has actually flipped a couple of fixer-uppers. And that's my dream job."

"I thought you were taking classes toward your degree?" Maggie said.

"I thought the most practical thing for me would be a teaching degree," Lola said. "I'm good with kids. And there's some security in teaching, not to mention a small pension. Plus, there's good vacation time—time I could put toward renovation. If I can find the right project."

"Let me show you the upstairs," Tom said. "We're finishing the bathrooms up there and when we're done with the tile and stone we'll paint and carpet. That'll go fast. We've got some new materials for the countertops and floors—not as porous, doesn't stain..."

He was leading her up the stairs and when they were out of sight, Cal turned to Maggie. He showed her a half smile and lifted brow.

"A shared passion for home renovation," Maggie said with a grin.

"They probably sound like us in bed," Cal said. "Oh, oh, oh, how about travertine on the front walk..."

She put her arms around his neck, pressing up against him. "Oh baby, show me that marble with the waterfall edge..."

He got kicked by the baby. "You're carrying a wild woman," he said. "Have I told you how terrified I am?"

"There's nothing to be afraid of," she reassured him. "Little girls always love their daddy best. Should we go upstairs and help Tom show Lola all his handiwork?"

"Give him a break," Cal said. "Did he seem awkward to you?"

"Not at all."

Cal's phone rang and he picked it up off the kitchen counter.

He looked at the screen and said, "This is work, babe. Make my apologies?"

"Sure," she said.

Cal went into their bedroom, which would become his office in just a few weeks. For the time being it was a bedroom that sometimes doubled as an office if he needed a room with a door that closed. This particular caller was a woman Cal had worked with when he was with the law firm in Detroit. Cal had reached out to her for help with Sierra's situation.

Alison started off as a paralegal before Cal met her. By the time he joined the Detroit firm, she was doing a lot of their investigating, which turned out to be her niche and her passion. Being in criminal defense, he had relied on her quite a bit. She was young, sharp, energetic and resourceful.

"Hey, Alison," he said. "What's up?"

"Quite a lot more than you might expect," she said. He scribbled on a notepad while she ran down a list of the information she'd gathered, ending with, "Finally, this Derek Cox, I can't locate him. Let me rephrase—I've located several, none in the Detroit area, none in the age range we discussed. If his name is Derek Cox and if he exists, he's in the wind. The police have listed Sierra as a person of interest in their investigation into a hit–and–run but she isn't a suspect, at least not at this time. They haven't issued a warrant. Frankly, they suspect foul play in the disappearance of Sierra and the abandonment of her car, the car notably involved in the accident."

"As I told you before, that's one of the many reasons I'm looking into this. She saw a man here who looked like him. She couldn't confirm that it was him. But it shook her up enough to come to me with her story. She's afraid of him. How did you get this information?"

"An accident report and a brief conversation with the sergeant in traffic. I don't get the feeling the case is getting a lot of attention. I hope I didn't stir things up by inquiring."

"How did you inquire?" he asked, not entirely sure he wanted the answer.

"Insurance companies always want a few clarifications about accident details. Is there anything else I can do?"

"You can keep looking for this Cox," he said. "It would help to know where he is. It would help to know where he isn't, for that matter."

"I'll need a little more information, Cal. If your sister could answer a few questions—where he worked, where he lived, where he's originally from. I need a little more to go on than he was driving her car that night."

"I'll talk to her," he said. "I'll get back to you."

He just sat for a moment after they disconnected. He was going to have to talk to Sierra. She had to know what he found out and if he was to help her, he would have to probe. He didn't look forward to it. He left a message on Sierra's cell phone. "We have to talk, whenever you're free. I have some information for you. Important stuff. Let me know when you have time. Time alone."

He tried to slap on the professional lawyer face rather than the worried brother. Not only did he have to face Maggie, there was company in the house. He gave himself a few extra minutes. When he walked into the great room, Maggie, Tom and Lola were all engrossed in studying the fireplace, something that had been installed before they'd moved in.

"This was one of the first things we added," Tom was saying. "Barns don't usually have fireplaces. Or so many windows..."

Cal wasn't listening.

Sierra worked at the diner in the morning and then hurried back to the Crossing for lunch and to meet Cal. When she'd returned his call last night she had asked him if it was about her car and Michigan, and he had said, "Yes."

"Is it all coming to a head now?" she had asked.

"All I have right now is information about the incident. The rest is still unknown to me."

She was sure then.

Sierra hadn't slept well. Her mind had been a little too busy. She'd spent years running away from things but sobriety made her see the folly of that. She'd learned many useful things, but high on the list were the benefits in facing your mistakes, taking responsibility and making amends. That was freedom. You couldn't run away to get free, you had to face the truth to be free.

When Cal arrived at the Crossing, he spent a few minutes visiting with Sully, then put his arm around Sierra's shoulders and walked her over to the front porch on Sully's house. Until the barn was finished, Cal met some clients at the Crossing, either at Sully's kitchen table or on the front porch where they'd have a measure of privacy.

"You have circles under your eyes," Cal said.

"I had a little trouble sleeping," she said. "Just lay it on me. What do you know?"

"There was an accident, just as you suspected and feared. A cyclist was critically injured, but he did make a full recovery. It's still a felony hit-and-run but they know it was a man driving. Sierra, I can only think of one way they could know that. There must be a witness. The witness could be the victim. I hired the detective I worked with at my old firm—she knows how to surf the public record documents, arrests and accidents, that sort of thing. She also knows how to finesse information by pretending to be an insurance agent, a banker, a lawyer—she's very good. And very sneaky. The police know it was your car, a man at the wheel, that your car was abandoned. And that you disappeared. There's even been some conjecture of foul play in your disappearance or the greater possibility that you and the driver ran off to avoid arrest. They want to talk to you. You're a person of interest in the case. Not a suspect, but a person of interest."

"Who could become a suspect," she said.

"If they have evidence to support that. They've been look-ing for the identity of a man. I suppose they're looking for this Derek Cox. My investigator couldn't find him. She needs more information like where he worked, lived, where he grew up, where his family is, anything at all to heat up his trail, provide a map of sorts. I hate to put you through this but can you tell me everything again? We need to have as many details as possible."

She closed her eyes and rubbed her temples. "He said so many things. He said he'd made money in real estate but I knew tons of people who were licensed Realtors and even busting their butts, it was hard to make money. He said he ran a messenger service for a couple of years and that's how he made all his con-nections. He also said he had owned a small valet parking ser-vice and made a bundle that way but before all that, he said he had been in the military and gone to Afghanistan. You know what I think? I think he was lying about everything. I think he was dealing. He always had something, usually pot. Sometimes he had ecstasy and oxy. He said he was from Maine, he said he was from California. I never went to his apartment. He said he lived three blocks from me but who knows if that's true. I didn't even date him. I hung out with him and other people, mostly—a bar crowd—and he came by work to take me to lunch. I'll give you the names of some of my so-called friends, but they weren't close friends. It's not like we knew each other's families; they weren't friends from school or anything. I just hung out with him at the bar a couple of times, talked to him on the phone, then we had one official date. I let him come home with me once. Just once. And that's when things got weird."

"Weird how?"

"I didn't get it until much later. He couldn't get it up. He had trouble. I told him it was all right and to just forget it but he was so angry. He wanted to keep trying. It was when I pushed at him and told him I was done, boing! Then he couldn't complete. He can't get it up in a normal situation. He liked that I wasn't into it. Then he didn't want to leave. He was rough. I couldn't get rid of him until morning, and then he showed up at the office where I worked with flowers. Flowers like we'd had a lovely, romantic evening, which we hadn't. He called and called. He said he was sorry and that's never happened to him before, which now I know is bullshit. I told him to settle down, we weren't engaged, just casual friends, and he got worse. Calling, showing up where I was, parking out in front of my house, hanging out in parking lots waiting for me. I finally got mad and told him I didn't want to see him or talk to him again but he didn't back off. Everytime I turned around, there he was. When I talked to the police and asked them if they could do anything they were perfectly nice, they told me to be careful, to stop answering my phone if it was him and to call the police if he became threatening. I blocked his number, I dropped Facebook, I deleted his emails and he couldn't get a text through. Then came that night."

"How long did this go on?" Cal asked, making notes.

"Only a couple of weeks, that's all. I talked to him at a bar, I gave him my number, I talked to him on the phone about three times. I saw him for lunch, at the bar after work a few times and there were lots of people around—people I saw after work all the time."

"People you worked with?"

"A couple of them came from the company I worked for. I hadn't had the job that long, didn't know too many people. I found the people who liked to go out right away. I had a talent for it." She laughed hollowly. "I was doing clerical work for Union Insurance."

"I need some names, Sierra."

"Sure. I can give you the names of some friends. My old roommate and her boyfriend. My old boss—but she was a battle-ax and I never shared anything about my life with her. She hated me. I wasn't crazy about her. I was... I wasn't the best employee."

"In those two weeks did you ever learn anything more about the guy? Can you think of anything?"

She shook her head. "Just the stuff I told you—he had a lot of stories. A lot of jokes. He buddied up to people. He gave them dope, like pot or ecstasy. They couldn't understand why I didn't want to hang out with him. After all, he was so much fun and he liked me. It was awful. I didn't want to explain why I knew he was bad news."

"Think about it and make me a list—any connections that could give us information about the guy because he's gone. And I'd like your permission to tell Maggie about this. She's very good at confidences, so don't worry about that."

"Why do you have to tell her?" she asked, feeling her eyes brighten with tears she knew she wouldn't be able to shed.

"Because, Sierra, we have to go back. You have to talk to the police. They're looking for you. They want to question you. I'm sure they want to know how the accident happened. Maybe they hope you can get them to the guy."

"Why? The guy he hit recovered. Can't we just stay away?"

"Here's the deal, Sierra. They know it was your car, they know you've disappeared, they know there was a felony hit-and-run. If you know they're looking for you in a felony investigation and you don't come forward, they can hit you with obstruction. Or you can wait till they find you, and it can sneak up on you. At the most inconvenient moment, you can find yourself taken into custody for questioning and I want to be with you. I don't want that to happen while I'm busy having a baby. Let me tell Maggie why I have to go back with you and let's get this done."

"And what if we get there and they lock me up?" she asked.

"Cooperating now is the safest thing to do. Once you tell the police where you are and how you can be reached, they probably won't restrict you. I don't think they will anyway. You're not their primary suspect."

"Who could be a witness?" she asked, frowning in confusion.

Cal shook his head. "Another motorist? Maybe even the victim?"

"Cal. He drove a red Nissan GT—a sports car. It was almost new. Candy-apple red."

"That might help, but it's a popular car. They're going to ask you why you ran if you weren't driving the car."

"Can they make me press charges against him? Seeing him again terrifies me."

Cal just locked eyes with her, looking at her steadily. "You might have to be braver than you've ever been. If I thought there was an easier way, I'd tell you."

She laughed without humor. "Eventually you always have to pay the bill."

"It was not your fault," Cal said.

"Oh, I know that," she said. "But running away made me feel like a victim. And by saying nothing, I hid him. And because I was too afraid of him to act, he might be getting away with everything. Now I have to ask myself—how many people has he hurt in this past year?"

"What are we going to do about that?" Cal asked her.

"I'm going to tell the truth. And pray."

All changes, even the most longed for, have their melancholy; for what we leave behind us is a part of ourselves; we must die to one life before we can enter another.

—ANATOLE FRANCE

Chapter 14

A YEAR AGO TOM HAD WONDERED IF HE WOULD
ever have a full life. He had four great kids and was certainly
blessed with work. While a lot of people couldn't find a job it
seemed like he had jobs coming out of his ears. He had even
accepted that he had a very unusual relationship with his wife.
His ex-wife. They lived apart and he raised the children, but
she was a regular presence for a few days at a time. Kind of like
being married to an airline pilot.

And then he had to face the hard truth—Becky was not just
a divorcée who had occasional boyfriends. She was a prostitute.
She called herself an escort, but the bottom line was always the
same—she padded her pocketbook by sleeping with men. He
conceded she was a pretty upscale hooker who made excellent
money. He was even grateful she didn't seem to fit the profile
he'd seen on most cop shows—she hadn't been driven into pros-
titution by a pimp or dependence on drugs. No, nothing as hor-
rifying as that. She was just a beautiful woman who had found
a way to supplement her income with sex. Which she enjoyed.

"Not with strangers," she'd argued. "They were all gentlemen
I was seeing, men I knew. If I hadn't taken money, I'd be just an
average woman—dating, having sex sometimes as adults do."

"I'm not buying it," Tom had said. "And the house rules

change, right now. The kids aren't going to your place anymore and you're not spending the night here."

"You can't do that," she said. "They're my kids, too."

"We do this my way or I'll tell them."

"No, don't! They're too young to understand!"

"Becky, I'm too young to understand!" he shot back.

"Fine. I've stopped that job anyway."

"I don't believe it," he said. "You've been lying to me for years, why would I believe you now? So here's the deal—you can visit the kids here, with my supervision, as long as you make plans ahead of time. No overnights."

"What am I supposed to tell them?" she asked.

"Tell them you're very busy with your second job. And if you run into trouble with that second job again, don't call me. Call your lawyer."

He knew that was the right thing to do but that action took some getting used to. Up to that moment, he'd had someone in his life, at least now and then. First he had to deal with the shock and hurt it caused him. Then there was the loneliness. Then the dread of telling his kids—they'd be devastated, he was sure. He knew he'd have to tell them someday.

But they barely noticed their mom was hardly around anymore. They were busy kids; they were a busy family! Every hour was accounted for. They had a lot of responsibility with school and their extracurricular activities.

He'd dealt with the disappointment. He'd always had a passion for Becky, but knowing the wide range her affections had traveled, his urges where she was concerned were gone. He'd finally adjusted to the shock. He could thank Cal for some of that. Cal, who had represented Becky in court, had a unique perspective: "Given my line of work, I've been professionally acquainted with a number of working women, you should pardon the expression. I've always thought the laws unbalanced in the emphasis, discriminating against women. They should be going

after the pimps, traffickers and johns before the working girls. I
don't care who an adult has sex with but I do care about human
trafficking, kidnapping, child abuse, extortion, human bond-
age, slavery, et cetera. A good old-fashioned hooker, exercising
some discrimination, her own boundaries, minding health and
safety..." He had shrugged.

"You'd care if you were her husband," Tom had said.

Cal had clamped a hand on his shoulder and said, for at least
the tenth time "Good thing you haven't been married to her
for about eight years, then."

So then Tom had to face the embarrassing truth—that he'd
been willing to forgive and forget anything because he wanted
his wife home, his wife who had not been his wife in years.

But now there was Lola. He'd known her almost his whole
life. She was a couple of years older than Tom, had been ahead
of him in school. Tom had grown up on a local ranch; his dad
kept cows and grew alfalfa. Her dad worked in the hardware
and farm equipment store. They'd both married too young, had
nothing much in common as couples, divorced and became single parents, too busy for much socializing.

Now he was looking at Lola in a whole new way. The reason
being, he was a one-woman man, period. When he thought of
Becky as his wife, even his part-time wife, his eyes just wouldn't
stray. Once he let go of that notion he realized how much he
liked Lola. Rather, he realized all the things he liked about
her. Her curly dark hair, her rosy cheeks, her pleasantly round
figure, her large dark eyes. She had red lips and a ready laugh.
She was funny. He'd always known all these things about Lola
but he hadn't appreciated them before. People loved her. She'd
been a fixture in the diner and Home Depot for so many years,
everyone knew her and everyone liked talking to her when they
stopped at the diner for coffee or an ice cream sundae, or maybe
Home Depot for paint or home repair supplies.

As far as Tom knew, there hadn't been a man in her life in

years. He started off with a potted plant, then a second, then a phone call. He'd had to think for hours and hours what pretense he would use for calling her. "There's a home show in Colorado Springs and I was thinking of going. Always good to keep up on that stuff, what's new, what's still popular, what's innovative. You have any interest in that?"

Now there'd been four plants, many phone calls, he'd taken her out to see Cal's house in progress, he'd shown her his house and they had a new hobby—looking at model homes and open houses. They could spend hours talking about construction, remodeling, new decorator items, paint. They invested almost an hour of porch time talking about sinks! That's when he held her hand. For the first time. And he laughed.

"What's so funny?" Lola asked him.

"I got butterflies," he admitted, adding a slight flush to the statement. "You know the last time I felt that? I was about fourteen."

"I think we should talk," Lola said.

"We've been talking nonstop," he said. "Almost every day."

"I think we should talk about this—you're courting me. I thought we were single parents who liked being independent?"

"Am I making you feel less independent by holding your hand?" he asked, giving her hand a squeeze.

"Just where do you think this is going?" she wanted to know.

"I have no idea, but I'm enjoying it right now. How about you?"

"I'm surprised, that's all. We've known each other for years and now, suddenly, we're kind of dating. Even if our dates seem to be on the phone or looking at new hardware. I grew up around hardware."

"That's what's so funny," he said. "I've known you for so long, I know your dad works in hardware and you work at Home Depot and yet I never considered we'd have this shared interest. That's very cool. What are you worried about?"

"Oh, I don't know. Getting too involved, I guess."

"Well, take it easy. We'll only get as involved as you want."

"Right," she said. "This is new territory for me."

"Me, too," he said, giving a nod. "I've hardly ever dated in my whole life."

"There was your wife, who is incredibly beautiful. I think she might be the most beautiful woman in the world."

Tom laughed. "You mean my ex-wife? Yes, Becky is very pretty. We've been divorced for eight years now."

"But you remained very...close."

"I'd say we get along pretty well, under the circumstances. But it's time for me to get on with my life. Becky has definitely gotten on with hers. Listen, if I'm making you feel uncomfortable or pressured or—"

"I'm not the kind of woman men pay attention to, that's all."

"I resemble that remark," he said, laughing. "I'm not exactly being chased down by women, but that's been okay by me. Four kids, a bunch of jobs... Until a couple of years ago when Jackson graduated from high school and Nikki started driving, I don't know when I would've found the time. Things are getting a little less complicated. Finally."

"Tom, you're a very handsome man..."

"Thank you, Lola. And you're a very beautiful woman."

She laughed at him. "Me? Please!"

He frowned. "I never suspected you for a lack of confidence. You always seem so sure of yourself."

"I am. But not in the looks department."

"Why the hell not?" he asked. "You're gorgeous!"

"Stop it!"

"I shouldn't be surprised," he said somewhat sadly. "Becky never thought she was pretty enough and there's no question about it, she's— Well, this isn't about her. Here's what makes you beautiful," he said. "Your hair is so silky...thick and curly and it kind of makes a guy want to dig his hands in it. Your lips, they're kind of heart shaped and I don't think you ever wear makeup—you don't need to. You have that beautiful, smooth skin, kind of like the sateen paint I like. Velvet skin, red lips, big, dark eyes, and you always smell a little bit like Ivory soap. I've always liked that smell so much, it's so clean smelling. And you're soft. I hope this isn't offensive—you're sexy and buxom in the most subtle, alluring way. I can't help but imagine what you'd feel like in my arms. That wasn't a pass, I just mean I can imagine you'd fill my arms and I bet that's the most amazing, beautiful feeling.

"And then if it's not enough that you look beautiful, you *act* beautiful. All the time. You're sweet and funny and so supportive— I bet it's just the way you are because it never seems phony or like you have to try. You're kind. You treat people with such consideration. But you're strong—there's something about strength in a woman that's enviable. Admirable. And you know what else I love—you seem fearless. I guess when a woman's been on her own with kids, she'd better be fearless or the earth would just swallow her up! Yes, Lola, you're sexy and beautiful and I love looking at you. Holding you is probably even better."

Her eyes welled up and tears spilled over. With a cry, she fled the porch. She ran into the house, leaving him alone.

He sat for a minute. "I guess I better practice my delivery a little," he said to no one.

Sierra was not entirely surprised when Maggie called her, but she was a little surprised by the request. "Can you come over? I have a couple of things to show you."

She went as soon as she could. She found Cal in the kitchen chopping veggies, marinating salmon filets. "Maggie's in the bedroom. Go ahead."

She gave a couple of taps before pushing the door open. She was immediately pulled into Maggie's arms for a loving hug.

"I guess Cal told you," Sierra said.

"Yep. I have some things for you to try on. I'm taller than you are but they might not be too big." There were clothes spread on the bed. She held up a black sleeveless dress and matching jacket. "We can have this shortened and taken in and you can keep it. I'm due a new one and I have no idea what size I'll be after the baby comes. Jaycee said to count on an extra size. Every woman needs a suit. I used to call this my funeral suit but it worked very well in court."

"Court?"

"Oh, I'm sure you heard. I was the defendant in a wrongful death suit. It was a nightmare, really. I was terrified I might lose in spite of the fact I didn't do anything wrong. I didn't make any mistakes."

"I think I know the feeling," Sierra said.

"Well, you're not going to court, don't worry about that. Then there are these," she said, holding up a pair of cream-colored dress slacks with a silky blouse and a matching vest. Next there was a pencil skirt and a sweater set.

"What's this about?" Sierra asked.

"Unless you're hiding something, your wardrobe is made up of jeans, shorts, sweats, T-shirts and so forth. You should go to the police department looking classy. Smart. Your lawyer will be wearing a suit. He's delicious in a suit—I live for those days he puts on a suit. You can't go to the police department to be questioned about a felony looking like a homeless teenager. Cal will take you by a store for the right shoes. My feet are more like paddles than feet or I'd loan you shoes."

Tears gathered in Sierra's eyes. *One of these days*, she thought, *I am going to actually break down and cry.*

"I want to come with you, but I can't," Maggie said. "But I bet I can help—I've been through about a million depositions as the alleged guilty party. It can be brutal."

"Oh, Maggie..."

"You're going to be all right," she said. "Cal is brilliant. He was one of the most sought after criminal defense attorneys in Michigan. Before Lynne died. He knows the ropes."

"I know," she said with a sniff.

"Well, come on, let's try it on," she said. She sat down on the bed, rubbing her belly. "I know someone who can make alterations for us in a hurry but we have a few days. I think he's got plane tickets for the weekend..."

"Sunday," Sierra said. "I took a week off at the diner—I said it was a legal matter, that I had an accident over a year ago and there's a deposition for a lawsuit, but that I wasn't in trouble. I hope that's true. A week. Those high school waitresses are getting all the time they need." She pulled her shirt off over her head.

"If they fire you, we'll find something else. Maybe something better," Maggie said. "Don't worry about stuff like that. This is survival. We're all going to back you up."

Off came the shorts. She slipped the little black dress over her head and turned around for Maggie to zip up the back.

"Wow," Maggie said. "That's close. I think we need to take it in a little bit, right up the side seams and raise the hem a couple of inches. It has to fit right and be the exact right length— you can't wear it too short or too long. Cal says when you're perceived as guilty, you don't go to court with tight, revealing clothes but it's even worse if you try to look Amish. Style and taste, that's the prescription. Whether people realize it or not, their first impressions are hard to erase."

Sierra put on the jacket which seemed to fit in the shoulders.

"A little hem in the sleeves—they're a little too long," Maggie said. "We might be okay on the length. What do you think?"

Sierra turned in front of the mirror. "It's beautiful, Maggie. Thank you. I never would have thought of this. What I'd wear was the furthest thing from my mind."

"I bet you're terrified," Maggie said. "I certainly was for my lawsuits. And I'm pretty brave."

"There are so many parts of this adventure that scare me, I can't even describe," Sierra said. "It feels like a problem with a lot of moving parts."

"Sierra, have you had counseling?"

Sierra nodded. "It came up in rehab. I cheated—I didn't tell the whole story. Well, I wasn't sure of the whole story. I suspected we hit something and he acted like we hit a person but I thought... I hoped he was just trying to terrify me. Sexual assault came up a lot in rehab." She shook her head sadly. "I never would have imagined how hard it is, how much shame is involved in rape."

"I haven't experienced it, thank God, but I've learned a lot about it. Sierra, I'm just so damn sorry."

"Thanks. But now it's time to be accountable. I'd rather not be, but I'm afraid there aren't any options."

"*He* needs to be accountable," Maggie said. "He's a criminal."

"Yeah."

She tried on the pants and blouse; only a hem was needed.

"Is Sully taking care of Molly? I would be glad to but I'll be in Denver for a couple of days..."

"I haven't talked to Sully yet but I'm sure he'd be happy to. He loves her. She's kind of a handful, though."

"What about Connie?" Maggie asked, her voice soft.

Sierra shrugged. "He knows about a lot of my checkered past, but I didn't have the nerve to tell him this one."

"Why?" Maggie asked.

Sierra lifted her chin. "I get that it's not my fault but it's very hard not to feel dirty. It's like he stained me and I can't get the stain off."

"Oh baby," Maggie said. "You have to live it off. One day at a time, just like everything else. But there's one thing I think you should consider. While you're going through this, while you're in Michigan, let's get you set up with some counseling. Cal knows who to ask, how to find the best person."

"That's worth considering, but I'm hoping not to be with the police too long," Sierra said. "Hopefully I'll spend a couple of hours answering questions and tell them where I can be reached, then come home." She smiled. "Home. I like thinking of this as home and I've only been here since March."

"Can I ask a personal question?" Maggie said.

"You think I have anything personal left?" Sierra asked.

"Did you have a full medical workup after...after the assault?"

"The very next morning I went to a women's clinic. They did a rape kit even though I had showered. Since I wouldn't go to the police, I have no idea what's become of it, but I was tested for STDs. If I'd gone to the police, the kit would have been preserved in evidence, but that didn't happen. I had a follow-up exam a few months later and was treated for an STD. Then there was a checkup to make sure that was taken care of. All clear."

"How about depression?" Maggie asked.

"I ran the gamut. Depression, anxiety, insomnia, you name it. It's the rare person who doesn't flirt with all the disorders. It's also the rare person who doesn't bring a lot of crap in addition to addiction to the program. I have a feeling that now I'm going to get to do all of that again. For a while anyway."

"I'll talk to Cal about lining up some counseling, just in case. You don't have to go through this alone."

Sierra folded up the clothes she'd be taking to the dry cleaner in Leadville who did alterations; Maggie had given her the name. She stayed for dinner with Cal and Maggie and learned that Cal had already put in a call to an old colleague of his, a woman who had an extremely good reputation in criminal law. "I'm going with you to the police, but I wanted to give her a heads-up. We won't call her unless we have legal issues. Normally I would advise any client of mine not to talk to the police, at least not without a lawyer, but under the circumstances I think the best course is cooperation. I'll be there to be sure the questions you answer are directed at solving the felony hit-

and-run, not at turning you into the suspect. We'll cooperate because you're the victim."

"Could they charge me with obstruction?"

"They could, but they'd have to prove you knew you were hiding something. You can't really obstruct if you don't know the facts yourself. You were very specific—you were fleeing the rapist, not the law. You can't tell them what you can't remember, what you didn't see."

"I'm so afraid I'm going to screw this up somehow," she said.

"I'll be right there," Cal said. "Just remember the four magic words. *I want my lawyer.* Don't take any questions, no matter how casual, without me present. If you run into a police officer in the ladies' room and she asks you a question, use the four magic words. No matter what."

"You've done this a lot, I guess," she said.

"It's been a while," he said. "But it's like riding a bike."

Sierra called Connie and she was invited over without hesitation. Molly started to wag and whine the second Connie's house came into view. As usual, he didn't even wait for her to knock. He opened the door, slid an arm around her and simultaneously gave Molly a pat. "I have ice cream," he said.

"Maybe we can have some," she said. "Something has come up. I'm going to have to be out of town for a few days."

"Oh?" he said, pulling her into the house.

"Get out the ice cream. I'll tell you about it."

"Bowls?" he asked, heading for the kitchen.

"You only use bowls with your parents and grandparents and with your warm cookies," she said. "With your girl, two spoons and a carton."

"In bed?" he asked hopefully.

"How about the couch," she suggested.

They settled in, her legs draped over his, the ice cream carton on a dish towel.

"So, I was involved in a car accident back in Michigan. Someone was hurt—a guy on a bicycle. He's fine now, I'm told. I wasn't driving but I guess the driver is still being sought by the police. I barely knew him and don't have much information but I'm one of the only people who did. I need to go back, answer questions."

"So was there a crime?" he asked.

Of course—he was a paramedic. He probably knew a lot about accidents. "I guess it remains unresolved and the driver is long gone. So, I have to go back, tell them anything I can, which is hardly anything. Cal is going with me to make sure I don't somehow get myself in trouble. I'll be gone just a few days. It shouldn't be too complicated."

"Do you have to pay a fine or anything?" he asked.

She shook her head. "I don't think so," she said. "Look, I told them at the diner it was a legal matter and I had to take a week off. I didn't want to mention the police. If you could manage not to mention this..."

He put a spoonful of ice cream in her mouth. "I don't talk about you. What aren't you telling me?" he asked.

"Can we wait on all the grim details?" she said. "There was a thing with the guy, the driver, that I still can't talk about, that I have trouble even thinking about. For right now all I have to do is tell the police what I remember of the incident. It shouldn't take long."

"And your brother is going to make sure you're protected?"

"Well, he's a lawyer. He's much smarter about things like accidents and laws than I am."

"Sierra," he said, filling her mouth with ice cream again, "are you coming back?"

She couldn't answer right away, her mouth full of ice cream. "Of course."

"Are you taking Molly?"

"I can't take her. We're flying. We're leaving Sunday and coming back on Thursday. I think Sully will be happy to watch her and Maggie will be around the Crossing some of that time but she has to go to Denver."

"I'll check in on them," he said. "Make sure they're doing okay with Molly. But, Sierra, listen, don't be afraid to tell me things. It's okay to trust me."

"I know."

"Let Molly stay with me," he said. "I'll take her to Sully when I have to work."

"She might get into mischief. She might chase the elk, if they show up."

"I'm going to have separation anxiety if both of you go."

"Well, Connie, it's not as if we're always going to be together 24/7, you know. I'm sure there will be times in the future when I'll want to go somewhere and can't take you."

"I know that," he said. "But this is different."

"Why is it different?"

"Because, for some reason you don't want to talk about, you're afraid."

Sierra stayed the night with Conrad, of course. He told her that just because he wanted to make love to her all the time, that wasn't all he cared about. "I care about you in a way so solid and sure, I don't doubt you at all. Not a shred of doubt. So you take all the time you need to get sure of me. I'll be right here when you are."

As she lay in his arms she decided. She loved him. She had since almost the beginning. She would go back to Michigan to see if she could clean up her mess, and then she would come back to him and tell him everything. It was only fair. He deserved a chance to decide if his feelings could hold up after everything was said.

What greater thing is there for human souls than to

feel that they are joined for life…to be with each other

in silent unspeakable memories.

—GEORGE ELIOT

Chapter 15

LOLA WASN'T SURE SHE WOULD EVER GET OVER the embarrassment of bursting into tears at a compliment. A compliment? It was practically a tribute! And then her behavior only got worse and worse. She wouldn't answer Tom's knock at her door because she was nearly sobbing. When he called her later that night, she begged him to forgive her but to let it go and not talk about it. Cole was working that night but Trace asked her what was wrong and she said she had a headache and wanted to go to bed early. Typical of a sixteen-year-old boy, he didn't push that excuse because he really didn't want to know if his mother had some kind of girl problem.

Lola had been enjoying Tom's company so much. It was all right with her that they were only going to be friends. In fact, it was better that way. They had plenty to talk about, laugh about, even argue about, though if they disagreed it was always friendly. They had shared interests. Having someone of the opposite sex to talk to met a need for Lola. She didn't need a lover or a partner or husband but she was human—it was nice to have a man for a friend. And if they were just friends, there was no room for disappointment or dashed hopes.

Then he held her hand and remarked on her attractiveness. He made her sound like a beauty queen when she really was a plain, unfussy, unremarkable, overweight forty-year-old woman with two kids. Alone with two kids and an irresponsible ex who had never been that much help. She didn't wear makeup, she cut her own hair and had lately been looking at the hair color section of the drugstore. She didn't have enough money to be getting fancy dye jobs at the salon. Her clothes were the nicest she could find in the discount store and she wore them long after the styles had advanced. She just didn't live up to all he was saying.

And no one had ever said those kinds of things to her before. Not even when she was a pretty cute, slim, smart high school cheerleader.

Maybe it would have been different if Tom was a dumpy, ordinary guy. But he wasn't. He was heart-stopping handsome. He had thick brown hair that showed no sign of getting thin. And he was a laborer with all the muscles and fitness of a man who used his strength every day. His smile melted her and he had dimples for the love of God! And if it wasn't enough that he could be in films, he wasn't that shallow movie-star or model type. He was kindhearted, funny, smart. Tom was a good father. A responsible man who put his family first and took very good care of them. She was in awe of him.

And being his friend was so lovely.

It had not been easy to train herself to not look for that one special person, that constant and loving companion, a man who would love her through thick and thin. A man who would stay. And now, by saying what he had said, she would get her hopes up and begin to dream of a beautiful man to wake up with, to go to sleep with, to hold on long, cold, winter nights. She didn't want those fantasies but she was only human.

Tom came in to the diner the next day and they talked of ordinary things. He told her what his kids had planned for after dinner; she told him about the kitchen remodel she'd seen on the Home Channel. "Are you feeling better, Lola?" he finally asked her.

"Yes, thank you. I apologize for the other day. I don't know what happened to me. I must have been emotional for no reason and didn't even know it. Besides, I think it's best if we don't talk about it."

"Maybe we should talk about it," he said. "I don't think it's okay that hearing nice things makes you cry. I'll get paranoid."

"We decided, didn't we, that we're just going to be friends?" she said.

"Well, I don't remember talking about that. But here's how I feel—I want to be *at least* friends."

"I can't complicate my life with romantic notions and ridiculous ideas..."

"Then don't," he said. "But, my gosh, let's go ahead and enjoy ourselves."

"You don't understand, Tom. I don't want to make a fool of myself by letting myself be taken in by a lot of sweet talk that isn't ever going anywhere."

"Okay. Understandable. But I can't imagine you ever being foolish. That's one of the best things about you—you're so sensible and smart."

She rolled her eyes. Another compliment and the kind that could really get to her—praising her practicality and brains. "You shouldn't talk like that. What if that kind of talk undermines our perfectly great friendship?"

"Why would it? I can't see how being admired can hurt you."

"I told you, you wouldn't understand."

She looked around the diner and saw they were mostly alone. If she kept her voice down, she could get away with speaking her mind. "All right, listen to me. I'm forty. I'm ordinary. I'm fat. I'm a single mother of two sons and have a useless ex-husband— lot of baggage there."

He laughed at her. "You're going to tell me about baggage? And you are not fat! Don't say that about yourself—you're perfect."

"Now see, stop that. Talk like that makes me uncomfortable and it's not going to get you laid."

He grinned. "Lola, you can't scare me with that. I've been *not laid* most of my life!" He let out a big laugh. "I can't understand why it makes you so unhappy to hear nice things about yourself."

"Because it's the first time!" she blurted. He tilted his head and looked into her eyes. And they got a little wet. "Damn it, I'm not going to cry! Listen, if we're friends, I guess I can be completely honest with you."

"Sure. Of course."

"I'm not used to that kind of talk, all right? Even my own husband didn't lay that kind of mush on me. I can count on one hand the number of dates I've had since my divorce, mostly first dates. They were very unsatisfactory dates. So maybe you can understand that I'm not likely to take it very seriously. And... and I really don't want to be let down. Okay? I just don't want to start to believe a lot of malarkey and then try to pick myself up and brush myself off, get emotionally strong again and learn how to like being completely alone. I've been through it."

"I understand," he said. "So have I."

"Then let's agree—no more of that bullshit. Let's at least be honest with each other."

"Do you like me, Lola?" he asked.

"Of course! Why do you think it's a struggle?"

"All right," he said. "I'll be more careful with what I say."

"Thank you," she said.

She didn't hear from him the next day and she was sad about that, but she admitted to herself that it was probably for the best. And the next day he didn't drop by Home Depot. And he didn't call that night. Well, she might have pissed him off. She was kind of rough on him, calling his sweet talk bullshit and telling him he wouldn't get laid. Maybe that wasn't his intention anyway; maybe she had offended him with her assumptions.

But she missed Tom and his silly potted plants. He was so sensible—just couldn't bring himself to waste money on fresh-cut flowers. Potted plants lived longer and could be transplanted. She missed his phone calls, which always started out with some contrived question. She wanted to go to home shows with him.

Then at about eight the doorbell rang. When she opened the door, he was there, a little dusty like he'd been working. He was slapping his cap against his thigh. "Hi," she said.

"Are your kids home?" he asked.

She shook her head. "Why?"

"Oh, I could probably use a little help. I brought you a plant."

She broke into an unexpected grin. He'd brought her a plant! Maybe they could salvage their friendship, after all. "A plant?" she said.

He stepped aside. His truck was parked at the curb and sticking out the back was the foliage of an aspen.

"That looks like a tree," she said in some confusion.

He shrugged. "I figured I'm going to have to up the ante. If I don't want you saying I'm just full of bullshit." He ran a hand down her arm until he reached her hand. He held it. "I thought the tree would look good on that sunny side of the house. You could see it from the porch. In fall when the leaves turn yellow, it'll make the trim on the house stand out."

"Tom..."

"It's fifteen feet," he said. "You'll have to help me get it out of the truck." He moved a little closer to her. "Kids aren't home, huh?"

She shook her head.

He lifted a hand to her hair and let his long fingers sink into her thick curls. "I've wanted to do this," he said. He gently let his lips hover right over hers. "I do think you're beautiful, Lola. Inside and out. Do not cry. My ego can't take it."

"You're courting me," she said.

"Uh-huh. It's not going to be that much of a courtship. We have six kids between us. Three in college so far. We'll be lucky if we have time to make out on the porch now and then." He gave her a brief kiss and she let her eyes drift closed. He kissed her more deeply. He let go of her hand and slid it around her waist, pulling her closer. It made him moan, a soft purring sound. Then she felt his tongue and she was the one who moaned.

She embraced him and moved under his lips. She thought, *I'm sunk now. It is now officially too late for me.*

"I love the way you taste," he whispered. "And you feel so good in my arms. Just like I knew you would."

"Hmm," she said, not opening her eyes.

He gave her another kiss, a very thorough one. Then a brief one. "Gotta stop now," he whispered. "Grrr."

"Me, too."

He pulled back slowly. "Should we pull that tree out? While I can still walk?"

"Okay," she said. "I'm a little weak in the knees, though."

"We'll be okay," he said. "Except, I'm going to want to kiss you every day."

"Okay," she said.

They broke apart and turned to go down the walk. Standing on the sidewalk was Trace. He was wearing cleats, carrying a bat and baseball mitt, all dusty and dirty and sweaty. His eyes were wide and his mouth was hanging open. "You're kissing Mr. Canaday," he said. "Why were you kissing Mr. Canaday?"

Lola shrugged and smiled. "Because I like him. And he bought me a tree."

"Wow," he said. He hit his cleats with his bat, knocking off some dirt. "Wait till I tell Cole." Then he walked up to the porch, passed them and opened the front door.

"Hey!" Lola said. "Go around to the back door and take off those dirty shoes!"

"Oh," he said. "Sorry. You kinda shook me up for a minute."

"Maybe you could give me a hand with that tree?" Tom said. "It's pretty heavy."

"Sure," he said. "Jeez." He dropped the bat and glove, heading for the truck. "Should you be kissing my mom?"

"Well, we're both single and over twenty-one. And we're good friends."

"Yeah, but she's my mom," he said.

Lola winced inside. Trace was a great big kid, as tall as Tom and almost as broad in the shoulders, but he was her baby.

Tom put a firm hand on Trace's shoulder and gave it a little shake. "Well, kiddo, she's not going to stop being your mom, so relax. Let's put the tree over there by the end of the porch. It's gonna look so nice there."

"You gonna plant it?" Trace asked him.

"Not tonight. Tomorrow. I have chores tonight. It'll keep till tomorrow. And you'll survive this crisis."

Sierra wanted a little fluff-up before traveling to Michigan. She thought it might help her in the confidence department. Maggie confessed that she liked to get her hair done by a favorite, pricey hairdresser in Denver, but in a pinch she'd been known to drop into the local beauty shop and they did a fine job at half the cost. She recalled a woman named Rhonda had done her hair.

"I could do that, but I don't know… Connie's ex-fiancée works in there," Sierra said.

Maggie got an impish grin on her face. "You don't want to get a look at her?"

"I've seen her! She's incredibly pretty."

"Well, you could spend an hour in the shop and see what she's like. But I don't think you should let her cut your hair!"

"She probably won't even know who I am. Connie hasn't mentioned telling her about me."

"Then do it," Maggie said, a little gleefully. "And report back."

She made an appointment for the afternoon with Rhonda. She asked for a few blond streaks and a trim of her ends. She was a little nervous about this bit of sneakiness. But she never could have prepared herself for what she found. Rhonda's chair was beside Alyssa's. And in Alyssa's chair was Neely.

"Well, hello stranger," Sierra said.

"Sierra! What a coincidence! I was just going to give you a call!"

"I guess you've been pretty busy lately," Sierra said. She was not nearly over being brushed off after that whole friendship seduction.

"I have, but I'm afraid it's been a real nightmare," Neely said. "A good friend's teenage son was in a terrible accident on 24. She lives in a little town south of Vail and it wasn't far from her house. He was just seventeen and was critical, taken to Denver by helicopter to the trauma center. Brandon barely hung on for two weeks before he died and I've spent almost all that time sitting by his bedside. I didn't think I'd ever recover!"

"I didn't hear a word about it," Alyssa said.

"Oh, you know small towns," Neely said. "They were barely aware."

"That's not what I'm used to," Sierra said. "I spent half my life in a really small town in Iowa and if there was a flat tire, everyone heard about it. A fatality would have been front page news!"

"Oh, there was an article, but it was small. He was the only injury and he was taken to Denver. And my friend, his mother, wasn't from that little town—she was just visiting friends. So—it wasn't like it was one of their own."

"But it was a horrible accident! If a helicopter rescue lands anywhere around here, we're all asking for details," Alyssa said.

"Well, it was the middle of the night," Neely said. "It was just so horrible, I'm happy it's over. But I did want to explain my long silence. I know I promised to call…"

"God, that's all right," Sierra said. "I'm so sorry you went through all that. By the way, what brings you to Timberlake? Do you come all this way to get your hair done?"

"No." She laughed. "I'm a walk-in today. I was in town looking at some property. There's a shop at the end of the street—Daisy's Menagerie. She's looking at selling. I just wanted to look it over, talk to the owner. I think I told you—I'm contemplating a specialty shop."

"What kind of shop?" Alyssa asked.

God bless her, Sierra thought. Was she going to get that I'm-not-ready-to-talk-about-it line?

"Possibly local art, not on a grand scale. But I must admit, I'm beginning to be seduced by the new marijuana trade."

Sierra almost choked and Neely laughed merrily.

"I wouldn't work with the product," Neely said. "I'd hire someone with experience in the industry. It's just that it's making so much money! Of all the privately owned small businesses in Colorado, marijuana is quickly leading the pack. Anyone with an interest in small business has to take that seriously." She turned in her chair to look at Sierra. "So, you live here?"

"Sort of. I live outside of town. So does my brother and his wife. I'm new in the area but I work part-time at the diner. And if everything works out, I'd like to stay. My brother's wife is expecting."

"Hey, what's the town where the accident happened?" Alyssa asked.

"I think it was Fairplay. Or it was a town right near Fairplay. I don't know—I never went there," Neely said. "When my friend called I went straight to Denver to the hospital." Neely turned to Sierra again. "So, do you have time to grab a cup of coffee after you get finished here?"

Sierra nearly shook herself in surprise. She did, in fact. But she said, "I'm sorry, I don't. I'm on the run today."

"And let's put you under the dryer for a few minutes to speed up this color," Rhonda said. "Girl, you do have the prettiest hair! And healthy! Want me to take off about an inch? Or less?"

"An inch is fine," Sierra said.

She got under the dryer and considered Neely. What a lot of drama, she thought. Then she felt guilty—after all, the woman had just been through what must have been a terrible experience. But Sierra had the worst feeling about her...

Ten minutes later she was being shampooed and when she got back in the chair, Neely was gone. "She said to tell you goodbye and she'll give you a call. She had to run," Alyssa said.

"Thanks," she said. Neely wanted to have coffee, but didn't even have time to say goodbye?

"Have you been friends for a long time?" Alyssa asked while she was sweeping up the clippings on the floor.

"No," Sierra said. "I just met her a month ago."

"Really? She said you wanted her to make a trip to Santa Fe with you but she wasn't sure how she'd find the time."

"She said that?" Sierra asked, dumbfounded.

"She sure did. Why? Was it a secret?"

"No, it was..." Sierra stopped herself. Better to not make this any more complicated. "No, not a secret. I don't think I can find the time, either."

"She seems like a lot of fun," Alyssa said. "Weird about that accident, though."

"What's weird?"

Alyssa leaned on her broom. "I've lived here almost my whole life. There were a couple of vacationers from somewhere back East killed on 289 a few years ago. A young couple. Their car was obliterated by a big rig. There were pictures in the paper and on the internet, it was on the evening news. Complete strangers put so many wreaths and crosses and stuffed toys by the side of the road it looked like a monument. Things like that just don't usually go unnoticed."

"Interesting," was all she said.

After her haircut she found herself walking across the street to the fire department. She was in a bit of a daze. This was only the second time she'd gone looking for Connie, and this time she found him. He had a rag in his hand and was polishing up the chrome on the fire engine.

"Well, what a beautiful surprise," he said, coming out of the open garage doors to meet her. He gave her a little kiss on the forehead. "I didn't expect to see you today."

"I was just getting my hair trimmed and the strangest thing happened." She told him the story.

Connie frowned. "She made that whole thing up," he said. "She know your boyfriend is a paramedic?"

"I told her I was seeing a fireman..."

"If there's a fatality anywhere near my territory, don't you think I'd know?"

"Well, I don't know."

"Rescue Flight was called out, Sierra. Sixty miles from here."

"Maybe she got the location wrong?"

"I'll check the logs on the computer. In fact, you can do that. It's a matter of public record and the Colorado State Patrol can confirm. What do you know about it?"

"Seventeen-year-old boy driving, his first name was Brandon, the car was supposedly hit by a truck, he lay critical in a hospital in Denver for two weeks before he passed away. A few weeks ago. And she said it happened on 24. Is that a highway?"

"Yep, the one most of us take to Denver. Come on in, have a water or soda or something. I'll look it up. It won't take two minutes."

"I'll just wait," she said. "I'm going to go pick up my clothes and get organized so I can be ready to go in the early morning."

"But I'll see you tonight?"

"Of course." .

Rafe came out to the front of the firehouse after Connie left and said hi. "Connie said he's looking up something for you. How you doing?"

"Great. And how are Lisa and the kids?"

"Excellent. Grandma's coming for a visit before summer's over. They'll shop for school clothes, she loves to do that. My mom likes to get in on some of that, too. I'll probably take 'em all out on the lake a few times."

They made small talk for a few minutes before Connie was back. "Will you give us a minute, Rafe?" Connie asked.

"Sure. See you later, Sierra."

"Nothing, " Connie said.

"Maybe it was farther away than she thought?"

He shook his head. "Statewide, no fatal involving a seventeen-year-old boy."

"What if she had his age wrong?"

"There were forty fatalities in the whole month and one sixteen-year-old boy died. In Pueblo. No seventeen-year-olds. That's as close as it came. And there's no obit for a boy named Brandon."

"Maybe I didn't get the details right," Sierra said, completely confused.

"She made it up, honey."

"Why would she do that?" Sierra said.

"Who knows why people make up wild stories. For attention? To get out of something they don't want to do? Some people just can't help it—they'd make up a lie when the truth is more interesting. I don't know about you but when someone flat-out lies to me, I don't trust them anymore."

"I just don't get it," she said.

"That's the woman you really wanted to be friends with, right? The one who let you down. The one who doesn't like animals?"

"Yep."

"Hmm. My advice? Back away slowly."

He who has a why to live can bear almost any how.

—FRIEDRICH NIETZSCHE

Chapter 16

SIERRA AND CAL LEFT FOR DENVER TO CATCH A plane early in the morning on Sunday. She left from Connie's house. A couple of hours after she left Connie decided, it being Sunday, he'd drive to Denver, too. But he was going to see his mother. He called her to let her know he'd be driving up from Timberlake. When he got there, he and Molly went to the door. Janie Chambers opened the front door and beamed.

"Well, now, who is this?" she asked, bending to pet Molly.

"Her name is Molly," he said. "I'm dog sitting for a friend."

"She's beautiful. She's very excited."

"It was a longer drive than she's used to, I think."

Only then did Janie hug her son. "It's been a while. I made us lunch. I'm sorry but Beaner said he couldn't come over. He had some plans he didn't think he should cancel. Just between you and me, I bet he's going to be out on the lake with friends."

"That's okay," he said. "I wasn't staging a family reunion or anything. I'll catch up with him. But he's okay?"

"He's great, Connie. He's so busy with work and school and friends that I hardly see him anymore. This house is just a stopping-off place for him. But come in the kitchen and tell me what you've been doing. Does your friend need a bowl of water?"

"Yeah. Thanks."

Janie set down a bowl of water and Molly went after it greedily.

"Now she's going to want to go out," Connie said. "What's up with work?" he politely asked while she fixed them a couple of drinks. She had coffee and got Connie a large cola.

Janie told him about some of the cases she was working on. She was an insurance adjuster; she surveyed accidents and other damage to try to put together estimates for their clients. Then she asked him about work and he told her about a few of their recent emergencies, fortunately all came out all right.

"Isn't it funny the way we both ended up in professions that deal with accidents?" she asked. "Want to go ahead and tell me what's on your mind?" she asked.

"There's nothing specific," he said. "The friend whose dog this is. It's a girl. A woman."

Janie smiled at him. "So, you're seeing someone?"

"Yeah. Her name is Sierra. She's awesome."

"Um, Connie," his mother said. "Why don't you seem particularly happy about it?"

"Oh, I am," he said. "I've never even known a girl like Sierra. Woman. She's thirty so she's not a girl, right?"

Janie laughed. "Some women get their undies in a twist about that. I might have even scolded you about that sort of thing when you were younger, but there are bigger fish to fry these days. If it's any consolation, I go out with the girls every other Friday night. The youngest of us is forty-five."

"Well, Sierra's really something. I met her back in March. Several months ago. Hard to believe it's almost fall. She's the sister of a friend from Timberlake. She lives at Sully's place and helps him out around the Crossing. Plus, she works at the diner in town a couple of days a week."

"Tell me all about her," Janie said.

"Well, she's pretty, of course. But not flashy at all—she likes jeans and shorts and stuff like that. She's probably the smartest girl I've ever met. She spent about six years in college. Part-time because she had to work. She's funny. She's always reading. She rescued Molly here from a jerk who was mistreating her. And… I don't know…"

"Connie," Janie urged gently.

"Listen, I'm probably in over my head already so advice is out the window. But I think she's in trouble."

"Oh no," Janie said. "What kind of trouble?"

"She's not coming right out with it. I mean, she's been letting information about herself, her past, dribble out a little at a time, like she's afraid one of these days I'm going to say I can't deal with it. And she's got some real challenging stuff, like her dad has been struggling with mental illness his whole life. Complicated, right? She got in some messes before she came to Colorado and she wanted me to know some personal stuff before we got, you know…"

"Yes, Conrad," she said, smiling. "I know."

"I guess you want to tell me to be careful here, right?"

She frowned and gave her head a slight shake. "What do you mean?"

"You and me, we both have had our issues with the opposite sex," he said. "You had two lousy husbands and I had one train wreck of a fiancée. Obviously we can't pick 'em all that well." He laughed. "And the funny thing is, Sierra thinks she can't pick 'em."

"Well, obviously her luck is changing," Janie said. "Now, Connie, are you going to blame me for your father and stepfather? Because I don't think it was my fault. You know I had a lot of counseling. I might not have had the best psychic abilities but those men seemed very nice when I first met them before they became verbally and emotionally abusive. I did my best but I couldn't stay with either one of them. And I'm sorry if that just makes you paranoid about relationships. It wouldn't hurt you to get some counseling. I've had a few nice relation-ships since then."

"What relationships? You didn't have relationships," he said.

"Okay, I had a few steadies along the way. You haven't lived with me since my second divorce, remember. And I doubt Beaner would consider his mother's dates to be interesting news. I've been seeing a very nice man for the last couple of years and Ted is a good, kind, respectful man and he makes me very happy. Believe me, my radar is on! I'm happy with Ted."

"Ted?" Connie said. His mother was fifty-seven. "You're just friends!"

Janie rolled her eyes. "I admit we're not a very exciting couple, but we're not dead yet. I'm just sorry I didn't meet a man like Ted decades ago. But then Ted even confesses he probably wasn't the best husband on record as a younger man." She smiled. "I kind of like that he doesn't blame his ex-wife for everything."

"Why don't you get married, then? Why don't you live to-gether?"

"Well, Connie, we might, now that you mention it. We talk about marriage sometimes. Maybe we're a little set in our ways and Ted has his own kids and grandkids to look out for. He helps them all out a lot. I've been in this little house for sixteen years, since Beaner was in elementary school. I'm not sure I'm anxious to share my space with a boyfriend."

"And I never lived here," Connie said.

"I know. That was kind of hard for me, but I think you made a good decision. The Vadas family was such a great family for you. Not just Rafe, but his parents, too. I was struggling to get on my feet and glad you didn't have to struggle, too. Can you imagine, changing schools your senior year? Plus, living with a recently divorced mother who was always an emotional wreck?"

"You weren't," he said. "You seemed relieved to be rid of that SOB."

"I was that, too," she said with a smile. "What's this all got to do with your girl?"

He took a breath. "She scares me to death."

"You?" she asked with a laugh. "You're not afraid of anything. And that usually scares me!"

"I don't want to make another mistake, but I think I'm too late. I don't think I have it in me to back away from her now— I'm pretty sure I love her. And I have a bad track record."

"Connie, it makes perfect sense for you to look at that last relationship and try to understand how you could've known it wasn't right for you. Or maybe there was something to understand about Alyssa that you ignored, something that might've saved you making the wrong choice. But frankly, I think it was Alyssa who made the mistake." She arched her eyebrows. "How's that working out for her?"

"She keeps trying to make up. As recently as a couple of weeks ago. But, never..." He swallowed. "All those feelings are gone."

"And you're moving on."

He thought for a second. "To what?" he asked. Really he was asking himself. It was the question he'd been struggling with. "When Alyssa broke the bond I was furious. I hated her. I hated him more, but I was the one who suffered. Chris Derringer sure didn't seem to suffer. And he didn't change his ways, either." He laughed without humor. "Oh man, did I suffer. No one wanted to come anywhere near me—I was loaded for bear. I was humiliated and betrayed and half-insane. I was so angry. I got depressed. I got out of shape and gained twenty pounds or so... So much for the divorce diet!"

"I remember," she said. "You always did take comfort in food. I can completely understand that you don't want to go through something like that again."

"But see, I wouldn't. I don't feel about Sierra the way I felt about Alyssa. In fact, if I were a real asshole I'd thank Alyssa for cutting me loose. When I broke up with Alyssa I didn't want to die. I wanted to kill someone. It's different with Sierra. She already feels so much a part of me, if I'm wrong and lose her, it would be so much worse. It would be like…"

He stopped himself. He was starting to feel like a wimp, like a weakling.

"You'll do the right thing," Janie said.

"How do you know?" he asked.

"Whatever you do, Connie, it will be from the heart. If there's one thing you have always been, it's honest. Sometimes too honest for your own good, but absolutely honest."

He was a little lost inside his head, hearing a conversation with himself that he wasn't likely to ever share with his mother. When Alyssa left he had said to her, "What the fuck? Wasn't I good to you?" If he somehow lost Sierra he would ask, "Didn't I love you with everything I had?" With Alyssa it had been pride. Sierra felt like the other half of his heart. He would do anything for her. He'd do anything to save her.

"Be sure to tell her how you feel about her," his mother said.

"It's not like I didn't love Alyssa," he said in defense of his own scrambled-up brain. "I tried to make her happy."

"I know," she said. "Connie, hear me on this. Things tend to happen the way they're supposed to. I tried very hard to make my marriages work. I did everything I knew how to do. It wasn't enough or it wasn't what was needed or it wasn't meant to be, I don't know. But I felt as though I'd failed. Now I feel as though everything went just as it was supposed to—I'm happy with my life.

"You just follow your heart," she said to him. "You'll do the right thing." Then she laughed. "There's no stopping you anyway. You're hell-bent."

He smiled in spite of himself. "I am," he admitted. "She was kind of mean to me at first. She doesn't put up with much. I think when she rescued the dog, she had me." On cue, Molly put her head on his thigh, ready for reassurance. "She'd never really had a dog before. She lived on a farm and said there were dogs but they weren't really pets. They were farm dogs. Not the same thing. But this dog... Sierra reads to the damn dog. And the dog loves it."

"You can tell a lot about a person by things like that."

"I think she's in trouble," he said again. "She went back to Michigan to straighten out something to do with an accident. She wouldn't give me the details but she took her brother with her and he's a lawyer, so I think it's sticky. I want to protect her if I can. I want to be there for her if she needs me. I don't want to let her down. I don't know what to do."

"You'll know," she said. "Listen to that inside voice. You'll know."

"I better go," he said, starting to rise.

"Sit down, Connie," she said. "You just got here. We're going to have lunch."

He left a couple of hours later. He took a picture of Molly and texted it to Sierra, but she didn't respond. Later he texted a selfie with Molly and said, We miss you. Nothing. The next day he drove out to the Crossing and asked Sully if he'd heard from either Sierra or Cal and he said he hadn't, but Maggie said they'd made it to Detroit safely. He wanted to ask Maggie for more details but used all his willpower not to—Maggie was getting very pregnant and he didn't want to act like they should be worried. But he left Sierra a voice mail. "I hope everything is all right. Call me if you need me."

Nothing.

It seemed as though there'd been a lot of tension surrounding Sierra's and Cal's preparation to leave town. Maggie bit her lower lip a lot and looked at them with worry. Sully was morose and frowning. Moody suggested she locate meetings in the area and pack her inspirational books. And Connie was a little too cheerful as if he was making a real effort.

"Why is everyone acting so strangely?" Sierra asked Cal.

"Maggie, because she knows how hard it must be to face this event from your past. The rest of them sense it's something more serious than a little car accident. We pick up each other's vibes."

"I better get a handle on that," she said. "I don't want the police picking up any vibes."

"Don't worry about it. The only one you've got going on is terror and it's all right if they know you're afraid."

They checked in to a nice Westin and Cal took her out to dinner in a classy restaurant, which she just couldn't appreciate under the circumstances. In fact, she was too gnarled up inside to even respond to Connie's texts. Monday morning, donned in her hand-me-down dress and new pumps, they headed for the police department. They had an appointment with a detective who was assigned the case.

They met with two detectives in plainclothes in an office. Detective Swenson was young, maybe thirty-five and the other, Detective Lundquist, looked like he should retire—he had to be in his sixties with silver hair and a grandfatherly paunch. It was the younger man who questioned her. The questions began slowly and were disarmingly superficial. *Full name? Date of birth? Where were you on April 22, 2015? Who were you with? His full name and address? Who were your friends? Their full names?*

Sierra didn't know where Derek Cox lived; there weren't too many friends during that time. She gave information about her roommate, her last address, a couple of people from work, several people she knew by their first names only because they were regulars at her favorite bar, Charlie's.

"Can we please get to the reason you wanted to interview Ms. Jones?" Cal suggested firmly.

"Why weren't you at your favorite pub that night, the night of the twenty-second? You were seen at Flynn's, is that right?"

"I was avoiding Derek Cox. He was pestering me and I thought he was following me. I just wanted to be left alone."

"But you were with him that night?"

"He was there. He was everywhere I went, it seemed like. I wanted to turn and leave, but he saw me and I didn't want him to follow me into the parking lot. I didn't sit with him. I picked a place in the corner, near the bar, alone."

"And you didn't talk to him?"

She shook her head and the detective said, "Verbal answers for the tape, please."

"No, I didn't talk to him. I almost left but I didn't want to leave alone because I was nervous and that night I didn't seem to know the people there. I mean, I knew the bartender, the waitress, but not the customers. I thought he might follow me out. I told you, I felt he was stalking me. But after about an hour he came over to the table and sat down and tried to make conversation."

"And you were drinking that night?"

"I wasn't drunk," she said. "I'd had a couple of glasses of wine and it hit me really hard. All of a sudden I was losing focus, getting really woozy, thinking about a cab, thinking about a cup of coffee and a cab."

"Did you usually do that? Drink coffee, call a cab?"

"I didn't usually get drunk on two glasses of wine! He drugged me. He must have put something in my wine because I hadn't had that much to drink." She smiled sadly. "I could really hold my liquor."

"Can you still? Hold your liquor?"

"I haven't had a drink in over a year," she said. "I'm in AA now. In recovery."

"How about your drug use?"

"You don't have to answer that," Cal said. "You're not on trial. These questions are supposed to pertain to a felony hit-and-run involving your car. Whether you ever took drugs is not relevant. That you didn't take drugs that night is relevant."

"It's okay. I rarely did drugs. A little pot here and there. And ecstasy once—I didn't like it. I admit that when the dentist gave me a Valium I loved it so I didn't do it again. No, I wasn't a druggie. Liquor was good enough to take me down."

"But back then, that night and before that night, you were drinking heavily?"

"Yes," she said. "I didn't think so, but…yes."

"Could you have stopped somewhere before going to Flynn's? Maybe had a couple of glasses of wine or drinks somewhere else first?"

Again she shook her head. Then she said, "Not that I can recall."

They asked her to look at a video. It was footage from a convenience store gas pump. A man got out of the car, put gas in the tank, smiled and then laughed at something. He got back into the car on the driver's side. The image was blurry but she knew it was him.

She was clearly sitting in the passenger seat. Of *her* car. The license plate was visible on the tape as the car pulled out.

"That's him. That's my car. I don't remember that. I don't remember a gas station. I don't remember stopping for gas. I only remember brief snatches. He must have taken me out of the bar to my car."

"Describe the day and night as you remember it," the detective instructed.

She went through it, moment by moment, explaining again and again that she was moving in and out of consciousness, that he had abducted her, he had stolen her car, somehow got her in it, took her back to her house, to her garage where he assaulted her.

"And when you hit the victim…?"

"I didn't know what happened. We hit something. I remember I got agitated and Derek looked to see what we hit. I think he hit me or I passed out again. I never saw anyone."

"Your car was damaged…the front right bumper and side."

"Could've been a rock or a branch or a— Look, I didn't know what it was. And even if I had, I was in no condition to help."

They made her retrace her movements for the past year and five months over and over again. Her fleeing to Iowa, her entry into rehab, her work history, her move to Colorado. Several times Cal suggested she didn't have to answer questions that didn't pertain to the accident for which she was being questioned. Almost every time she answered anyway, trying to give them what they wanted, what they needed.

They brought lunch, right when she was in the thick of it and she couldn't have eaten if her life depended on it.

"I'm about to end this interview," Cal said. "Let's move this along quickly."

"It's probably in the best interest of your client to be patient for these questions and get it all behind her."

"The client is also my sister," he said, scowling.

"It's okay," she said. "I need it to be over. If it can ever be over."

"I put a call in to the sexual assault unit," the detective said. "We have to establish whether there was another crime."

She looked through a bunch of pictures and bingo, there he was. She identified him and they told her he had a record; quite a few felony arrests for everything from robbery to battery to sexual assault.

She told them he had given her the creeps but he didn't fit her image of a career criminal; he was so clean-cut, so preppy. After she'd spent a little time with him she knew he was wrong. She never anticipated how wrong.

The sexual assault sergeant introduced himself simply as Charles. He asked her to explain how she knew he was a deviant or maybe just explain why she was dead set against seeing him. So she told them about that one night he was invited inside, how enraged he was with his dysfunction, how difficult it was for him to successfully complete intercourse.

As far as they could determine, his name was actually Craig Dixon. They showed her an artist's rendering too, a pencil sketch. "That's him," she said. "Why do you have this?"

"He's committed other crimes. He has other victims."

They asked her seven times where he was. Seven times she told them she had no idea, that she ran from *him*, that she feared *him*.

Charles was incredibly tall with giant feet that made her think of Goofy, the Disney character. He folded his legs uncomfortably under the desk. Detective Lundquist left the office briefly, while the remaining two detectives questioned her. "You know it's best if we locate him and bring him in," Charles said.

"If I could help you do that, I would. But I don't know where he is."

"Is it possible you got drunk and you and your boyfriend ran down a cyclist and left him by the side of the road, critically injured?"

"No," she said much more calmly than she felt. "He's not nor was he ever my boyfriend. I'm telling you, I didn't even know where he lived. We had one official date and he was stalking me after that. I'm afraid of him."

"Have you seen him at all since that night?"

"I think I see him a lot, but it's just my nerves. It always turns out it's not him. It must not be him—he hasn't bothered me at all. Why would he come all the way to Colorado if he didn't intend to hurt me again?"

"Wait? Colorado?"

"I thought I saw him in a mall in Colorado Springs, but he didn't see me. He finally turned and I don't think it was him. His nose was too big."

The sergeant fished out a more mug shot—profile and forward—that was newer than the photo and the pencil sketch.

"Oh God," she said.

"Is this the man you saw in Colorado?"

"Maybe it was. He was kind of far away. But I followed him for a while because I thought it might be him and I had to know. But I was on crutches. I had a sprained ankle. I wasn't moving very fast."

"He didn't approach you?"

"No. And he was gone before I could verify it was him. The story of my life—seeing my nightmare over and over and never being sure."

"Did he say anything that night? Anything memorable?"

"I asked him what he hit while we were driving and he said, 'Don't worry about it. I wasn't driving. *You* were driving.' But I wasn't. I couldn't have driven if my life depended on it."

"I believe that's enough for today," Cal said. "Ms. Jones is not under arrest and doesn't have to—"

"We could arrest you for obstruction," the detective said. "You were with him in the car and it was 1.7 miles from that gas station that the cyclist was hit. He might've died but for the fortuitous presence of a passerby with medical knowledge who came along less than a minute later."

"Obstruction from a girl who was drugged and raped? That will never get by a judge," Cal said. "Her head is clearly lolling on the tape and he gets behind the wheel."

"I have medical records," she said. "I didn't report it to the police but I went to a clinic. I was bruised and injured and afraid of disease. I had showered but they did a rape exam anyway. Since the police weren't involved they didn't have evidence. But they have records. It was the Macmillan Women's Clinic."

The detective looked at his watch. "We've been at this all day and it just occurred to you to mention medical records?"

"I talked all day! I answered all your humiliating questions in front of my brother!" She looked at him. "Cal, I've had enough."

"We're done here. We won't be answering any more questions without a warrant. You pretty much squeezed her dry. If you have any more questions, we'll be in Colorado."

He took Sierra's elbow to lead her away.

"Wait a minute," she said. "My turn. You've been looking for him? For the hit-and-run?"

"Among other things," the detective said. "You're going to have to be very cautious, ma'am. Craig Dixon is a dangerous man."

"Why are you looking for him?"

"Rape, for one thing."

"But I don't want to testify against him! He terrifies me! And if for any reason he isn't put in prison..."

"Let's worry about that when we have him in custody," the sergeant said. "For now, my advice is, caution."

"Well, he was certainly right about one thing," she said. "I'll never forget him."

The detectives sat stone-still and silent. The sergeant from the sexual assault unit leaned forward. "What were his exact words, please?"

"He said, 'You'll never forget me now.' And then he walked away."

The men looked at each other. "That's a wrap. You can go. Make sure we're able to reach one or both of you. If you change cell numbers, please contact us. Thank you for your cooperation."

Cal led her away. "You all right?"

She shrugged. "A little beat up. Why were they so hard on me if they know he's the bad guy?"

"They had to be convinced you weren't a co-suspect in that hit-and-run but, more important, they want to know if you can lead them to their suspect."

"Lead them! Don't they understand I'd be running in the other direction?"

"I'm pretty sure they understand that now. I wondered why this much energy was being spent trying to find him for a hit-and-run when the victim has made a full recovery. Sierra, the man has obviously raped other women. They connected the dots—found his face on that hit-and-run film. They might never have found him if there hadn't been a felony hit-and-run. That tape would never have been viewed in the first place if there hadn't been a crime and investigation. That's why they were looking for you. They tied your car to their suspect. I have a feeling, based on what you've said and their questions, they're looking for a predator. A serial rapist. Or worse."

She couldn't speak. Finally she said, "Won't the other victims bring him to justice?" she asked.

"And what if they can't?" Cal said.

"Can't?" she repeated shakily. "Dear God."

The privilege of a lifetime is to become

who you truly are.

—C. G. Jung

Chapter 17

SIERRA WAS JUST TOO TIRED TO CALL CONNIE.
She wasn't about to explain all this over the phone. But she saw
his texts and he'd added another one with a picture of him with
Molly. She finally wrote back, I miss you guys, too. Sorry, I'm
exhausted and hungry. Tomorrow will be better.

He must have been sitting on the phone. He texted back instantly. If you needed me, I would come.

The sweetest man alive, she thought. She didn't think she deserved him. She texted back, I'm okay. I'll be in touch tomorrow. Thank you for being so wonderful.

They went out for dinner in the hotel, then to bed. She slept
incredibly well for someone who had just surmised that the only
way this monster would go to jail was if she faced him and ac-
cused him. And she was sure she wouldn't be able to.

But God was watching out for her. She didn't even dream.

The next morning they picked up a copy of her medical records. Cal called Charles—Sergeant Tilden—who had inter-
viewed them and arranged to have the mug shot of Craig Dixon
emailed to him. Then they headed for the airport. Cal changed
their flight, but they weren't going right home. They flew to
Des Moines and rented a car, making the two-hour drive to the
little farming village where Marissa and Jed Jones lived. Given

their parents were overly sensitive to drop-in guests, even their own children, Cal called and told his mother that he and Sierra were passing through and wanted to stop by and say hello in the morning.

"Say hello?" Sierra asked with a laugh. "Is that what we're doing?"

"We'll say hello, ask if they need anything, ask Marissa if the man whose picture I have on my cell phone was the one who came to the farm looking for you."

"You think she'll even remember? It was over a year ago!"

"I'd be satisfied with her best guess."

Sierra held her breath. She didn't even want to see the farm. It was the farm where she hid for three months prior to rehab; it was the farm where she had started to fear she was crazy like her father. She didn't want to know if the bad man had followed her there.

"I'm not for certain," Marissa said. "But I think that's him. He was wearing such nice clothes and he said he worked for a special department of some kind. I wish I could remember. But it didn't matter because I just said you hadn't been around in a long time, you were in Michigan. Or you could have gone off to California." Then she smiled with satisfaction. "And look, I was right. Wasn't I."

On their way back to Des Moines, they were both completely silent.

"She might be mistaken," Cal finally said after a very long silence.

"She's not mistaken," Sierra said. "He followed me. I bet he did have some kind of tracker in my phone."

"Well, the phone is gone," Cal said. "How long after he visited the farm did you check into rehab?"

She laughed, an almost hysterical sound. "Twenty minutes," she said. "Okay, not quite that fast, but fast."

"And they took all your personal items, including your phone, and turned it off and locked it away."

"Yes, and when I asked my group leader if it was possible there was an app in my phone, he said he'd take care of it. He had the phone wiped, got a new number for me, and I was able to use it again after three weeks. But I had to check it out before I could have it. I couldn't just have it in my possession. If you can believe it, there were people making drug buys from inside, if they could."

"I believe it."

"I got rid of the phone anyway," she said. "I couldn't chance it."

They got into Denver at seven o'clock and instead of driving home, they stopped at Maggie's house, now a very stylish crash pad for those nights she spent in Denver so she could work. It was then that Sierra finally caught up with Connie. "We're in Denver, staying overnight so Cal can sleep with his wife and unborn baby, but she has surgery early in the morning so we'll be up and on our way."

"I have to work but I'll try to sneak away just to see you," he said. "Then on the weekend, I'm all yours. Or maybe you're all mine."

"Is Molly okay?"

"I think she misses you," he said. "She keeps looking out the living room window. I'll be taking her to Sully in the morning before work so she'll be waiting for you."

"I can't wait to see her. Has she been a good girl?"

"She found herself an elk cow and calf. All survived..."

"I'm looking forward to a quiet weekend."

"I just hope that whatever was upsetting you is past," he said.

"What if it's not? What if it's never past?"

"Then I'll comfort you as much as I can," he said.

Sierra had no doubt where Connie was concerned. Of course he would be supportive and comforting; of course he was brave and loyal and wouldn't falter. But what if it turned out to be more than he signed on for? What if she one day saw regret in his eyes?

"This is as much time as I've spent with you since I was a little kid," Sierra told Cal when they got back to the Crossing.

"I was thrilled by every second of it," he said. "And I hope we don't have to do it again anytime soon."

"Ditto," she said.

Her reunion with Molly and Sully was perfect; Molly attacked her with excitement and Sully showed one of his rare, toothy smiles. Cal dropped her and took off, eager to get back to building. She suspected he needed the work to clear his head. She had a cup of coffee with Sully on the porch.

"Get everything taken care of?" he asked.

"As much as possible," she said. "It's complicated. Let me just say there are still a few messes from the past that have to be attended to."

"Girl, not a person alive who doesn't have messes from the past that could use cleaning up."

"This one is pretty awful."

"I meant awful messes," Sully said. "Might be time you figured something out. Your life hasn't always been a bowl of Froot Loops, but you're smart and strong. And I don't know a single person who gets through this with nothing but giggles. Frank went to war three times, then he got cancer. Twice. He sent a son to war and buried him. And at my age you start to realize someone like Frank isn't a rare thing. It's par for the course. It turns out the mark of a happy life isn't staying just one step ahead of the grim reaper. It's knowing you're strong."

"Is that your best advice?" she asked.

"Nope. My best advice is this—by the time you meet your Maker, and may it be a long, long time from now, I hope you can close your eyes on a life where you did your damn best and tried your damn hardest. It's not winning that's really winning. It's never giving up."

"Your life hasn't been easy, I know," she said.

"Much of it my own making," he said. "But there were a few times I was flawless and I ran into some rotten luck anyway. If there's any way I can help you with anything, you'll let me know."

But he never asked what it was.

She talked to Connie twice but he was so busy at the firehouse, she didn't see him. He wasn't working the weekend and she made plans to go to his house after lunch, after helping Sully a little bit in the garden. She told Connie to get a little rest; the firehouse had been hectic.

When she got to his house she found him waiting, freshly showered and shaved. Molly ran around in circles and then to her water dish but Connie pulled Sierra into his arms.

"It was so hard being away from you," he said. "I'm afraid I'm going to suffocate you, be too possessive, scare you away."

"Oh, Connie," she said. "I have so many secrets."

He put her back on her feet. "You want to talk?"

"I do. I have to talk."

He shook his head. "Don't be afraid of me, Sierra. You know it's okay to talk to me. Nothing will chase me away. I love you."

She thought her heart might explode. "You were going to let me say it first."

"I couldn't wait," he said.

"You might run for your life," she warned him.

"Sierra, listen to yourself sell me short. I go into burning buildings for a living. I dangle over sheer cliffs to help people. And that's the half of what I do. What've you got to compete with that?"

"I was raped," she said.

He actually jumped in surprise. He grabbed her upper arms. "Recently?" he asked in a hushed tone.

"About a year and a half ago."

"They catch the guy? Lock him up?"

She shook her head. "Not yet."

"Okay," he said, a little out of breath. "Sit down. Tell me everything. I mean, tell me what you want to tell me. Just please tell me. How can I be there for you if I don't know what's going on?"

It took her longer to tell him all about the day with the police than it did about the actual assault, but she didn't leave anything out. At least not intentionally. It was a lot of conversation, a lot of questions. Connie got up from the living room chair to get them bottled water from the refrigerator. He leaned his elbows on his knees, hands clasped to keep control. He scowled and even growled at times.

"You thought you saw him?" he asked.

"Several times but I was never sure. I thought he was a nightmare mirage," she said. "I thought I saw him in Iowa and I actually chased him down and grabbed his arm. It was like temporary insanity—I had to know. It wasn't him. Up close it didn't look anything like him. A bunch of times I thought I spotted him and held my breath, but when he turned I realized the guy didn't look that much like him."

"Every time?" he wanted to know.

"I'm pretty sure the man I saw in Colorado Springs really was him. And I think the man who went to my parents' farm was him. Connie, I think he's around. I think he found out where I am. Maybe not exactly where, but approximately. The police told me to be very observant and very cautious."

"I don't know very much about rape victims and what they go through," he said. "We made love. If there was anything wrong about that, I couldn't tell. If you don't like the way I touch you or hold you or—"

She shook her head. "You were the first since and it was nice. It was epic," she added with a smile. "The rape counselor said

I'd know when I was ready. For a while right after it happened, when I ran to the farm, I was a mess. I couldn't sleep or eat. I slept with my shoes on! Couldn't leave the house after dark and even at the house, I'd have these major anxiety attacks. When I did go out in daylight, like to drive to work, it was the country. I could see for miles. I could see no one was following me. Then I went into treatment and they got me set up in some counseling groups. I stayed in one after I was out of rehab, living in a kind of halfway house. I got stronger, very slowly. I even took some self-defense but probably not enough. But I have PTSD, there's no question about it. I can't park in a garage again. I can't even go to the car wash. I can't even think about going to the movies—there could be someone behind me in the dark. But I can walk on the trails behind the Crossing. In daylight. And I like it inside my little cabin, but I admit, before Molly came along I used to stack things in front of the door. I get freaked out at the weird-est times. I like to get up before the sun's up and have coffee with Sully but that walk from my cabin to the store…it's a very long walk. I usually jog."

"Oh baby," he said, stroking her arm. "They need to find him, lock him up…"

"You think that'll take care of everything? I'm sure there are other psychopaths out there. I'm going to be afraid forever." She swallowed. "I want to be free of him. He took away my tears. I can't cry anymore. I haven't truly cried since…"

"Come here, Sierra," he said, pulling on her hand. She let herself be drawn onto his lap. "I'm proud of you," he said. "But will you let me take care of you a little bit?"

"What can you do?"

"I can't take the fear away but I'll do anything you ask." He pushed her hair back and kissed her neck. "Anything."

"I wanted to tell you," she said. "I always intended to. If all this is too much of a load for you, let's decide now."

"It's not," he said.

"I'm pretty screwed up," she said.

"That's the thing—you're not. I know people who haven't been through half of what you have who are wrecks. You're so strong."

"Stubborn," she said. "That bastard is not going to get any more of my head."

"You didn't tell the police when it happened," he said.

"I didn't then, no. I wonder if I was in shock. I went to the doctor, I ran away, I stayed petrified until…until rehab. I went into rehab because he couldn't find me there. That's the only reason I went—I fully intended to ride it out for a month while I thought of how I'd press on. I had no intention of giving up alcohol. I had no intention of changing my life. It all started because I was so afraid of him."

"They're going to find him," he said.

"They're going to want me to testify against him and I've been saying for a year and a half that I won't. That I can't. But I don't think I'll ever be free until I face it head-on," she said. "I don't know if I'll get through it, but I think I have to try."

"I'll be right there," he said. "A lot of people will be right there. You have a lot of fans."

"Oh, Connie, I'm such a load…"

"Don't worry about me. I have pretty broad shoulders."

"I missed you so much," she said. "I love you, you know."

"I know," he said. "You didn't even have to tell me."

"How could you know?"

"Oh, I must be psychic," he said with a smile. "Or maybe you treat everyone like you treat me?"

"I might give you some priority," she said. "Because you're good to my dog."

"I'm going to get you some pepper spray," he said. "And one of those alarm buttons they advertise on late-night TV. It's loud enough to bring down buildings."

"I have pepper spray. But I'd really like one of those alarm buttons."

"See? We make a good team. We'll be okay."

For a few days Sierra was tense and worried; her visit with the police brought the whole event to the surface again, made her feel like a victim again. She called Sergeant Tilden of the sexual assault unit four times and each time she got a little more information. The latest news was that, because the suspect was in the wind and they had excellent probable cause to arrest him and prosecute him, they were getting a little help from the FBI. Colorado's state police were also notified. "Should I be calling the FBI for information?" she asked.

"Nope," he said. "I'm still your point man. Call me anytime."

She began to calm down. And she had a pair of strong arms around her. Connie brought her comfort and solace.

Connie was also on a mission. He took her rock climbing a couple of times, which she found exhilarating. He took her to a gym in Denver where there was a self-defense instructor to give her a refresher on some of the moves she'd learned over a year ago. He also introduced her to a couple of new techniques.

"Why are we doing all this?" she asked.

"Because, Sierra, you need to bolster your confidence. That's half the battle."

He supplied the alarm button she could attach to her key chain. They took it out in the country to test it and it was deafening. It also alerted his cell phone with her location.

A couple of weeks had passed since she'd been to Michigan when she told Sully about her situation. The hardest part was seeing this tough, cynical old guy shaken by the information. Later that same day he presented her with a bat. "I thought we could use two bats on the job."

"Did you go buy this for me?" she asked.

"I did," he said. "Sleep with it under your bed. Put it in the backseat of your car when you're out."

"Thank you," she said. "Please, don't be upset. I'm working through it."

"Of course you are," he said. "Don't aim at his head. If he's got reflexes worth a damn, he'll stop it with his hands. Aim at his knees. Be crafty—make it look like you're trying to hit him in the head, then swing lower. Fast. You have to be fast."

She smiled at him.

"Practice," he said. "And on those nights you're not with Connie, would you oblige an old man by staying in my house? Just until we can safely put the matter of that bastard's whereabouts behind us?"

"I can," she said. As much as she longed to establish her independence, now might not be the wisest time to push something like that.

Sierra, with Sully, Connie and Cal all looking out for her, felt a growing sense of confidence. Not enough to relax but enough so that not quite fifty of every sixty seconds was dedicated to the tension and fear of feeling hunted. Then even that began to give way.

The month of August was busy in every possible way. She was picking up time in the diner as some of the high school waitresses were looking for more afternoons to accommodate their school schedule and there was heavy tourist traffic in the campground, in the town, on the lake, on the trails and roads. The campground was teeming with people and the store was busy; Sully was grateful for Sierra's help and Sierra was glad to be distracted by the activity. She felt a little safer, never being alone. The last days of summer would peak with Labor Day weekend and after that, life would be quieter.

"Except for the rut season," Sully said. "You'll hear a lot of bugling among the bulls, a few fights over especially attractive cows. Rut season peaks around the end of September. We'll be seeing some hunters—bow season first, starting in September. And then come the rifle hunters. Around here, mostly bow. At least it's quieter. And along with the archery season, the leaf peepers show up."

Sierra looked forward to observing some of that, at a safe distance.

The last weeks of summer brought other changes to the little town. For one thing, Connie was so present around Sierra, so affectionate and tender, there was no longer any question as to the disposition of their relationship. He either held her hand or had an arm around her shoulders. She was just leaving the diner when he was returning to the firehouse and he gave her a brief kiss. Across the street Alyssa was standing on the sidewalk in front of the beauty shop and saw them. Her mouth fell open. She whirled and fled back into the shop.

"Oops," Sierra said. "I guess she wasn't expecting that."

"I told her I was seeing someone," he said with a shrug.

"I don't think she believed you," Sierra said. "You didn't tell her it was me? Why not?"

"Because I'm not going to discuss my love life with her. I don't owe her any explanations."

"I heard her mother passed away last week," Sierra said. "Was there a funeral or celebration of life of some kind?"

"A funeral. Alyssa left a message for me at the firehouse. I sent a bouquet and made a donation to cancer research but I didn't go."

"I hope you didn't skip it because of me," she said. "I wouldn't have questioned that."

"No, babe, not because of you. Because of me. I'm not mad at Alyssa anymore but I don't want to be any closer than we are right now. And I thought what mattered was visiting Rachel when she was alive. I'm glad I did that. The only thing left was to pay my respects to the family when she passed. I did that, too."

There were other things going on in and around Timberlake.

That small shop of Daisy's was changing owners in a few months and there was talk of it becoming a commercial marijuana dispensary. A pot store. The local business owners were gossiping about it a lot. Some were up in arms; they worried about drawing a lot of heavy drug users to the town. Others were thrilled to have a moneymaking venture on the main street. No one seemed to know who was buying the store.

Sierra suspected Neely but said nothing. And she had not heard from her.

Labor Day weekend was a madhouse of campers, hikers, boaters. The camps across the lake were filled with people, as well. Sully said they would continue to do a decent business through September but not seven days a week and not in numbers like the holiday weekend.

The leaves had barely started to turn and wouldn't come into their full glory for another month. The air was taking on a crispness and Sully's fall melons and pumpkins were just about ready. The long-distance hikers had come and gone because the higher elevations of the Continental Divide Trail were starting to get cold and there would be snow on the mountains before October.

The camps across the lake would close in November for winter. Sully stayed open but they would only see a few RVs and occasionally rent the cabins. He said it was extremely rare to see any tents. Cross-country skiers and ice sailing skaters would be evident with the snowfall and freezing of the lake but maintenance on the grounds would be greatly reduced. That caused Sierra to think she probably should scout around for a real job, something full-time with benefits, something with potential.

In early September an RV towing a Jeep came into the park. The RV was outdated and the black Jeep, new. Checking in for a week were Clyde and Priscilla Snowdon, originally from England. He was a professor of history from the Midwest and she was a high school drama teacher who loved photography. Priscilla hoped to get in some hiking and photographs of early fall in the mountains. They had taken a semester off to do some traveling, and with the RV they could stay in each place they visited for a week or more, really get to know their adopted country. Two days later, a couple of archery hunters arrived with a toy hauler that carried a couple of ATVs, perfect for getting around the back roads. Pete and Lucas from Phoenix. And then the next day, being Friday, the camp began to welcome some new weekenders.

For the next several days, Sierra noticed their British campers and archery hunters making the most of the area—the ATVs on the back roads, walking along trails, in town, checking out the shops and the local tavern.

The following week Cal called Sierra and asked if she could come to the barn, he had something to talk to her about. When she told him Connie was at the Crossing, Cal said, "Bring him. I want to talk to him, too."

When they got to Cal and Maggie's it appeared they were ready to lay carpet and the interior of the barn was looking fantastic. There was a large roll of foam padding and a larger roll of carpet.

"You're almost finished!" she said excitedly.

"Very close with some detail work left that I'll probably keep seeing for months, but once the carpet is in the new living room and dining room, furniture and the bar stools can be delivered. I have a couple of walls to paint and paper to hang in the nursery. Maggie!" he called.

She popped out on the landing at the top of the stairs. "Hi," she said. "Want to see the master and the nursery?"

"Sure," Sierra said. "You're sleeping upstairs now?"

"Wait a minute, I wanted to talk to you about something, then you can have the grand tour. Dakota called. He's deploying again—in two weeks."

"How long has he known?" Sierra asked. "I mean, it doesn't surprise me, but he could've given us some notice."

"I take it it's very short notice. Maggie's headed to Denver on Wednesday morning, home Friday late afternoon so I'm going to pack a bag and shoot down to Fort Hood to see him before he goes. I'm going to make it a real quick trip—I want to be back here when Maggie gets back. If she weren't working this week, I wouldn't be leaving but she'll be in Denver with her obstetrician. No safer place for Maggie these days."

"My last week until after the baby," she said, giving her big belly an affectionate rub. "I'd work up till the end but my OB doesn't like that idea. I think it's as much the two-hour drive as the working that's bugging her. But—Jaycee is a mother herself and she said I'll thank her someday for insisting I take a month before the baby comes to rest and get ready. So, I'll have a month before my due date. Any more than that and I might go stir-crazy."

"Do you want to go with me to Texas?" Cal asked Sierra.

"I'd kind of like to, but it's too short notice for me. I'm scheduled to work. I know it's not much of a job but someone has to do it. And Sully has hunters and leaf peepers around—I should spend time there."

Cal looked at Connie. "I probably don't have to ask but will you look out for her?"

He put his arm around her shoulders and pulled her closer. "You don't have to ask. I'm working one twenty-four-hour shift this week and Sierra promises to sleep in Sully's house while I'm not around. They both have baseball bats now, you know."

"I heard," Cal said. "I'm leaving tomorrow. Just a couple of days."

"Be sure to ask him how is best to communicate," Sierra said. "I'll write or Skype him every day while he's deployed. Ask him if he knows how long this deployment is. And tell him I'm sorry—a good sister would go see him."

"Don't kick yourself," Cal said. "Chances are he told me so

late so he wouldn't have to be bothered with coming out here before he leaves. Or, God forbid, Iowa."

"He won't see them, then?"

"I don't think he's seen Jed and Marissa in a few years. I'll be back on Friday. I think Tom and Jackson are going to try to get the rest of the carpet in while I'm gone."

Sierra let Maggie lead her around the upstairs—they'd moved into the master bedroom and the baby's room was right next door. Maggie had a big box of letters and pictures for the walls, plus a crib yet to be assembled. There was a dresser-changing table and the closet was outfitted with shelves. And there was an adorable wooden pink rocking horse. "I couldn't resist," she said.

"It's really happening," Sierra said. "We're having a baby."

"We sure are," Maggie said.

Quite beyond her deliberate control, Sierra took such comfort in these small things—a new niece making ready for an appearance, a brother and sister-in-law who were thrilled she was near and always looking out for her, a strong boyfriend and a welcoming and bucolic setting in which to live. The end of summer brought later sunrises so she was having her morning coffee with Sully on the porch, in the dark. The approach of dawn brought out those campers who thrived on the early, early morning—the photographers and the hunters—who brought their coffee to the porch before 6:00 a.m. for a visit. They were friendly, outgoing folks, typical of campers she'd gotten to know over the summer months. Private, standoffish people didn't seem to frequent campgrounds like the Crossing.

Life really did seem so mild, safe and carefree. Sierra nearly forgot there was anything to worry about, any unknown threat of any kind looming in the back of her mind.

Until she was driving to work early Thursday morning.

Life is either a daring adventure or nothing. To keep our faces toward change and behave like free spirits in the presence of fate is strength undefeatable.

—HELEN KELLER

Chapter 18

THERE WAS A CAR BEHIND HER AND SHE FELT THE hair prickle on the back of her neck. She frowned into the rearview mirror, not understanding where that car could have come from. It hadn't come from Sully's and she rarely passed or was followed by another vehicle this early in the morning. She thought about turning around and heading back to the Crossing, but that would be difficult on this road.

But surely that was just an innocent car. Hunters? But hunters almost always had SUVs or trucks and this appeared to be a small sedan. As it gained on her she realized that no, it was not just an innocent car. It was someone who had been waiting for just such an opportunity. And that could only be one person. Instantly, her foot hit the gas and she sped away. The driver was a man. She could not make out his features in the rearview mirror but as he accelerated, there was only one possibility. And his car almost caught up to her so easily because she was in the pumpkin and the poor, dear pumpkin just didn't have the kind of power most late model cars had.

And she was still so far from town, unsure she'd make it before he could crash into her or run her off the road.

On a whim, she took the turnoff to Cal's barn. It was closer than town. There was no one there unless Tom was getting a very early start since he wouldn't be waking the occupants. But she could get inside and lock herself in. She had a key to Cal's house right on her key ring. And once in the house she could call for help. She could press her alarm button—the noise wouldn't serve any purpose, lost in the countryside, but it would signal Connie's cell phone…if Connie even had his cell phone nearby. For all she knew he could be out on a call, some early-morning heart attack out on a ranch.

But never mind, it was only important to get herself into a safe fortress and hope to be able to hold him off until help could arrive. She roared down the road toward her brother's house. Mother Nature was trying her best to foil her—the road was blocked by a small herd of elk and she laid on the horn with all her might. They barely moved and she scooted that little pumpkin onto the shoulder and wove carefully through them. Seven of them, one bull. And apparently in no hurry.

She heard a horn and looked into the rearview mirror—they had closed ranks around him and he couldn't move. She sped down the road, digging in her purse as she drove. She grabbed her cell phone and her pepper spray and less than five minutes later, pulled right up to the door and ran from the car so fast she didn't even put it in Park. He was just pulling into the clearing as she fumbled with the keys. A small squeak of panic escaped her as she tried to get the key in the lock, the door open. Just as she was getting inside she saw him running toward her and yes, it was him. Derek or Craig, or whoever else he was now pretending to be. She whirled inside and locked the door behind her. She depressed the alarm button and sent the noise screaming into the air.

He rattled the door immediately. She backed away from it. She went as far back into the house as she dared to get away from the noise and yet be able to see the door. She dialed 9-1-1.

"Emergency," the operator said.

"This is Sierra Jones and I'm being pursued by a rapist. I think his name is Craig Dixon and the police are after him. He followed me and I'm locked in my brother's house."

"Address?"

"Crap," she said. "I have no idea! Conrad Boyle, firefighter in Timberlake, he knows. Please! Please! He's trying to get in. Please!"

"Where is the house, ma'am," the operator asked.

"It's a barn turned into a house and it's in the country, isolated, right between Sullivan's Crossing and Timberlake. Crap." She shoved her phone in her pocket and ran to the kitchen and lifted the cordless. She dialed 9-1-1 again.

"Emergency," the operator said.

"Help! Help! The house is on fire and I'm trapped!" Then she laid down the phone with the line still open and grabbed her cell phone just as the door was kicked open. She hit the speed dial for Connie's number but she didn't have time to say anything. She put the phone down in the shrieking din of her alarm and backed away, holding her pepper spray behind her back. Terrified, she knew she'd have to let him get close for it to be effective. And his approach was so slow. Her alarm stopped. The silence almost echoed.

"Well, clever girl, you tricked me," he said.

"No," she said, shaking her head.

"How do you expect me to find you if you stop going to bars?" He turned around, kicked the door closed and then methodically pushed the heavy picnic table against the door. She noticed his strong arms, his muscled back and shoulders and was terrified. For the first time she found it strange that he didn't seem to carry a weapon. But his strength was his weapon. Oh dear God, don't let Connie get hurt, she prayed. She was backed right up against the kitchen counter.

He turned toward her again. "I guess we're going to spend a little time together, my little bitch."

She just shook her head and reminded herself not to let him get close enough to touch her.

"I couldn't find you," he said. "You gave up the bars and you threw away your phone, naughty girl."

He was six feet away. Then four feet. Then she pulled out the small canister and fired right into his face. He cried out and with lightning speed his arm shot out and knocked the canister from her hand, but not before he'd taken a hit in the face. Maybe not as much as she'd hoped, but he'd been hit. And she'd gotten a little overspray; she felt the sting in her eyes immediately.

Though half blind and disoriented, he grabbed her and slugged her in the face so hard she fell. He kicked her out of the way and she couldn't breathe. She thought she was doomed but then he went to the sink and flushed his face with water. She wasn't sure she could stand so she crawled away from him as quickly as she could.

When she had a little distance from him, she pulled herself upright but looked despairingly at the picnic table against the door, her eyes tearing madly. If she broke a window, could she somehow outrun him? Was his vision bad enough to give her a chance? Because after being kicked in the stomach, she wasn't going to be very fast.

She couldn't afford to think about it for long. She took to the stairs. She would be cornered up there but her only hope was to stay alive long enough for help to come. She'd made three calls for help. Cal's house wasn't close to first responders and it would take them a little while—ten or fifteen minutes—but she was banking on this man's pathology. He wasn't going to kill her until he tormented her. She'd survived him once, she could survive him again.

She ran to the master bedroom and closed the door but of course there was no lock on the door. She gave the bureau a tug but she couldn't budge it. She looked around for something to bar the door, something to hit him with. She looked in the master closet, so large it was almost a room unto itself. Cal and Maggie hadn't moved their things into the closet yet because Tom was still in the process of finishing it with custom shelves and hanger rods. The finished wood was cut to the right sizes, stacked and about half the closet finished.

She heard some powerful pounding coming from downstairs and she tried to imagine what he was doing. Breaking up the place? Destroying it?

On top of the pile of boards sat the nail gun.

She had to search for an outlet and plugged it in. She lifted it to turn it on and it was so heavy she could barely hold it. She'd been around Cal's house when some of the building was going on and she knew from observation you couldn't fire nails out of the gun by pulling a trigger—the later models had been improved and were much safer than the earlier nail guns. It had to be pressed against something to work. And it was too heavy for her to hold behind her back like a small canister of pepper spray.

She heard breaking glass and wondered what it was. Was he trying to make his escape through a broken window? She sat atop the stacked boards, the nail gun in front of her and the outlet behind her.

Then, without warning, he was standing in front of her in the closet doorway. She nearly jumped out of her skin. His eyes were red and already swelling, his burned cheeks wet with his tears. And yet the sneer on his face was so awful, so sinister. She remembered—this was what he liked! A victim who fought!

There was a shout from inside the house.

"Craig Dixon, you're surrounded! You have no exit route—come out now—hands in the air!"

"So, you told," he said. And yet he grinned a sick and evil grin. "And here I thought you'd learned your lesson."

Suddenly she laughed. "You wish," she said, matching him for bravado.

"You're a bitch," he snapped.

"And you're an impotent loser!" she flung.

He lunged at her, his hands around her neck, a growl coming from deep inside him. He squeezed and shook her, her head slamming against the closet shelf. It took enormous willpower not to grab for the hands that choked her but the self-defense training kicked in. The nail gun was almost too heavy to lift with one hand, so it was slow and she prayed not to lose consciousness before she could at least do some damage. She pressed it into his side and fired—*crack, crack, crack, crack.*

His eyes were wide and startled as he looked into her eyes, but he didn't lessen the grip on her throat.

She pressed the gun into his side and fired again. *Crack, crack, crack.*

An inhuman yowl escaped him, the cry of a wounded animal, and he resumed choking and shaking her and her peripheral vision began to darken. She saw stars for a moment.

Then suddenly he let go and she was dimly aware of some kind of struggle but she couldn't focus. She fell off the small stack of shelving to the floor, straining to take a breath and to focus. Her hand rose weakly to her neck and she thought, vaguely, *I don't think the police had time to respond...*

Then there was a face above her. Pete. The bow hunter. Oh man, he must have found her elk in Cal's pasture! She had been rescued by an elk hunter. She let her eyes close.

"Medical is on the way, Sierra," he said, brushing her hair back from her face. "We got him. He's in custody."

She looked at him. "Cus..." she tried lamely. Then she coughed. She could breathe better but her throat was certainly damaged. "Custody?" she asked again.

"Yep, in handcuffs, in custody. You're safe. I'm not leaving you and Medical is on the way." She could hear a siren in the distance, still a long way off. She closed her eyes again.

"Pete?" she whispered. "Were you shooting elk?"

"No," he said with a laugh. "I'm hunting more dangerous game. I have a lot to explain to you. After you've been to the hospital. Better make sure he didn't hurt you too badly. Stay awake now. Stay with me—you took some hard knocks to the head—don't go to sleep on me."

"He hit me and kicked me," she said. "Is he dead? Did I kill him?"

"He's not dead," Pete said. "But he's done. You took a little blood out of him."

She sighed. "Is he going to the hospital, too?"

"Not the same one you're going to, don't worry. He's going to have a couple of FBI agents and some state troopers with him."

"God, I wish I'd killed him," she whispered.

"Nah, you don't want that burden, too. But you gave him to us—you're a hero."

"No, I'm a survivor," she said in a hoarse whisper. Again, her eyes closed. Pete was moving around.

Then there was a new presence. She opened her eyes to look into the piercing beautiful blue of Conrad's eyes. "Hey, baby," he said. "Open your eyes and let me look at them, okay? Good, good," he said, shining a light in them. "You still need a head CT but I think you're going to be okay." He took her blood pressure. "Yeah, you'll be okay now. Sorry I couldn't get here any faster," he said, wiping off her face. Coming into focus now, she noticed the wipe he used was bloody. "Just a few battle scars."

She smiled into those remarkable eyes. "Connie," she whispered. "I nailed him."

Sierra went all the way to Denver by ambulance so her sister-in-law could examine her and read the head CT. She would have been taken by medical air transfer if Connie had found anything in her preliminary exam that was questionable. Maggie chose to keep her overnight for observation and Conrad stayed with her, wouldn't leave her side. Then in the morning before she was discharged, she had more company. Cal was back, as he had intended to be, but with him was Dakota.

"Boy, what some chicks will do for attention," Dakota said, taking her into his big arms and hugging her.

"Don't call me a chick," she said. "I'm dangerous."

"So I hear. Good for you."

"Aren't you late for a war?" she asked.

"I'm not late yet. All your drama kind of demanded a visit before I head out again. I thought maybe you could give me some tips in kicking ass."

"You came to the right person," she said.

He touched her cheek. "You have a wicked black eye."

"I didn't say it was easy. Do you want to come to the Crossing with us? It turns out some of Sully's campers were actually FBI agents and I've been promised a debriefing, which is dangerous-chick talk for an explanation as to how all this crazy shit went down."

"Oh, I wouldn't miss it. And that's all I've got—the day. I have to get back to Fort Hood. I can't let them leave without me. They made the mistake of putting me in charge. I'm going to rent a car so I can come back to Denver later tonight."

"Forget about it," Cal said. "I'll take you back. I don't want you alone and getting tired. You're jet-lagged and worn-out. I'll stay at Maggie's place and rest before I drive back."

"I think he's going to be a little overprotective as a father, don't you?" Dakota asked Sierra.

"No help for it," she said. "Number one sibling put himself in charge many years ago." She smiled at Cal. "I don't think he'll do any real harm."

They worked it out so that Conrad drove Cal's truck with Sierra and Dakota because he couldn't stand to be away from her for five minutes. And Sierra and Dakota were due a visit. Cal drove back with Maggie. Of course that meant Connie sitting through another recitation of all the events that led up to the capture of a serial rapist named Craig Dixon. Fortunately for him, Sierra was not quite as graphic with this brother.

"Are you going to be all right now?" Dakota asked.

"One in five women is sexually assaulted. Some figures claim one in four. Yes, I'm going to be all right. It stole a year and a half of my life. I'm not letting it have any more than that."

"Plus, she got a little payback," Connie said.

When they got back to Sully's there were four campers waiting for them. The first thing Pete wanted to show Sierra was the inside of Priscilla and Clyde's RV. Even though there was quite a crowd waiting for an explanation, only Sierra was taken inside the RV. Behind a closet pocket door were some computer screens that were operated by electricity and WiFi, controlled by laptop computer and tablets and smartphones. "This is a surveillance van," Pete said.

"You had him under surveillance?" Sierra asked.

"No, we had you under surveillance," he said. "Our suspect had a pattern. He picked up strangers in bars all over the map, played the role of a rescuer in taking them home when they appeared to have had too much to drink, brutalized and raped them, threatened their lives if they told anyone, stalked them, and then to be absolutely sure, he found an opportunity to assault them again, proving to them he was in control and they would be punished for going to the police. At last count we know he assaulted seven women in three states. I'm sure there were more, probably at least twice as many. His first known victim was fifteen years ago when he was a heating and AC repairman, aged twenty. But, you were the only one who ran, that we know of. And you ran far and deep. You really threw him off his game.

Not only did he have trouble finding you but when he got in the general vicinity, you were never vulnerable. You didn't live alone, you didn't go out to bars, you were always one step ahead of him. Sierra, we think he was obsessed with carrying out his ritual, for lack of a better word."

"So you were stalking me?" she asked.

He nodded. "Priscilla and Clyde took turns watching the screens. We had a tracking device on your car, cameras in a few of your commonly visited locations—the Crossing, Conrad's house, the street outside the diner. It wasn't just to keep you safe, I'm afraid, although that was intended to be a fortunate by-product. We knew he was in Colorado—we had positive ID. We couldn't locate him or his vehicle but he'd been seen and identified. We thought he'd eventually find you and we were going to be ready for him."

"You didn't have a camera at Cal's house," she said.

He shook his head. "But we had your location. You were traveling at high speed, changed your direction abruptly and stopped. We knew where you were but didn't know why, since your brother wasn't there. It looked like it could be a confrontation with Dixon."

"He must have been lying in wait for me," she said.

"I think once he learned where and when you worked in town, that was his only option."

"Has he murdered anyone?" she asked.

"Not that we know of but after we have him in custody and conduct a thorough forensic investigation at the federal level there's no telling what might turn up. Each of the states in which he committed crimes has his DNA from the few victims who came forward." He put a hand on her arm. "Let's go have something to drink with your family. We can answer a few of their questions, and then I'm afraid we have to leave."

"Where's he going? Dixon?"

"He's going back to Detroit. Federal agents there will book him and the federal prosecutor will press charges and take him to trial, unless there's a full confession. In which case he'll go to federal prison. It's a much more secure and punitive establishment than state or county detention."

"I wish you had told me you were watching me," she said. "I was terrified and had no idea help was on the way."

"If we'd told you beforehand, everything might've progressed differently. I haven't seen a criminal as slippery and invisible as Dixon in my career. If you had known, he'd have smelled it. I'm sorry it had to be that way. I'm glad the plan worked."

There was something comforting about all the questions Sierra's friends and family had for the agents. There were ten of them in all—four agents, Sully, Maggie, Cal, Sierra, Dakota and Connie. Some of their questions had to go unanswered—police procedure that wasn't discussed or the future of the prosecution that was at best unknown.

She learned that Lucas and Pete got around the back roads and through fields on those ATVs, often sitting near roads that led to the Crossing or into town or that long, isolated road to Connie's house. It had seemed she'd seen these agents around town because she had. While she was working, they were poking around town, looking for familiar faces. And she also learned that Pete was well-known as Sneaky Pete, a seasoned undercover agent.

The agents praised her for her quick thinking and resourcefulness. She did some damage, it turned out. "Too bad that nail gun didn't hold the four-inch nails used for framing. But you did pop a couple end for end and drive 'em deeper," Clyde said. And Clyde and Priscilla no longer had those lovely British accents!

They didn't stay long. They had some coffee and sandwiches and by two in the afternoon they were ready to be on the road. Priscilla and Clyde were driving the surveillance RV back to

Chicago, where it had come from. Detroit didn't have one but they were quick to point out they had an army of FBI SWAT vehicles and equipment. Lucas and Pete were going back to Detroit where they were currently assigned.

There was a lot of hugging when they were leaving. Pete held her close for a long moment. "Thank you," she said. "If it wasn't for you, I'd be dead now."

"You know what, Sierra? I don't know about that. You've got some amazing fight in you. Not to mention smarts and incredible instinct. As long as you remember that, you're safer than ninety percent of the world. You trust your gut and you fight, young lady. Big battles, little battles, you refuse to give up, you hear me?"

She bit her lip and nodded. Her eyes welled with tears and a couple spilled over, running down her cheeks. "I haven't been able to cry since that night," she said in a soft whisper.

"Well, now you can. The danger from that night is gone. And once he's locked up, we're throwing away the key."

"I think I'm changed forever," she said tearfully.

"I want you to remember something, Sierra. It was something that happened to you. It's not who you are. Permission to move forward." Then he smiled and said, "Yes, Sierra. You're a badass. Own it."

Jackson Canaday showed up at the Crossing to work and Sully happily left him in charge. The family and dogs went to Cal's house to find Tom was there, a screwdriver and tube of caulk in hand. He'd replaced the window that had been kicked open by federal agents and repaired the lock on the door.

"They said it wasn't a crime scene anymore or anything, so I thought I'd fix it up before you got back. Jeez, Sierra, you're the fricking talk of the fricking town!"

"Great," she said, but she laughed a little in spite of herself.

"Um, there's some blood on the floor of the master bedroom closet. I'll replace the carpet before I finish the built-ins," Tom said.

"A lot of blood?" Maggie asked.

"Nah. Some good quarter-sized spots, though—very noticeable."

"Oh hell, I'll have those out in fifteen minutes. Hydrogen peroxide."

Tom's eyebrows popped up. "You're kidding! After all those bloody noses at my house, I could've used hydrogen peroxide? How'd you know that?"

"I'm a surgeon, Tom," she said with a laugh. "We're very closely acquainted with blood."

"Gee, I should've asked you how to get out blood a long time ago! Well, if there's even a shadow left, tell me and I can switch out that carpet really fast."

Cal asked Tom if he could stay for dinner, but he was off to feed his kids and check homework. Maggie and Cal got busy in the kitchen. Since they hadn't been prepared for a big crowd they'd pillaged through Sully's refrigerator, their freezer and the last of the garden.

They sat around the picnic table for a pizza dinner with bruschetta and salad. What was left of the baguette was sliced and slathered with garlic butter. It was a celebration.

When the meal was almost done, Connie clinked his glass. "I have a request, since everyone is gathered. I don't know when I'll have Sierra's big brothers in the same room together again so I'm sorry if this seems a little unusual." He looked at Sierra, an arm around her shoulders. "Sorry, honey. Nothing required of you—this is between me and the big brothers." Then looking back at those men he said, "I'd like your blessing to ask Sierra to marry me. I haven't done it yet, but I've wanted to. Now, if you give your blessing, I'll ask her when she's had a little more

time to recover and a little more time with me. You know—
not too long, not too fast. So?"

Dakota shrugged. "Okay by me," he said.

"I heartily approve, if that's what Sierra wants," Cal said.

"Nobody asked me, but I like the idea," Sully said.

"I'm in," Maggie said. "I've known Connie since he was a
kid and he's okay. I mean, he's really okay."

"That's nice," Connie said, smiling. Then he looked at Sierra.

"Well?" she said. "When are you gonna ask me?"

"I don't want to rush you."

"You don't want me to get tired of waiting, do you?"

"Never thought of that! Will you marry me, Sierra? Because
I love you a lot. More than you can imagine."

She grinned hugely. "I absolutely will. I love you a lot, too.
More than I thought possible."

"Oh God! Really?" he said.

"Oh yes," she said. "You're one of the greatest men I know.
I want to be with you forever. Then some more."

"Oh man," he said. Then he grabbed her and planted a big,
deep, sloppy kiss on her to the cheers of everyone in the room.
When he broke that lip-lock he still had a hand on her cheek,
holding her face close to his. "I love you so much," he whispered.

"Me, too," she whispered back.

"Well," he said, straightening up and looking at the dinner
table. "We hate to eat and run, but—"

The room dissolved in laughter as Connie pulled Sierra along.
She broke away just long enough to hug Dakota and tell him
she loved him and would miss him and would email every day.
Then she hugged everyone else and was literally whisked out
of the house by Connie.

Her future husband. The man who believed in her and was
truly her knight.

If a book is well written, I always find it too short.

—JANE AUSTEN

Epilogue

WHEN THE FALL FOLIAGE WAS IN FULL GLORY IN mid-October, Maggie and Cal drove to Denver together. She was in the very early stages of labor but a long drive in advanced labor would be too uncomfortable. So, she called her dad and explained they'd be waiting it out in her Denver house. Cal called his sister with the same message. They called Maggie's mom and stepdad, Phoebe and Walter. Everyone asked for an update call when they went to the hospital. And they happily obliged. "Elizabeth Margaret Jones will be arriving sometime today. First babies are in no hurry so be patient."

Patience, it turned out, was not a common trait among Cal or Maggie's family. Without conferring with each other, they fell like dominoes. Sully called Enid and Frank and Jackson Canaday— there were only some leaf peepers and two hunters in the campground and the store was not at all busy. It could be closed at six. And Sully headed for Denver to meet his first grandchild.

Sierra and Connie tried to distract themselves by putting on a good movie, but it wasn't working. Connie had two days off anyway so they took Molly to Rafe's house to play with Rafe's kids for the day and off they went to sit baby watch in Denver.

Phoebe and Walter didn't even try to wait.

And of course when word got out that Dr. Sullivan and her

husband were in the labor and delivery suite, her best friends and biggest fans gathered.

"You're at eight centimeters," Jaycee said. "Nice work. And they're all here."

"All who?" Maggie said with a groan.

"Everyone. Sully, your sister-in-law and Connie, your mom and Walter, half the ER staff and some neurosurgery folks. Waiting. Partying out in the lounge."

"Oh God," she moaned.

"You want anyone in the room?"

"Only California Jones!" she said. "Cal, go talk to them, tell them you'll let them know when the baby is here. Oh God," she groaned again. "And hurry back!"

Thus it was that an hour and a half later a very sleepy Maggie with swaddled Elizabeth in her arms welcomed what seemed like a throng of well-wishers and relatives. They all congratulated the mom and dad, gave Maggie a kiss and were slowly leaving.

"Sierra, wait a minute," Maggie said.

"Sure. Can I get you something?" she asked.

"Pull up a chair," she said. "You've really had a wild ride the past couple of years."

"Oh yeah," she said. "Only to get crazier. I've agreed to testify when he's brought to trial. That man has to be put out of business."

"Are you afraid?" Maggie asked.

"It doesn't matter," she said. "It has to be done and I'm the one to do it."

"I've watched you evolve into the most amazing woman I know. A hero. A wonder woman." She lifted the baby and passed her to Sierra. "My daughter needs a guardian angel, mentor, teacher, friend, a role model. Someone who is her strength. Someone she can always depend on and look up to. I'm so glad she has you."

Sierra took the baby so carefully, holding her close. "Wow. Maggie. No one's ever said anything like that to me before."

"They're all thinking it. I'm so proud of you. I'm in awe of you. Will you be Elizabeth's godmother? And her fairy god-mother? Protector and nurturer?"

"I will always be there for her. I give you my word."

Maggie smiled fondly. "I'll never lose a minute of sleep, then."

Sierra's heart was as full as her arms.

She was home.

★ ★ ★ ★ ★